Blue Dreams

Reclaiming Wonderland #2

Taila Cantrell

Tails Tales

Contents

To the dreamers and the survivors. More often than not we are one in the same. Don't let anyone stop you.

Quote

In a Wonderland they lie, Dreaming as the days go by. Dreaming as the summers die: Ever drifting down the stream- Lingering in the golden gleam- Life, what is it but a dream?

-Lewis Carroll

Characters and Their Code Names

Caterpillar (Cater)- Roman Ainsworth

Hatter- Hayden O'Hare

March- Maxton Danara

Cheshire (Ches)- Sinclair Malone

White Rabbit (Rab)- Jonah Ainsworth

White Queen- Alcinda Young (Cinda, Cindy)

Duchess- Vivica Rose

Red Queen- Penthea Rose

King of Hearts- Frederick Rose

Dodo- Gavin Danara

TweedleDee- Idalia Tallant

TweedleDum- Ilaria Tallant

Jabberwocky- Dnais Umbrell

Sectors of Wonderland

Sector One: The Red Party's base (formerly the White King's home), home and offices of the high-ranking members of the Red Party.

Sector Two: The business quarter, offices, banks, etc.

Sector Three: The Grove, theaters, museums, galleries, etc.

Sector Four: Department store, electricity hub, etc.

Sector Five: Middle class apartments and jobs.

Sector Six: Uninhabitable due to the destruction during the final days.

Sector Seven: The Hearts Club and other night life.

Sector Eight: Inhabited by animals, avoided by most citizens of Wonderland.

Sector Nine: Suit barracks and training center.

Sector Ten: The mental hospital and other doctors' offices. Many buildings in this sector were destroyed before The Dome was in place.

Sector Eleven: Dodo's store, the bistro, as well as other shopping and fast food.

Sector Twelve: Hatter and Dina's apartments. Lower class living area and jobs, heavily policed but not well maintained.

Prologue

Taken from the dream diaries of Eumonia Lyon, 2017

"Eu, we can't hold much longer. Let this city go, you cannot fight nature!" Nudd had been screaming various things at me but that clanged through my pounding head. The magick that flowed through my body was reaching its limits. My golden glowing skin burned from the pressure as I pushed harder and faster, as I built a shield hundreds of miles wide to protect the entire city. I had no doubt I was reaching the end of the well of power I held inside me; I'd already depleted my team's power reserves. If I couldn't close the shield, the entire city would fall soon enough. The ground was shaking. I'd felt more than seen buildings crumbling, vines and plants were beginning to wind and choke any surface they could climb. The sun was sweltering, I couldn't distinguish its burn from the burn of my power. I had to block out horrified wails and screams of innocent people dying. I'd long become numb to the death surrounding me. A single-minded focus to save the population of the last standing city on Earth drove me higher. I mentally spiraled down into my power. It cooled me, I could almost feel it lapping against my legs, comforting me, drowning out the sounds. The pain I was feeling. Insatiably, I became the power I carried. I was no longer in my body. I floated high above the city, watching as the faint golden shield raced to close the final hole. At the top, I could see the dome closing. If I could hold for just a few more moments I would accomplish my goal.

I slammed back into my body with so much force I crashed to my knees, sweat poured down every inch of my body. I collapsed forward, unable to hold my own weight, my cheek rested against cool concrete. I took in as much oxygen as I possibly could, trying to cool the burn in my lungs. I could hear footsteps running toward me. The city had gone surprisingly quiet, the cries were distant now. Strong arms lifted me, my husband's voice was warm in my ear, "You did it, my queen, you did it. You can rest now." With no further prompting, I fell into a deep sleep.

The house I found myself standing in was unfamiliar. I floated through, taking in the understated décor, white stag statues beckoned me toward an ornate door. My phantom body entered the room with no issue. I found myself staring at a middle-aged man. He was hunched over his desk, writing somewhat frantically. I leaned over his shoulder trying to make out the words he was writing. When a wet drop of red liquid fell onto the paper I backed away. A bad feeling filled me, immediately the man turned toward me, making eye contact. I held my breath; a vision had never interacted with me like this before.

"I don't know who you are, seeing this moment, but I can feel you. Feel the magick in your blood. It feels so familiar to me." His voice was hoarse, and I took in his face. I gasped when I saw my own bright blue eyes staring blankly toward me. Instantly I knew I was looking at a man who was related to me. I

reached toward him, desperately wanting to ease the pain that was so clearly etched onto his face. Instead, he began speaking again, "Something horrible is coming. I believe it is my own fault, something I've played a hand in. Nothing I do now will change what is to happen next. I'm not sure if you can either, but I've seen something I must share."

Suddenly, his hand gripped my bicep as if I was standing in the room with him. I could almost smell the magick as he shared a vision of his own with me. I saw a beautiful, blonde woman, her hair was loose flowing behind her wildly. Her blue eyes were fierce, a snarl curled her full lips, a familiar glow alight in her skin. I gasped when I saw the sword she held aloft, pointing toward some unseen enemy. I would have known it anywhere, tears filled my eyes. I never imagined I'd see it again in this lifetime. A scream I could not hear left her throat as a bright green light surrounded her. I yanked away from the man, pulling myself from his vision.

"I think that girl will save my home from what is coming." He collapsed back into his winged back chair, panting heavily. The vision began to darken, and I clawed desperately to hold onto it, I needed to know more.

I awoke to sunshine on my face but clamored out of my sleep-prone position. I searched desperately for my journal. Once I found it, I wrote frantically, trying to catalog every moment of my vision. A door opened, but I didn't look up, unable to pull myself away from my writing. "The people need to see you, Eu." Nudd's hands lay on my shoulders as he pressed a kiss to my head.

"They are not my people; they have no need of me. I have done my duty." I responded absent-mindedly, I couldn't stop thinking of the vision I'd just seen.

"We are all they have now. You know as well as I do that, we cannot return to Undraland. Let us make a home here, lead these people to prosperity. We can settle into a comfortable life, my queen." I knew what he said was reasonable, but his mention of my home caused tears to prick my eyes.

"I will think about it, my love. I am not ready to face reality yet." I whispered, closing my journal. I would come back to that journal entry many, many times over my too-long life. However, what I had seen that day was not something I'd ever see come to fruition.

Chapter 1

January 14th, 2159

"Drive faster, Ches." I shouted, digging my nails into the soft leather seat. It may have been freezing outside but sweat dripped down my spine. "I'm already going eighty-five, woman." He growled back. I turned around in my seat, watching the three black SUV's following us. "I swear to the Creator, if you tell me they're gaining on us. This is not an action movie Alice." He said, his voice pitching higher as he took a hard-left turn. My head hit the roof of the Hummer as I moved into the backseat. I reached into one of the duffle bags in the back, searching until I was able to pull out a large shotgun. "What the hell are you doing, Al?" Cheshire asked, fear in his voice.

"Open the sunroof." I commanded. He did so without question. I slid my body up through the small hole, carefully aiming the shotgun in my hands at the wheels of the closest SUV. I took a deep breath before taking the shot. My ears rung as I watched the vehicle twist as the tire blew out from under it, crashing into one of the other vehicles. I tossed the gun down, before climbing back into the passenger seat, and buckling my seat belt. I sent a quiet thanks to Rab, he'd been working with me on my aim with guns ever since the wedding. We'd all started training again. Cheshire had figured out recently that non-magick users couldn't detect him at all if he focused. Caterpillar and my mother refused to let Hatter train at all, insisting that his healing abilities should only be used in an emergency.

They still couldn't figure out why his hair had started to turn white. It had taken him several days to recover after healing me. March kept a lid on what he was working on, and I forced myself to respect that even if I wanted to know more about his magick.

"I think that might be the hottest thing you've ever done," He chuckled, but his knuckles were white from their grip on the steering wheel. We barreled down the dirt road. I shrugged my shoulders, glancing in the mirror to see that one of the black vehicles was still in pursuit. Cursing silently, I picked up my phone.

Alice: Ches and I were caught. Trying to lose the last car. Might need back up on the side road.

The lack of immediate response set me on edge, I hadn't heard from anyone in several hours. A simple drive out to the boonies to check in with Sammy and Patrick shouldn't have ended in a car chase. The Queen of Hearts had found any person who was still loyal to the Red Party and hid them. She sent them after us in various different ways as often as she could. We'd been careful not to go anywhere alone. We'd become so easily recognizable none of us were safe. Caterpillar and I most of all since we'd become the faces of change in Wonderland. Our responsibility as elected leaders of the city had weighed heavily since it was decided that we'd take over.

The Hummer jumped hard as the black SUV slammed into the back of it. Metal on metal caused my head to pound as Cheshire stepped on the gas pulling farther away from the vehicle. The tires squealed as he took a hard right turn. I took a deep breath, my muscles tense from the implant, when my phone finally dinged.

Boss Man: Headed your way, we'll cut them off.

"Roman and Rab should meet us halfway." I glanced behind us, wishing I could see into the tinted windows. We were having a hard time identifying the people who'd sided with the Queen of Hearts. Cheshire focused on the road, barely registering what I had said. When I glanced back again, the

SUV was gone, "We must have lost them, try to skirt around, I don't think they know—"

I screamed as the SUV jumped right in front of the Hummer. I felt like I was floating, as the Hummer spun out, hitting a tree. Cheshire had been driving too fast for the hit to stop our momentum. In slow motion we slammed into another tree. My eyes swam as I reached toward him, hoping he was okay. Something wet came away on my hand after I laid my hands on his arm. I groaned as I saw the blood coating my fingers, I tried and failed to unbuckle my seat belt. The sound of slamming doors was the last thing I heard as I faded into blackness.

"Damn, damn, damn," My ears were ringing, but I could hear Hatter's curses as I felt my body being lifted out of the car.

"They've got to go, they took Hatter's baby from him," Cheshire's weak joke wasn't funny, but I heard Hatter scoff.

"I can try healing you, sweetheart. Give me just a second," He laid me down gently, but I began to protest immediately.

"You will do no such thing," Caterpillar appeared in my line of vision, "It's just a surface level wound. We can take them both to Cinda."

"If I never test it out, we will never know if her theory is even correct," Hatter snapped back.

"Here is not the place to have this argument. We need to get out of the open, and I need to join Rab tracking the one who got away."

Hatter sighed, "Go. I'll get them home."

I didn't hear Cater's response before my vision swam and I blacked out again.

"Have I mentioned how fucking sick I am of blacking out? You'd think at this point my head could take more of a hit," I bitched as Mom bandaged a cut on Cheshire's hand.

"H-head injuries are the most dangerous, Ali. Sit down," March chimed in, pushing gently on my shoulder to stop me from pacing around the room. I did as I was told, huffing as he carefully wiped blood away from my hairline. I studied his features, he was biting his pouty lips in concentration, a quiet hum vibrated in his chest. His honey brown eyes met mine, and he gave me a small smile, pressing a quick kiss to my lips. It instantly made me feel better, and I accepted his soothing magick. He'd really honed his skills, but I'd noticed a slightly strained under current to his voice. Almost as if controlling it put him under constant stress. I'd tried to bring it up a couple of times, but he'd shut me down at every turn. I knew soon enough we'd have to address what was going on inside his head, but we'd all been distracted by the Queen of Hearts constant attacks. There had been twelve attacks since our botched wedding. A sense of sadness filled me as that day played out in my head. Hatter had insisted that we should have immediately completed the ceremony, but Caterpillar and I agreed that we should wait until things had settled down. We had defeated the Red Queen, surely the Queen of Hearts wouldn't be too difficult. I was learning quickly that simply was not the case.

"You don't have a concussion, I've got you c-c—" I watched as March gritted his teeth together. Recently it seemed like anytime he stuttered it made him angry. I took a deep breath, hoping he'd mimic me. I smiled up at him, waiting for him to speak again, "You can g-go shower up."

I stood, pressing a kiss to his cheek, before whispering in his ear, "Would you like to join me?"

He grinned and took my hand. I waved goodbye to Mom and Cheshire, allowing March to pull me toward our bedroom. Our apartment had become home base for everyone. We'd purchased an old office building in sector two. It hadn't been too hard to convert into several apartments with all the facilities we needed to function. So far, I'd refused to take over the large mansion that the Red Party had made its base. Even though my mother had explained several times it was the home she grew up in. I felt that the horrors my aunt had committed within its walls would haunt us all if we moved into it. As we entered the bedroom, March turned, pressing his lips to mine, as he unhooked my jeans. We walked toward the bathroom that way, shedding each other's clothes. Once we were both naked, we separated. March quickly turned the water on, and I ran a brush through my hair, wincing when I ran over the cut on my head. March wrapped his arms around me from behind, his eyes meeting mine in the mirror. We watched each other for several moments, before I asked, "Are you okay?"

I watched a look I didn't understand cross his features, but when he spoke my heart broke. "I am so angry, Ali... I can't even tell you why. I believed it was over when you took down your aunt. I thought I could f-f-finally have just a little peace."

"We will figure out a way, Maxton. I promise, we will find our peace," I turned, laying my hand against his cheek. "I will tear the entire city to shreds if it will make you happy. I will bring her head on a spike to you if you want."

"I always knew you were blood thirsty, sweetheart, but that may be the hottest thing I've ever heard," Hatter's voice caused both of us to jump, "But let's try to keep the blood spilled to a minimum. I don't know if the citizens could take another show like last time. They're already a little afraid of you."

"I didn't even hurt her in the square," I argued, crossing my arms over my naked chest.

"No, you just stripped her of all of her magick and revealed her darkest secrets." He shot back, though I had to admit I became distracted when he began stripping his clothes off.

"How are you feeling? Cheshire said the Hummer was totaled." March changed the subject.

I could see Hatter deflate a bit at the question, but he said, "It's just a car, I'm thankful everyone survived."

"We can find you another vehicle." I stepped into the hot spray of the shower, followed quickly by March. We'd ensured at least three of us could easily fit into the shower.

"Ali, we both know vehicles are hard to come by... especially anything like the Hummer." He responded as he climbed in behind March. I turned, reaching for my shampoo bottle which was quickly pulled from my hands. March began washing my hair as I mulled over Hatter's problem. I knew he was right; the bright yellow Hummer had always been a strange luxury for him to have. I doubted we could find an exact replica, but I wanted to replace what he'd lost. "Stop thinking so hard," Hatter whispered in my ear, startling me. They'd switched spots, and I turned watching as March soaped himself up. "I can almost hear you thinking about how to replace the damn car. It's fine, Alice. Nothing matters to me more than you."

I ignored the feeling of tears pricking my eyes, reaching to wrap my arms around Hatter's neck. He picked me up, burying his face in my neck. "I still feel bad. I know you loved the Hummer."

"Not nearly as much as I love you." He whispered.

My heart warmed, no matter how many times one of the guys said they loved me it would always give me butterflies. "I love you too."

"Can y'all hurry up. I know shower sex is fun, but I'd like to wash up and sleep off the pounding headache I have." Cheshire's voice was muffled through the door.

"You're just jealous we didn't invite you, Cat." I yelled back.

"No shit." He muttered just loud enough for us to hear.

The three of us finished our shower, stepping out, and helping each other dry off. My nipples stood at attention as I exited the bathroom, walking toward our shared closet. I grabbed one of Caterpillar's shirts, pulling it over my body. Cheshire was laying on the bed with his arm thrown over his eyes. I crawled on top of Ches, ignoring the dirt that covered him. "You can go shower now."

"Not with you on top of me." He snarked back, but his hands landed on my hips.

"Are you complaining?" I ground against him, feeling as he hardened.

"You're an evil woman, Alice Young." He flipped me over, hovering above me. "Tonight, we're going to discuss—"

"Caterpillar just texted; we've got a meeting with everyone at nine." Hatter once again interrupted my fun, and I pouted as Cheshire rolled off of me.

"Who is everyone?" I asked sitting up.

"The entire team." I sighed at his response. I wanted to spend some time with the guys tonight, but I knew this meeting was going to be hours of planning.

"I'm taking a nap until it's time to go." I grumbled, crawling into the middle of the bed, and pulling the covers over myself. Hatter and March both pressed kisses to my forehead, murmuring their goodbyes as they left to prepare for the meeting. Cheshire disappeared into the bathroom, complaining under his breath. I swear I heard him call Caterpillar a cockblocker. Slowly I drifted to sleep, still thinking about how I could make up the Hummer's loss to Hatter.

Chapter 2

"What the hell do you mean you're not going to continue to try to track her movements?" Caterpillar's shouting pulled me out of the absolute boredom I'd been experiencing ever since I sat down at the large round table in the office space we'd claimed for meetings. Leading Wonderland had a lot more to do with paperwork and keeping the citizens alive than I'd ever expected. I wasn't suited to the work at all, but Caterpillar had done a great job organizing everyone.

"We're chasing our tails, Roman. There is no reason to pretend we have any idea what she's up to." Ilaria snapped back, flipping her long red hair over her shoulder. She and I had become close over the last eighteen months.

Ilaria had been at the forefront of many of our missions, helping plan and execute things when Caterpillar and I were busy with other things. I knew she didn't intend to be rude, but she wasn't handling this situation well. Caterpillar gritted his teeth, sitting down. I could tell he was trying to calm down enough to give a reasonable response, so I jumped in. "There's no point in us fighting each other. That's exactly what she would want. If we're divided, we're much easier to defeat."

"I agree with Ilaria. We need to find a way to get ahead of her. We've found no information on her other than what Duchess could remember. At best we're playing a guessing game, at worst we're doing exactly what she expects us to." Hatter piped in.

I cringed. We always tried to ensure the four of us were on the same page in front of everyone else. I glanced toward Caterpillar who looked defeated. He met my eyes, a questioning look passed between us. He sighed when he realized that I agreed with Hatter. We'd spent months trying to find any sign of the Queen of Hearts. Any idea how she was hiding the former members of the Red Party and whoever else she had on her side. We'd had no luck, and things were escalating more and more.

"What do you suggest we do instead?" Caterpillar asked, glancing to each person in the room.

I looked over each person cataloging their reactions. Tilly and her two husbands, Jackson and Cahir, looked about as bored as I had been feeling. Idalia and Lily were whispering to each other, every once in a while, they'd glance toward Ilaria with concern. Rab sat in silence, clearly deep in thought. My mother was pacing behind him, I could see her lips moving but no sound left her mouth. Dina was bouncing her daughter on her lap, who gurgled and smacked at the table. Griffin seemed to be asleep in the chair next to her. March and Cheshire were ignoring the tension in the room by playing some kind of card game I couldn't follow. I snorted. We were the leaders of the city, and we clearly had no idea what the fuck we were doing. Duchess met my eyes when I looked her way, a small, but encouraging smile gave me enough confidence to speak. "Let's go over what we know one last time."

"We think she is my father's sister, because I was always told to refer to her as Aunt Rose." Duchess was the first to speak. Her input had saved our lives several times as we tried to protect ourselves from the queen's minions.

"We can assume that means her real name is Rose," Cheshire pointed out.

"No assumptions. Only the facts we know." Caterpillar said, he had a notebook before him and was furiously writing.

"We've seen no sign of magick or fighting skill from her," Idalia pointed out.

"She could be hiding any skill she has to keep us guessing. We knew exactly what Penny could do, and it gave us some advantage over her." Mom spoke up.

"She has access to vehicles, weapons, and people with no sign of a homebase. She was also completely anonymous until she revealed herself at the wedding." Dina continued.

"She knew exactly where we would be, and continues to have information about our movements." March whispered, and silence filled the room.

"So, we have a mole?" Hatter asked, sharp intakes of breaths and gulps could be heard from almost everyone.

Caterpillar and I looked at each other. We had discussed the possibility in private a few days ago, but we had decided not to make that accusation to our comrades yet. Caterpillar gave me a reassuring nod. They had planned to reveal the knowledge tonight. I hoped they found what they were looking for, but I couldn't believe for a moment that any of our friends would help the Queen of Hearts.

"Maybe she has some kind of tracking magick," Rab said, his voice was gruff causing him to sound as tired as he looked. He'd grown more greys since Mary Anne's death, his age more clearly showing now. I knew some of that had to do with running around helping to raise Lewis. Many discussions had happened after the Red Queen was defeated about how to handle the young boy. We had searched for his father but came up empty at every turn. Letting Rab and Mom handle the boy for the most part hadn't been a purposeful choice at first, but they both seemed to enjoy having a child to care for.

"We can't rule that possibility out, but if someone is feeding her information... We need to be more careful about what we share." Silence reigned for a long time after Lily's comment.

"I think we have to assume she does not have any magick. I don't and neither does my father," Duchess piped up, changing the subject, "Also, I've only met her four times. Always at night...." Duchess trailed off. I waited with bated breath for the thought that was clearly churning in her mind. "Have we ever seen her during the day?"

Our wedding had been at dusk, March wanted to watch the sunset together before we said our vows. I ran through every other encounter we'd had, "No..."

"What does that mean?" Dina asked.

"I don't know, maybe nothing. She could just be hitting us at times she thinks we will be least prepared." Hatter responded, but there was a hesitation in his voice. There were very few coincidences in our world, if we'd never seen her during the day there had to be a reason for it.

"Maybe she's vampire," Cheshire joked, trying to lighten the somber energy of the room. "I refuse to rule that out. Look at the magick users in our presence. Why couldn't vampires, werewolves, and fairies be real?"

"Hatter's right, nighttime is when it's most likely for us to have our guard down." Caterpillar brushed Cheshire comment off, "If we're trying to get ahead of her, what types of traps can we set for her?"

"Another wedding," March said, looking to me.

"She wouldn't fall for that." I dismissed the idea. It wasn't that I didn't want to marry them, but I hated the idea of our wedding being a trap for our enemies.

"A public, high-profile event? She's going to make her presence known." Duchess argued. I glared at her.

"Alice, they're right. You want to be married anyway, if she doesn't show up, then you can have the redo you deserve." Dina reached across the table, laying her hand over mine.

I sighed, sinking further into my chair. "Can we discuss other ideas as well? I need time to think about it."

And so began a long discussion about any and every way we could trap the Queen of Hearts and end her rebellion. I wondered for a moment if there had been discussions like this among the Red Party leadership when the Resistance had gotten close to winning. If my aunt had sat at a similar table surrounded by people wondering if she was making the right decisions. I knew beyond a shadow of a doubt that we were morally and ethically doing the right thing where she was not. However, the irony of us being the governing body was not lost on me.

Three hours later I collapsed into bed, drained and exhausted. I couldn't believe the Hummer had been totaled just hours before the meeting. It already felt like days ago.

"We need to discuss if we are going to follow through with a second wedding." Hatter said, arms crossed over his chest as he watched me.

"I told you I need more time to think about it," I snapped.

"No, you don't," Caterpillar growled as he dropped onto the bed beside me, yanking me into his lap in one smooth move. "You want to marry us, it's that simple. You're just scared after what happened last time."

I hated how well he was able to read me, "Our marriage shouldn't start out like that. We shouldn't have to sacrifice one of the most important days of our lives for her."

"We have the rest of our lives together. If this puts an end to the Queen of Hearts little game, it's worth it." Cheshire said.

"Where do the sacrifices end? Our marriage, our souls?" A tear ran down my face, "We didn't defeat the Red Party and get peace. We inherited a city full of problems. We will never know a day without sacrifice."

"It's okay to be scared, Ali. I am t-too." March said.

All of the guys had found spots surrounding us, March was pressed into Hatter's chest beside us. March's fingers had entangled mine, and he gave me a comforting squeeze. Cheshire was rubbing my back on Caterpillar's other side. Tears streamed down my face. The day the Queen of Hearts had walked into our wedding had been a rude awakening. I had convinced myself that things would only get better now that we had some control of Wonderland. The Red Party had not been close to the only issues within the city. The Suits had done a good job controlling crime. We were still trying to establish a fair way to handle the more egregious crimes. Idalia had made several suggestions that had been extremely helpful. I had begged her to come up with laws and some sort of council to judge these situations, she was still hesitant. We didn't want to scare anyone, but we did need to protect the peace within the city. There would always be a few bad people who would do anything they could to get what they wanted.

"It's going to be okay, princess. If you don't want to go through with this plan, we will figure something else out." Caterpillar said, his lips pressed against my head.

I watched Hatter tense at his words. His face had been strained since the conversation had come up, but he had yet to speak his mind, so I asked, "What do you think, Hatter?"

He didn't respond immediately, staring up at the ceiling for a long moment. "I want you to be happy, but it hurts me that we didn't get married immediately after the wedding fiasco. I'm willing to risk the plan actually working, not that I think it will, if it means we will finally be married. You are ours, sweetheart, and I want everyone to know that."

Hatter had become much better at communicating how he was feeling. I was so incredibly proud of him, but he still struggled with expressing himself without being directly asked. "You don't care if we get attacked again and don't actually complete the ceremony?"

"I will complete the ceremony standing in her blood if I have to, Al," He responded. Something about his tone flooded my core with heat. I remembered that I'd been interrupted earlier when I'd sought release, so I sat up, grinding in Caterpillar's lap.

His face darkened as he realized what I wanted. "Always a little vixen. Do you think you're going to distract us from the topic at hand?"

"Convince me it's a good idea, Rome," I shot back, stripping out of the shirt I was wearing.

"I thought you'd never ask," He attacked me like a mad man, sucking one of my already hard nipples into his mouth. I felt hands pull at my pants, stripping them off of me, hands gripping my ass as a hot mouth met my neck. A hard smack clued me in that Cheshire was behind me. He had such an obsession with my ass. I glanced toward Hatter, who was already hard, guiding March down on his cock. I never considered how much watching the two of them together would turn me on, but my pussy was immediately flooded as March's plump lips wrapped around Hatter's cock.

"Pay attention, princess. You'll play with them when I'm done with you," Caterpillar gripped my face, forcing my eyes to his. The swirling grey pulled me in as it always did, and I fell into him with a hard breath. I felt Cheshire's clothed erection press harder against my ass with the movement. So I pushed back into him, mentally begging him to take me.

"What do you want, pretty girl, you're going to need to use your words." Cheshire taunted me, another smack landing on my bare ass.

"Fuck me, Cat," I hissed.

Several hard slaps rained down on my ass, "Ask nicely,"

"Her mouth is going to be too busy to speak, Ches. I think she needs a reminder on how to be a good girl," Caterpillar gripped my hair, lowering me toward his cock. I hadn't even noticed him shedding his clothes. I licked his tip, aiming to tease him since they'd wanted to play games, but his grip on my head tightened, forcing me to take his entire length. When he hit the back of my throat I started to gag, "Hm, what was that princess? I couldn't hear you."

I whined, tears starting to prick my eyes, but I didn't pull away, loving the feeling of his cock in my mouth, like warm steel against my tongue.

With one final smack, Cheshire finally decided to reward me by sliding into my dripping pussy. I moaned around Caterpillar's cock. Cheshire's rhythm pushed me up and down on Caterpillar in a punishing pace. I could tell he was getting close, so I began sucking in earnest. I looked up to meet his stormy eyes, the pleasure there caused a flood inside me. His deep grunts turned on me endlessly. "Are you ready for my cum, princess?"

I nodded as vigorously as I could with his cock in my mouth. Within moments the salty taste of cum flooded my tongue, I licked and sucked him until he pulled me away. "Always such a good girl for us. Are you ready for her, Hayden? Our girl needs to cum after her day."

Cheshire was still pounding into me as Hatter appeared before me lifting me slightly, to where he could suck one of my nipples into his mouth. I looked to March who was sprawled out, clearly recovering from Hatter's attentions. He grinned when he saw me watching and crawled toward us. Hatter moved, allowing March between us.

"Cheshire, lift her up, I-I want a taste," I whined as Cheshire pulled out of me, but I was quickly lifted, my legs spread wide, before he was back to fucking me. It didn't take long before March's tongue found my clit, licking and sucking in just the way I liked. Hatter found a new position torturing my nipples. I was seeing stars when I heard Cheshire curse, spilling himself inside of me. The feeling of his hot cum was enough to finally send me over the edge.

Once the orgasm had subsided, I was laid down gently. A warm cloth wiping me gently as the guys took turns kissing me and whispering their praise and love. I was floating away in the afterglow when Hatter pulled me to his naked chest and whispered. "Do you have your answer now?"

I looked up at him. I could see the pain in his eyes, and without another thought, "Let's try again. Anything for you." The last thing I saw was the grin that spread across his face at my words.

Chapter 3

January 23rd, 2159

It didn't take us very long to get a small, but extremely publicized wedding together. Mom and Rab had been spreading the news. I was convinced they had created flyers, telling everyone in Wonderland that the leaders were marrying,that the Queen of Hearts was no concern to us, and we would no longer allow her to prevent Wonderland from thriving. It was an absolutely genius plan. I had to admit if the Queen's ego was as large as I expected, she would jump at the chance to ruin this day for us. I stood in our bathroom, staring at the floor length pale blue gown I wore. The deep plunging neckline accented my chest nicely, but also showed off just a taste of the muscle I'd built training in the last few months. It was nothing like the pure white, fluffy minidress I'd worn to the first ceremony. It had been completely ruined after I was shot, but at least I liked this dress even better. Dina had picked it out for me, and apparently had ensured it was tailored to my exact measurements. I wasn't sure how she knew what my measurements were. I was convinced she snuck into the apartment while I slept and measured me, but I really couldn't complain.

"You look beautiful, Alice," Rab appeared in the bathroom door.

"Thank you, Jonah. Is everyone ready?" I asked, trying to push away the panic that was bubbling under the surface.

He nodded, "Armed to the teeth and waiting for you, darlin,"

"Do you really think she's dumb enough to show up?" I looped my arm into his, letting him lead me out of the apartment.

"I'm not sure. If she doesn't, you'll have a beautiful ceremony, and we will figure a new plan," He opened his truck door for me, helping me into the cab.

As we drove toward the town square, I watched the people milling in the streets. Children ran around, their parents laughing at their antics. Even with the threat of the Queen of Hearts, the city had an air of peace that I had never experienced before. For all of them to have enough faith in their leadership to defeat this threat pulled at my heart, but a seed of doubt existed in me. I felt my magick rise at my anxiety, electricity jumped out of my fingertips. I lifted them watching the bluish silver energy wrap itself around my hand. It nuzzled me, almost as if it was trying to comfort my inner thoughts. It had taken months for me to fully recover from absorbing Penthea's powers. I'd felt exhausted and drained, nightmares had haunted me, showing me all the things her magick had done. Thankfully, the guys had been at my side the entire time, comforting me, and ensuring I had everything I needed. Now, my magick was the strongest it had ever been, but I felt the weakest I ever had. I glanced up, catching sight of the statue in the center of the city. I often found myself staring up at it, wondering who the woman was. The plaque had been rubbed away long ago; she was the biggest mystery in Wonderland.

The car stopping pulled me out of my thoughts. I glanced toward Rab, his face was serene, a warrior's calm had taken him over. He looked at me, and I nodded, "Let's do this,"

As we stepped into the event center that had once held meetings for the Red Party I found the room filled with unfamiliar faces. Every eye in the room swung toward me as the door closed. With my arm still looped through Rab's we began the slow, but extremely long walk down the aisle. I ignored the stares and whispers of the strangers, random citizens of Wonderland who had been invited in. It seemed like an extremely dangerous choice to me, but I hadn't made the decisions around the plan here. I finally met the eyes of my men. One by one they gave me reassuring smiles, and I took them in. Caterpillar had chosen a dark blue suit, with a grey tie the same color as his eyes. Hatter stood next to him, a black suit hugging his body in the most delicious way, a light blue tie complimented the dress I was wearing. March had tears in his eyes when I looked to him. He'd chosen a white suit with a dark blue shirt underneath, a white bow tie at his throat. Cheshire always had to make a statement, so he wore a velvet suit in a purple so dark it was nearly black. His undershirt was slightly unbuttoned, forever my rebel. Slowly we climbed the steps that would lead toward them, excitement finally lit in my chest, I loved these men with every fiber of my being.

My mother stepped toward as Rab and I came to a stop across from my men, "Hello, everyone. We invited you here to help us celebrate the marriage of my daughter, Alice." She reached out gripping my hand, "We all need things to look forward to. After the incident at their last wedding, we wanted everyone here to know that we will not give up until Wonderland is a safe place for each and every citizen." Cheers went up across the crowd, stopping her words, "Let us take this opportunity to band together. To show those who would try to disrupt the peace we're building that the people of this city are strong. Nothing will stop our joy." Her words echoed through the building as I admired her. Even with the horrors she'd experienced at the hands of her sister, she had never broken, only bent to survive. No one would know the torture she'd experienced for ten years now. Aside from the deep scars hidden underneath her long sleeved green dress she was every bit the same woman who had raised me.

When the uproar of the crowd stopped, Sammy stepped forward. He rested a hand on my shoulder, and I looked toward him as he squeezed. I could see the slight tension in his body, he was prepared for the fight we were all expecting. Sammy had refused my offer to move into the city proper and take a more active role in the inner workings of Wonderland.

He'd said he was at home in the boonies, that those people needed him far more than we did. I respected him so I'd never brought it up again. Thankfully, he'd agreed to marry us today and bring a few of his men to watch over the innocents in the crowd.

As he began to speak, an overwhelming emotion swelled in my chest, I couldn't pinpoint. Without thinking I reached out to grip Caterpillar's hand, he squeezed my hand, looking at me with concern. I gave a slight shake of my hand, and zoned back into what Sammy was saying. "I have witnessed the five of you grow together, fight not only for each other, but for every person in Wonderland. I could not be prouder that you are leading this city into a time of peace," Sammy stopped speaking, wiping a tear away, causing a tear of my own to fall down my face, "Sorry, sorry folks, Alice has become a bit like a daughter to me... Let me get myself together." Sammy leaned into my ear and whispered, "I just received a message. One of the men stationed outside believes he just spotted Jabberwocky. Do you want me to continue?"

I chewed my lip; Jabberwocky had been the scariest member of the Red Party. His escape had haunted all of us for well over a year, but I was realized a spotting could just be a distraction, "Yes."

Sammy took a deep breath, "I guess we better get to the marrying part now, huh?" Laughter came from the crowd. "Roman, Hayden, Sinclair, Maxton, do you promise to care for Alice in sickness and in health, to love and cherish not only her, but each other as well?"

The chorus of I dos from them caused my heart to beat faster. I believed for the first time we might actually be able to successfully marry. "Alice, do you promise to care for Roman, Hayden, Sinclair, and Maxton, in sickness and in health, to love and cherish them so long as they draw breath."

Just as I was about to answer, the doors of the building flew open. A figure covered in shadow stood between them. Every armed person in the room stood, reaching for the weapons hidden on their bodies. I saw Lily's golden shield reach out, protecting the people around her. She still hadn't been able to have it reach across more than a six-foot area, but she was training every day. I let electricity spark around my fingers, each of the guys pulled a gun from a hidden holster on their body. Silence reigned as the figure walked into the light, what stood before us was not what I expected. A tall man sporting a long, unkempt beard and dark brown hair braided down his back stepped closer toward us. He was covered in grime; a trail of dirt followed him up the white runaway I had walked just minutes before. As he approached, I saw startling, hard green eyes meet mine, a sneer formed on his lip. I continued to take him in, and when my eyes finally reached lower, I gasped, his pants were tied off just below the knee. Part of his leg was missing, a gnarled wooden stick assisted his walking. "What the hell is this?" His deep raspy voice asked, it sounded as if he hadn't spoken in years.

Everyone was silent, confused as this stranger stood before us. "Really not the welcome I was expecting home, son." A strangled sound came from my left, and I turned slightly, finding Hatter, mouth agape staring at the man.

"Dad?"

And with that one word my world descended into an entirely new level of chaos.

Chapter 4

I paced outside our apartment, the slap of my bare feet on the marble floors the only sound to be heard in the hallway. Hatter, my mother, and his father had disappeared into the apartment hours ago, locking the door behind them. Cheshire had escorted March down to our training room. He'd been unable to contain himself so we'd hoped some exercise would distract him from his thoughts. Caterpillar hadn't come back home with us, coordinating with Sammy to see if the Jabberwocky sighting had any credibility. I was still in my wedding gown, it's silky material now felt itchy against my skin. I knew it was just the nervous energy racing through my body, but nothing I did helped me to relax. Which is exactly how I'd ended up here pacing in front of my home for what felt like hours. I heard the knob turn, and rushed to the door.

My mother's golden head peeked out, and she motioned me inside. "They're still talking in the guest room, but I could hear you out here. Go and change. Try to relax." She whispered.

"Relax? He's been outside of Wonderland for how long? I need details." I spoke through my teeth.

"Alice, you need to give Hatter time…" She trailed off, looking away from me. "This is not an easy situation you've found yourself in. It needs to be handled delicately."

"Fine," I breathed, stomping toward our bedroom.

I threw open the closet doors and began digging through the clothes. I couldn't claim the five us kept an organized space when it came to our clothes. More than once one of us had walked out wearing something that wasn't ours. Cheshire had accused Caterpillar of stretching out his shirts more than once. I snorted, the memory cheering me up. I found some comfortable, but decent looking work out clothes, and began trying to take my dress off. It was much harder than I expected, but after several minutes of contorting I was able to get it unzipped. I kicked it across the room, my frustration building with every passing moment. Once I was dressed again, I sat down on the bed, staring off into space. I hadn't been able to gather my thoughts since Hatter's father had appeared in the middle of our wedding ceremony. Loud voices pulled me out of my head, I jumped up, making my way toward the sounds.

"You don't get to show up here and act as if you're still his father," March's tone shocked me, he was nearly growling the words out.

"Maxton, you have to understand just how unhealthy this situation is for all of you. It's understandable that you've trauma bonded—"

"You d-don't know a goddamn thing about what we've been through the last ten years, Joshua," He snapped back.

"March, take a breath, he's just worried for us, we can explain—"

"You're an idiot, Hayden. When you r-r-ruin our lives, it'll be your own fault,"

I raised my eyebrows at March as he stormed past me, but he ignored me. "Alice, I want to introduce you to my dad." Hatter waved me toward him, He wrapped an arm around my shoulders and giving a small smile to his father, "Dad, this is Alice Young. Our fiancé—"

"Multiple people cannot be married, Hayden. I've explained my thoughts on this situation to you already." Joshua interrupted him, dismissing me.

I gritted my teeth, "I understand that our situation is somewhat unique, but we aren't the only people in Wonderland with this type of arrangement, sir. In fact, I can introduce you to at least two people right now. Tillie lives right down the hallway."

"You seem like a perfectly nice young woman, but I don't care what your excuse is. My son isn't going to continue to participate in this sham." He responded.

"Now, Dad, I've already told you. I love Alice and March. Caterpillar and Cheshire are my brothers, our relationship isn't up for discussion." Hatter said. I breathed a sigh of relief; happy he was standing up for us.

"This isn't pertinent right now, though we will most certainly be continuing the conversation at another time. Alcinda said she would explain more about what has happened since my… unfortunate departure. We'll catch up further another time." Joshua dismissed his son without another thought, exiting our apartment before either of us could respond.

I wrapped my arms around Hatter, knowing he needed some comfort, the tension in his body was visible. "Has he explained where he's been?" I asked quietly after a few moments.

"Outside the city," Was his only response before he left me confused.

"You need to give him time to get used to the Wonderland of today. He's been through an extremely grueling and terrifying few years. He just wants to be with his only remaining family." My mother was trying to be reasonable, but I didn't have the capacity for empathy at that moment.

"I don't really care if he's been probed by vines while hanging upside down from a tree. He's not going to treat Hatter and March like that," I growled back.

"Don't take that tone with me," She snapped.

"Sorry, Mom." I grumbled, "But you have to understand. He left Hatter when he was only seventeen, how dare he come back here and start imposing his opinions on us."

"It's the only way he knows," She closed her eyes, clearly trying to choose her words carefully. "Joshua O'Hare is the product of a different time. He remembers the days your grandfather had control of Wonderland."

I snorted, "That's no excuse."

Mom pinched the bridge of her nose, trying to keep her cool, "You cannot handle this like he's an enemy. He is Hatter's father. Hayden needs that relationship, just like you need a relationship with me. Just because you are adults doesn't mean you don't still need your parents."

I thought for a moment, I knew she was right, but I was so angry I could hardly think straight. "You didn't see March's face, Mom. I've never seen him this angry."

"March has a lot of things he needs to deal with, baby. He's hurting over more than either of us can understand. Joshua's appearance has triggered a lot of feelings for him."

"What can I do for them?" I asked, feeling hopeless.

"Be there to support them. Between you, Caterpillar, and Cheshire they both have lots of support. Not to mention the rest of us, who love you all," Mom laid a hand on my arm, "You aren't alone Alice. You don't have to take everything on by yourself. You have so many people rooting for you."

"I love them so much, I don't want them to hurt," I argued, weakly.

"You can't stop the people you love from experiencing pain, that is just a part of life. If I could have protected, you from all the pain you've dealt with you wouldn't be the person you are today." She responded. "Now,

I'm going to go check on Jonah and Lewis. Lewis was tearing the house apart last time I was over there. Jonah gives that boy far too much leeway."

She was grinning as she spoke, which sparked a small amount of jealousy that I pushed away. I was glad Mom had found purpose in watching over Rab and Lewis, but I wished I had gotten more of her time. I would always hurt over the years we lost because of my aunt.

"I'll see you soon. Caterpillar wants us to have another meeting tomorrow." I walked her to the door, giving her a hug before she left.

March and Hatter had had an argument the moment his father left. Now they had locked themselves in different rooms to cool off, leaving me to try to talk sense into them. I rolled my eyes and sent a text.

Alice: Joshua is kind of a dick, could have used some warning.

Sexy Cat: I only met him once, plus we all thought he was dead.

Boss Man: How is Hayden doing?

Alice: Joshua has a problem with our relationship. March has a problem with him.

Sexy Cat: So, not great.

Boss Man: I'm headed back.

Alice: Any update on Jabberwocky?

Boss Man: Talk when I'm home.

Sexy Cat: Uh oh, bad news.

Alice: Shut up, Cat.

Sexy Cat: You know you being mean turns me on. Stop it.

I snorted at Cheshire's text. He always knew how to lighten the mood. I gained enough courage to walk toward Hatter's room. We had ensured that we all had a space to get away from each other in. Cheshire's room was a dim office space. Caterpillar's looked just like his office at the warehouse before it burned down. March and Hatter shared the other room since neither of them used it much. A light knock before I entered was all the warning I gave him.

"I'm not ready to talk," He was lying on the bed, an arm thrown over his eyes.

"Well fine, you can listen," He snorted but didn't stop me, "No matter what your father has to say, we love you. Nothing anyone says is going to stop me from being here for you. But I know you're processing a lot, I'm not going to push you to talk about it, make any decisions—"

Hatter was off the bed before I could finish my sentence, "There are no decisions for me to make. You belong to me. I don't care if the Creator comes down here themselves. There is nothing in this world that could stop me from being at your side."

"What about me, Hayden?" March was standing in the doorway.

"Oh, Max..." Hatter crossed the space between them, "I have loved you almost my entire life. I know I haven't always treated you the way you deserved, but nothing is going to get between us now."

"He's your f-father. If my biological father showed up, searching me, loving me...." March trailed off, his eyes far away, "I would do anything to have a parent that loved me,"

I rushed toward him, seeing those first tears fall. "I can't take away your pain but know that I will always be here. I will always be here." I pulled him down, hugging him close to my chest, forcing him to bend down to me. I continued to repeat the words as sobs racked his body. Hatter joined us, pulling us down toward the bed, whispering his own words. I could feel the drips of both of their tears falling on my exposed skin, and soon my own mixed with them. We had all been through so much, and at every turn a new challenge appeared, but these moments... the moments where we could hold each other, suffer together. They were the most important. I could almost feel our souls melding, our hearts beating the same rhythm.

"Oh, better not interrupt the tear fest," Cheshire stood awkwardly in the door next to Caterpillar who immediately slapped the back of his head. Caterpillar crossed the space, wrapping his large arms around all of our shoulders, a kiss pressed into the top of my head, and a whispered, "I'm sorry." Was all he had to say.

Cheshire joined our huddled, and we all stood, holding each other. No words were spoken as we soaked in the comfort of each other.

Eventually, it all had to end, a sharp knock on the front door pulled us out of the moment. Caterpillar stomped off, I heard his muttered annoyance as he opened the door, "Guys... you need to come here now."

The urgency in his voice had us all nearly running down the hallway to see who was at the door. Duchess stood in the doorframe. Her usually tan face almost white, eyes swollen from shed tears. "We have a huge problem."

Chapter 5

"I-I-I found it when I got home," Duchess was shivering so hard the cup of tea I'd shoved in her hands was shaking dangerously. Brown droplets dripped over her hand, but she didn't move to wipe them away. I used the sleeve of my jacket to wipe them away

"I sent Griffin over to clean it up, Viv," Cheshire laid a hand on her shoulder, trying to comfort her.

A butchered rabbit had been found hanging from her apartment door with the word 'traitor' written in blood. "It screams something my mother would do," She grimaced as she spoke.

This wasn't the first time that Duchess had been accosted or threatened since she joined us. It was certainly the most cruel and violent. "I'm working on moving you into this building. There's an empty apartment directly below us. We're getting it habitable for you." Caterpillar chimed in.

I breathed a sigh of relief. I didn't want my cousin to be stuck alone in that building after some crazy person did this to her. No one other than us should have even known where she lived. "You'll stay in the guest room until your new place is set up. I don't want you alone for a few days at least. We'll send the guys over to get your things." I said to her; a yawn left my mouth immediately after the words. I mumbled, "I'm sorry."

"I know I interrupted your night, I'm sorry," Duchess said, standing, "I'll go to the guest room—"

"You are fine, we're here for you. I know you have to be terrified," I tried to comfort her.

"We both know my mother did far worse to prove a point or trigger magick in me." She trailed off, a haunted look in her cognac eyes. She stood, leaving the room before I could say another word. I looked toward the guys, hoping they had some wisdom on how to help Duchess. Unfortunately, all I found was exhaustion in their faces.

"Why don't you all head to bed? I'm going to talk to her." I sighed. Duchess was hard to connect with, but I wasn't going to give up on her.

They didn't try to argue as I left the room. I stood outside the guest room for a moment before knocking, a muffled response had me opening the door. Duchess was sitting on the edge of the large bed, staring at her feet. "You don't have to pretend you care, Alice."

"I'm not pretending," I shot back, taking a seat next to her. "I can't pretend I know what you've been through with your mother, but I want to. We're family."

"Our mothers were half-sisters, and we didn't meet until you removed mine from power. You've done enough for me, giving me some kind of life in the city." She argued.

"I didn't do that because I felt bad. I did it because I see who you are Vivica." I paused, thinking, "We aren't our parents."

"Says the one following the exact life path her mother planned for her." Her words cut deeper than she intended, and I inhaled a sharp breath. In a way, she was right. My mother had known I would be the one to put an end to the Red Party. She had made plans for me to do so before I could even properly wipe my own butt.

"I'm going to let that one go because I know you are hurting, but don't ever say some shit like that again." I thought carefully on what I was going to say next, "I wanted to open a bakery."

Duchess looked at me confused, so I continued, "I never intended to lead Wonderland. All I was trying to do was save Lily and Dina. I didn't expect anything that followed."

"Oh, poor pitiful Alice, has to marry four men and be the leader of the city. Must be so hard," She stood as she ranted, "My parents had me by accident. You know they didn't even want children. When I wasn't ignored, I was bullied. The only potential love my mother could have had for me was if I had any power. I'm completely powerless, not an ounce of whatever genetics our mothers share passed onto me. My father at least tried to pretend he cared with lavish gifts, but I've never been loved a single day of my life." I sat in silence for several minutes, trying to find words. I knew she'd been treated badly. Before I could find my words, Duchess continued, "I envy you. Everyone loves you. You're the most powerful person in Wonderland. You'll never understand what I've been through. What I'm still going through." A sob cut off anything else she wanted to say.

I rushed to pull her into a hug, not letting her words bother me. "I can't change what they did to you, but I'll do anything I can to make your life better now. If you'll let me. I care about you." I spoke as she cried in my arms.

"I wish I could believe that." She pulled away, "I'd like to go to bed now."

With those words, I was dismissed. So I wandered toward the living room as I thought on her words, knowing sleep wouldn't find me now. Duchess wasn't entirely wrong, I had so much good in my life. It would be blind of me to ignore all the blessings I'd been given by the Creator, but things were far from perfect. My relationship with my mother had always had an undercurrent that I couldn't explain. She looked at me sometimes as if she was both terrified and awed. A look on her face I could remember as far back as my memory would go. I didn't dare bring it up, too afraid of what her explanation would be. At least my mother loved me. She'd suffered years of torture at her sister's hands just to protect Lily and I. I couldn't imagine how Penthea could treat her daughter so badly. I flinched as my mind conjured images of her, of her memories. I still woke up from nightmares sometimes. Images of my mother's torture, of the sheer number of people my aunt had killed and maimed without remorse.

"Those are some pretty deep thoughts you must be having," Cheshire's voice startled me.

"Duchess got me thinking." Was the only answer I provided.

Cheshire sat next to me at the kitchen table, intertwining our fingers. "Just remember, she's been through a lot."

"I know. I wish there was more I could do for her. For everyone. Did you see how exhausted Hatter looked? How are we going to deal with his father?"

"Together." He sighed, "We're going to do it together. That's all that matters."

"I wish I could believe that, but I have a terrible feeling I just can't shake."

"Please don't say that." Cheshire whined, "I trust your instincts, and if you feel like bad shit is coming... it probably is."

"I'm sorry, Ches. I shouldn't be stressing about an imaginary problem when we have enough to worry about."

"Don't apologize. You know you can tell me anything." He kissed my knuckles. "Let's go to bed, a fresh day will bring fresh eyes on our situation."

"You go ahead. I need some more time."

"No room for argument, Al. Let's go. I need my beauty sleep. If you're not around, Caterpillar will keep me up all night. You know how handsy he gets in his sleep."

I choked out a laugh, giving him the chance to yank me up from the table and toward our bedroom. A yawn escaped me, and I decided not to fight it anymore.

January 24th, 2159

I woke up alone. The silence of the apartment was oppressive, forcing me out of bed. Before the Queen of Hearts made her appearance a few months ago I hadn't woken up alone since we moved in. At least one of the guys had always been in bed with me, but now... sometimes it felt like we were right back in the fight with the Red Queen. Only now we had gotten so close to each other that it almost physically hurt when we didn't see each other enough.

I stood in our kitchen, staring at the note on the counter:

Sorry to leave you alone Al. Hatter's Dad showed up this morning. He's gone off to talk with him. March and I are going to Vivica's apartment. Caterpillar grumbled and left without an explanation. Love always – Cheshire.

I sighed. This was our life for now, but things would change, things would be peaceful eventually. I had to believe that.

"Oh..." Duchess's voice startled me, "I-"

"It's fine. I was just going to make some breakfast. Would you like to join me?" I stopped her, the awkward look on her face made me cringe.

She sat down at the island, watching me as I quickly threw together some yogurt with fresh fruit and honey. When I sat it down in front of her, she stared into the bowl as if it would bite her.

"I didn't poison it," I joked.

"I can't remember the last time someone made me food," She whispered.

My heart sank, "The joke was distasteful. Please eat and enjoy."

I didn't make eye contact with Duchess, but I did watch as she picked up her spoon, taking her first bite of food. A quiet moan slipped out, and she met my eyes, giving me a small nod. I smiled at her and began to dig into my food with vigor. Our food was eaten in a comfortable silence, and I appreciated her company. "I can't believe you liberated all those people, and they still agreed to keep the city running with their magick." She finally spoke.

"Honestly? I was shocked, but I think they knew the city would crumble without them. Plus, we gave them every comfort we possibly could. They get plenty of rest now… No one makes any demands of them."

"I'm just glad we have fresh food to eat." She responded.

"Me too." I said, "What are your plans for the day?"

"I am off today. It's Ilaria's day to handle the paperwork." She responded.

I thought for a moment, sifting through my mental calendar, and realized I didn't have anything to do today either. "Would you like to have a girl's day? I have coupons for a spa day at the Porcelain Mouse."

"How did you get those?" she asked, shocked.

"I have my ways." In reality, the owner had been so grateful for being allowed to work again after the Red Party had shut her business down. She still sent me coupons every couple of months. I think she just wanted to be on my good side, but I wasn't going to let them go to waste. I always tipped everyone well enough it made up for any discount she gave me.

Duchess snorted, "You are a dork." I laughed, looping my arm through hers as I led her out of the apartment.

A groan left my lips as the masseuse rubbed her hands up and down my calves. Duchess groaned next to me as well. I turned my head slightly, watching as the buff brunette man used his elbow to massage down her spine.

"This is exactly what I needed," She said to me, "Thank you."

"Anytime. Dina doesn't feel comfortable getting massages, so she refuses to come with me." I responded.

"Dina is a sweet girl..." She trailed off, "I am sorry for what my mother did to her. I've heard the two of you talk about her nightmares."

"You aren't to blame— "

Duchess cut me off, "I knew what my mother was doing, and I made a choice to do nothing. You and the guys are the only people in all of Wonderland who don't blame me."

"You tried, Vivica. The information you fed Cheshire helped us stop her." She didn't respond, and I went back to focusing on the feeling of the stress leaving my body. I knew Duchess had been harassed by her old friends and random citizens since we had brought her into the fold. I didn't realize until last night how much she was going through. Of course, I didn't know how to truly help her, but maybe she just needed a friend.

"Will you ladies be going to the mud baths today?" The woman asked as she stepped away from me.

"I'd love—" My phone ringing cut me off. I answered it, "Alice."

"Meet me at the Grove. We've got a big problem." Caterpillar was nearly growling into the phone.

"Be there in fifteen, I've got to put clothes on." I rushed to say.

"You're not home? Where are you naked?" If it was possible his voice lowered even more.

"Decided to take a girl's day with Vivica," I responded, reaching down to pull my pants on.

"How is she doing?" He asked. I glanced toward her watching as she stood, a towel wrapped around her lithe body.

"Not good, but better than last night." I tried to be cryptic as I responded.

"Good. See you soon, princess. Love you." He had hung up before I could respond.

"You need to leave." Duchess looked disappointed.

"Yes, but please stay and enjoy all the spa has to offer. It's already paid for."

"Are you sure?" She asked.

"Absolutely. Call Lily and she will pick you up. I don't want to risk you walking home alone." I instructed her.

Suddenly, she threw her arms around me. "Thank you for doing this. I am so sorry for what I said to you last night. I'm a bitch sometimes."

"Don't worry about it. Runs in the family." I grinned as she pulled away.

I finished dressing and rushed out of the spa. It wasn't a terribly long walk from the spa to the Grove, but I'd promised I'd be there in fifteen minutes, so I broke into a sprint. Weaving around crowds of people, some shouted in greeting, but most were just careful to get out of my way. I ran through all the possibilities of what could be wrong. There was enough going on right now I couldn't be certain what had happened. I slowed down as I approached the metal building, vines creeping up the side. It was much busier than it had been the last time we'd been here. I had insisted that businesses could no longer deny anyone service so long as they could afford the product. Elitism wasn't going to continue to poison Wonderland if I could help it. I took a deep breath, preparing myself as I pushed the door open. All I could see was chaos, voices overlapping as they shouted at each other. I searched for Caterpillar, as all the sound began to give me a headache. I tried to make out what they were saying, catching a few snippets.

"It can't be,"

"What if he's right?"

"They're too young to deal with this."

I weaved through the crowd, finally finding the source of the panic. Hatter's father was standing at the front of the room looking smug. Caterpillar was off to the side, clearly having a heated argument with my mother. I approached cautiously, trying to hear exactly what they were saying.

"Roman, you cannot send him back outside the city. He has created a panic, if he disappears, no one is going to trust that we didn't end him. They will assume we are just like the Red Party."

"The fact he's created panic is exactly why we need him gone," Caterpillar growled.

"Think of Hayden!" My mother was seething, "How will he feel if you banish his father?"

I finally stopped eavesdropping, making my presence known, "What the fuck is going on?"

"Joshua has revealed that just outside the city, there are some concerning signs of natural disasters." My mother said.

"We've known that Earth has been resetting itself. That's how we ended up the last human city a hundred and fifty-two years ago." I furrowed my brows; all this panic was over information we already knew.

"He's implied that something is causing it, and it's going to begin to affect what is inside the boundaries." She spoke quietly.

"How could he possibly know that?" Fear gripped me. If the magick that clearly protected the city failed, how could we possibly survive?

"I'm not sure. He's refused to explain anymore until the rest of our counsel is here." Caterpillar growled. I stepped into his arms, hoping I could help him calm down.

"Where is Hatter?"

"On his way. They got into another argument." He took a deep breath, "I think that's why Joshua has done this. He wants us to know we aren't in control."

"I'll fry him where he stands if it would make you feel better," I offered. He looked at me disapprovingly, "Just a little zap?"

Caterpillar finally smiled, "As much as it would satisfy me. Your mother is right. He is Hatter's father. We have to try to get along."

"To what end? It's clear he's trying to hurt all of us." He shot back.

I didn't have an answer for him. I stared Joshua down, he met my eyes but didn't acknowledge me. I heard more than saw Cheshire arrive, "Move it, people. Really, folks. Why are you all acting like panicked children?"

March and Cheshire both stepped into the corner we'd taken over. "What's the rub?"

"More of Joshua's bullshit," I said, simply.

"Joy of joys." March rolled his eyes.

More and more people filed into the Grove. Lily waved to us as she found a seat, Idalia standing behind her. Those two were seldom apart, although they still hadn't made anything official.

"I'm here, Dad. Can you please explain what the fuck is going on?" Hatter was nearly yelling when he finally made his way in.

Joshua cleared his throat, "Many of you may know that I left Wonderland many years ago. I was seeking answers about the world outside the city. It's been so long since the supposed end," I caught the glare he leveled at my mother, though I didn't understand why. "Surely, if there was any extinction event the world outside would be safe by now." He paused before continuing, I was certain it was for dramatic effect, "I found it is not. Predators roam barely tolerable conditions. I explored, unable to find home again." He bent down, bringing attention to his missing leg, "I lost my leg to a wolf triple the size of the largest dog in the city. When I finally started to make my way home, I was fighting through earthquakes, dangerous heat, and cold waves. As I got to the edge of the city, vines were climbing over some invisible shield. It's clear to me they were trying to pull it down."

Silence reigned over the room as he finished. Without thought, I stepped up next to Joshua and began speaking. "We cannot thank Hatter's father enough for bravely fighting to share this information with us. Currently, we've seen no signs inside the city of this danger, but I want each and every one of you to trust this. We will do everything we can to protect this city. If the shield on the city was created by magick, we will find a way to reinforce it. Wonderland will always be our priority. Don't doubt Roman and I will do anything to protect this city and all of you."

Caterpillar stepped up next to me, effectively drawing any attention away from Joshua. "We will keep everyone updated on any information we find. This will be our second priority after protecting the city from the Queen of Hearts. Please, go home, and hug your families. Don't let this information prevent you from living your lives as normal."

The entire room breathed a sigh of relief, and slowly people began to leave. A few stopped to speak to us, but most filed out silently. Eventually, we were left with our core group, in an empty restaurant.

"What the hell was that, Dad?" Hatter was seething as his father came toward us. He grabbed him by the shirt, "You could have created a mass panic. What was your goal? To undermine us?"

"Hayden, baby, it's okay." I laid a hand on his shoulder, gently pulling him away. I glared at Joshua as I pushed Hatter away from him, "Let me make something perfectly clear. I don't care about your feelings about our leadership skills, relationship, or frankly anything else. If you ever risk this city again, I will end you."

"Okay, Al. Not any better than what Hatter had to say," Cheshire yanked me away, then smoothed his shirt as he turned to speak to Joshua. "Sorry, they're all a little protective of Wonderland. You don't know the sacrifices we've all made to bring peace to this city. I'm sure you can remember how bad it was getting when you left. The effects of the Red Party haven't been completely eradicated. These people are fragile."

"That has nothing to do with me. They have a right to know what is coming," Joshua snarked.

"You are absolutely right, but in the future if you would please talk to us. We are reasonable people, we want to protect the city, but there is a safe way to go about that." Cheshire was calm. I was shocked at how reasonable he was being.

"Joshua, I've tried to tell you. Join our group, help us lead this city to the very best it can be." My mother chimed in.

Hatter's father stood silently, taking all of us in. "For the record, I'm with Alice. I think we should fry him now and damn the consequences." March spoke, quietly.

Joshua turned a surprisingly hurt look to him, "Maxton, I'm sorry for whatever harm I've caused you. I'm just worried for you and Hayden both. Everything I've seen... it's deeply concerning. You are like my son too. I want what is best for both of you."

"And it's not even a little homophobic?" March shot back.

My eyebrows raised into my hairline. Joshua gritted his teeth, "Your sexualities have never been any of my business. I just worry that you have never healed from what happened to you as a child. If you had been willing to see a different doctor—"

"Dad, drop it." Hatter said, quietly, "Please...just stop."

"Hayden...." Joshua reached for his son, but when Hatter brushed him away to move toward March, I saw pain in his face.

"I love these people. I know you don't understand it. I've already told you I don't care. Why can't you respect my choices? I am not a child." Hatter snapped at him, a note of begging to his voice.

"I-I..." Joshua was lost for words.

Lily was the one who spoke. "I think we all need to part ways for today. You've given us a lot of information to absorb sir. We appreciate the warning, and I truly hope you'll join us as we investigate and seek a solution."

Joshua nodded, and without another word, picked up his walking stick and exited the room.

"That was fucking intense," Cheshire breathed.

"I have s-s-something I need to tell you all," March said.

"What's going on baby?" I asked, reaching to pull him into my arms, resting my head against his shoulder.

"I... I know I shouldn't have kept this to myself..." March was choking on his words, "D-Dodo got my mother out."

"Fuck..."

Chapter 6

❧❧❧❧❧ ❧❧❧❧❧

Hatter

March was collapsed on the ground of our apartment sobbing. Nothing any of us had done calmed him down since he dropped the news at the Grove. My head was spinning, I couldn't process everything that had happened over the last few days. I hadn't even dealt with crashing the Hummer. I grimaced at those thoughts, bringing forth blurry images of my mother. I had chosen the Hummer because I vividly remembered my mother playing with me, racing little cars together. One of them had been a bright yellow truck. I couldn't be mad at Cheshire or Alice for wrecking it. The blame lay solely with the Queen of Hearts. I hated that our plan to draw her out hadn't worked. Maybe it would have if my dad hadn't shown up. Thinking of him caused my fists to curl. How dare he barge back into my life and upset all the people I loved.

"We aren't going to let them hurt you, March. They have no power over us." Alice had been trying to soothe March for an hour. I could see the strain on her face as she rubbed her hand on his back.

The only response March gave was several sniffs and a slight choking sound. Cheshire glanced toward them from his sprawled-out position on the couch. Caterpillar was stooped over his notebook, writing frantically. I'd noticed him doing that more and more, but I hadn't considered actually asking him about it. We all had so much going on, I don't think we had the time to communicate all of it.

"Can we eat some dinner?" I could tell Ches was trying to distract everyone from the news, but he was failing. Alice sent a glare his way, before turning pleading eyes to me.

"Maxton, other than knowing Dodo got Claudia out has anything else happened?" I asked.

"N-n-no." He responded, looking up at me as I approached him.

"Then we are not going to create problems that don't exist yet. If they come looking, we will handle it. For now, you are not to go anywhere alone. That will protect you from them catching you alone." I had to be stern even domineering with March. I enjoyed that in the bedroom, but there were times it exhausted me. Alice was the only person I could be gentle with, "Is that okay?"

I could see him thinking through my words, weighing them. Finally, he nodded. "I think Cheshire is right. Why don't we have some dinner, and try to relax."

Caterpillar stood and silently entered the kitchen. He had become our primary chef. After March was tucked into my side on the opposite couch from Cheshire. Alice exited the room following after Caterpillar. The two of them bonded over cooking. A sad smile curled up on my face, I thought back to our first night in the warehouse, the first time I tasted Alice. I hardened at the thought but adjusted quickly. Now was not the time for any sexual behaviors.

"Hatter, what's really going on with your Dad?" Cheshire blurted out.

I gritted my teeth at the question but stopped myself from lashing out, "I don't know. Most of our conversations have revolved around relationship drama and where the hell he's been for ten years."

"His explanation didn't make much sense, right?" He countered.

I hadn't considered that, but I ran through his speech mentally and came to the same conclusion. "He's definitely not being entirely truthful…" I trailed off unsure what to take from that realization.

"How do you feel about what he's saying about us? Don't lie. I know you have to feel something about it." Cheshire asked.

I chose my words carefully, glancing down at March before I began speaking. "My love for you all trumps anything my father has to say."

"That's good to hear, but honestly… it's bullshit. The rest of us either have dead or deadbeat parents. Well… Alice and her mother are close, but," Cheshire lowered his voice, "We all know there's some tension there."

I couldn't argue with that. Alice adored her mother, agreed with most of what she had to say, and sought her out for comfort. I'd give Alcinda, she was a fantastic support for my girl. Something still felt off about it. In well over a year I hadn't been able to put my finger on it. At first, I thought it was just her mother's guilt for Alice growing up without parents, but it was something more than that. I shook my head, it wasn't any of my business what their relationship was like. At least Alice had her family. "At first I was in disbelief, now I'm just… sad." I stopped for a moment, absorbing the truth of that statement. "I was an adult when he left by every technicality, but children still need their parents at any age. Being freshly eighteen and him choosing to leave for such a dangerous mission for seemingly no reason. I don't know that I can ever really forgive him for that."

"You don't have to," Alice said, leaning against the door between the kitchen and living room. "Feel what you feel about it. It was his choice to go off on some half-cocked adventure."

I could feel the indignation coming off of her from here. Alice would always wear her heart on her sleeve, no matter the subject. I took her in; she had her hair pulled back in a high ponytail drawing attention to her sharp cheekbones and piercing blue eyes. She was wearing one of my shirts, it was falling over her shoulder, revealing her collarbone. My eyes trailed to her exposed cleavage. For her stature, she had average-sized breasts, but they were perky and always bouncing around when she walked. Looking down her body to the curve her hips had me imagining the feel of my hands gripping them as I slid into her.

"Fuck…" I muttered, once again having turned myself on. I cleared my throat, hoping no one noticed, "I know you're right. I just need some time to figure things out."

"I'll be here to support you no matter what conclusion you come to," I ignored the slight pain in her eyes. Alice would end our relationship if she felt it would be best for me. The thought had anger rising in my chest. I stood, marching toward her. "Do not ever doubt that you are more important to me than my father. My family is in these walls. If he threatens that…" I trailed off again. I didn't know exactly what I would do if he put me in that position, but I meant every word I had said.

"I love you," She stood on her tiptoes, pressing a quick kiss to my lips.

"You are my world," I whispered into her ear.

She crinkled her nose, a grin on her face, "Don't be gross."

"Tell them dinner is ready, or I'm going to eat all of it," Caterpillar shouted from the other room.

"No blowjobs for a week if I don't get any dinner," Alice shot back.

Caterpillar rounded the corner like lightning, grabbing her around the waist, "Oh really? Maybe I should just feed you cock for dinner tonight." He backed her into the wall, towering over her.

She smirked, "Oh, should I get 'eat me' tattooed over my pussy?"

"If you mar your pussy with a single dot of ink. I… Well, I'll find some way to punish you." He was clearly at a loss for words.

"Terrifying Cater baby. I'm shaking in my fuzzy socks." I glanced down to her feet, confirming that she was wearing bright purple fuzzy socks. She ducked under his arms and entered the kitchen. I could hear the sounds of her setting the table.

"She's going to be the death of me," Caterpillar mumbled as he followed after her.

I smiled, I couldn't have been more pleased with the people I shared my life with. No matter what happened I knew I would always be safe and happy with them.

January 25th, 2159

I turned, pulling a warm body into my chest. "As much I love you, Hayden. Please stop cuddling me." Cheshire's voice woke me up.

"Where's Alice?" I asked, groggily. I sat up, finding that we were the only two still in bed.

"No clue. I heard Caterpillar wake March up for training a couple of hours ago, but I never heard her leave." He responded, rolling out of bed, and stretching.

I picked my phone up, checking for any texts. Unfortunately, the only one I had was from Dad, asking to meet and chat again today. I groaned internally, debating on if I should respond. I typed a quick response and slammed my phone back down.

I padded toward the bathroom, taking care of business, and taking an efficient shower. I searched the apartment after, looking for a note from Alice. When I found nothing, I sighed and decided to make my way toward the gym in the basement. I found Caterpillar holding the punching bag as

March rained punch after punch into it. Sweat was dripping down his face, his chestnut brown hair hanging into his eyes. I could see a few tears mixing with the sweat, but tried to ignore it. March had things he was working through, and while I would support him, I was going to wait for him to come to me to talk.

"Sup, Hayden?" Caterpillar grunted as March landed a particularly hard hit.

"Have you seen Alice?"

"Nah, she was in bed when we came down here." He quirked an eyebrow at me. "Maybe she's with Dina? Elsie was fussy yesterday, they probably need a break."

"Thanks. I'll check there." I left the room. It was good for Caterpillar and March to bond. They'd never argued, but I always thought Caterpillar felt March was weak. He'd never outright said anything, but it was clear he didn't expect much of anything from him. Even before Alice came around, Caterpillar had kept March at a distance. He's always given him less to do than Cheshire and I. I climbed the stairs, knocking as quietly as possible on Dina's door.

Griffin answered, shirtless and groggy. "What?"

"Is Alice here?" I asked.

"No. You need anything else? This is the first time Elsie has been down since yesterday morning. I need sleep." I waved, walking away so they could rest.

I was out of ideas, so I decided to shoot her a text.

Maddie: *Where were you this morning* □. *I needed your attention.*

I leaned against the wall outside our apartment waiting for her response. I didn't have anything pressing to do today. None of our people had gotten back to Caterpillar yet about the Jabberwocky sighting so I was twiddling my thumbs for now. Last night after the debacle with my father, I'd quietly asked Patrick to investigate the edges of the border in the boonies. If he found any evidence of any weakening he was supposed to get back to me.

My phone dinged, and I was disappointed to find my father had finally responded.

Dad: I could go for coffee. Meet now?

I sighed, deciding it was at least kill some time to talk to him. It wasn't a long walk to the café down the street. He was standing outside when I approached.

"Thanks for seeing me. I wanted to apologize for yesterday. I didn't intend to upset your friends—" Dad started.

"They're my life partners, Dad." I sighed as I corrected him.

"Right. Right." He rubbed his neck awkwardly, "Your...partners. I was genuinely concerned when I brought up what I saw outside the city. I don't want anything to happen to you."

"You left me in a city with a corrupt government, while you galivanted to Creator knows where. I have a hard time believing you're overly concerned for my safety." I snapped.

"I deserve that. I didn't consider when I left that you would be alone... I am glad you have people that have supported you." Even though I could tell the words were hard to say I did appreciate them.

"I'm not trying to be snappy. Your arrival came at a bad time. We're dealing with a new threat, and we are at a loss." I admitted.

"How can I help?" There was hope in his eyes as he clasped my shoulder, leading us inside.

Once we'd sat down with our coffees, I started talking and didn't stop until I was out of breath. It felt good to get everything off my chest. To finally have a parent again. Dad sat staring at me over the top of his coffee cup. I glanced down at the swirling brown of my coffee, suddenly regretting all of the information I'd just given him. If he wanted to hurt all the people, I loved he now had all the information he would need to do that. I looked up, he must have seen the panic in my eyes, because he said, "I'm so proud of the man you've become."

Against my will a tear slipped down my face. I swiped it away, "Seriously Hayden. You have so much on your shoulders. I'm not sure I could handle everything that you've taken on. I'm sorry for the stress I've caused."

I was speechless, staring into green eyes that looked just like my own. "Please stop discouraging my relationship."

His eyes widened, "You have to understand—"

I held up my hand, "I do. I know who you are, and I've heard your opinion. I know how you feel. I am telling you man to man, this isn't something I am going to do any differently. I love Alice and March. I care for Caterpillar and Cheshire. This isn't up for negotiation."

We sat in silence, a clear line drawn in the sand. Eventually, my father cleared his throat. "We need to focus on what I've seen outside the dome anyway."

"Why do you call it a dome?" I asked, glad he changed the subject. At least we had an understanding of some kind.

"Outside of the city, a sheer golden dome shimmers over the entire area. It prevents anything out there from getting in here. Trust me, I tried to get back in for years and couldn't. Obviously, something has changed, since I'm here." My mouth dropped open at his explanation.

"It's magick..." My brain ran through every possibility. We already knew that, but it being so visible. I never expected that. "I need to bring Alice into this."

He inclined his head, and I typed on my phone calling her number.

"I was wondering when one of her little harem would call. If you want your bitch back, you'll do exactly as I say. I can't promise she's going to stay in one piece for much longer. I want to sample what she has to offer so badly."

"Jabberwocky," I growled. I felt nauseous at what he was implying. How the fuck did he end up with Alice's phone. I couldn't believe he really had her.

"You'll be hearing from me again soon. Bye-bye for now." He hung up before I could say anything else.

I gripped my phone so hard I heard it crack. I stared down at the busted screen. "Hayden, what's wrong?"

"I-I..." I couldn't think, the panic welling in my chest was taking over, "They might have her. They might have Alice."

Before he could respond, I broke into a run. Racing toward home, praying this wasn't real. That my girl was laying in our bed curled up with March.

Chapter 7

Caterpillar

I slammed my fist into the nearest wall as Rab continued speaking, "We're scouring the city, Roman. There's nothing more we can do until he calls, or we find them."

"If a single hair on her head is hurt, I will burn the entire city to the ground to make up for this," I growled. How could we have missed Jabberwocky grabbing Alice? I can't believe I wasn't concerned when none of us knew where she was. I'd find a way to track her every movement from now on. I'd never let her out of my sight when I had her back.

"She's fine. I'm sure of it. Remember, Cater she's stronger than all of us." Cheshire gripped my shoulder, "You need to rinse your hand, you're bleeding all over the floor."

"She is just one woman." I was nearly yelling. Alice wasn't some invincible goddess. She may be powerful, but she wasn't the Creator. It was our job to protect her, and we had failed. Too focused on other bullshit to pay attention to the most important thing in our lives. "You need to get on your Creator damned computer and figure this out, Sinclair." I knew using his real name would spur him to get away from me. I needed to be alone to think.

"Fuck you." My eyebrows shot up at Cheshire's tone, "You act like everything is on your shoulders. Or that you are the only one that cares for Al. She's my wife too."

"She's not our wife yet." March's dejected voice piped into the conversation. I swung toward him, seething, but when I saw his face, I paused. I'd noticed a fire in his eyes recently. A monster was lurking under March's skin, and if we didn't nurture it... March was so close to a breakdown. "Go to your corners b-boys. Arguing isn't finding her."

My respect for the skinny man rose. I'd never been particularly close to March until I noticed that monster. I saw it in training one day, a strange light in his eyes as he pummeled a training dummy. Since then, I had started paying more attention to him, trying to grow our relationship. He needed real support. I understood better than anyone the violence he was craving. Alice saw it too, we'd talked about it a time or two, but she was worried. I wasn't. I knew what was coming. When March blew it would be fiery, I needed to be there to extinguish it. Hatter would never stop babying March. While I respected their relationship, March needed to be treated like a grown man. Running steps had me turning quickly, Hatter was panting and holding his broken phone aloft. "I've got him."

I snatched the phone away from him, putting it to my ear, "Dnais."

"Ainsworth. I should have known they'd get you. Their mighty leader." I could hear the sneer in his voice. It was easy to imagine the curl of his lip. Rage ate me alive inside, but I forced myself to respond.

"Where's my wife." The phone creaked in my ear as I gripped it.

"Oh, that's not how this is going to work. You have twenty-four hours to meet my demands, then I'm going to start slowly tearing parts off of her."

"When I find you, Dnais, I'm going to take my time peeling your skin off," I growled.

"Ah ah. My demands." He reminded me, his amusement clear.

"I need proof you have her before I do a goddamn thing." There were several noises in the background, before a very groggy female voice spoke, "When I get done with you. I promise you'll wish you'd never been born."

A slap rang out through the phone, "She's awfully insolent. You really didn't train her well."

"I trained her perfectly." I couldn't see I was so angry, "What the fuck do you want?" I would break every finger that had touched her.

"Five thousand dollars, an escort out of the city, and your best guns." Silence reigned as he spoke. "I'll call again in a couple of hours to get your answer. Better hurry, I might have to punish the little lioness."

The line went dead before I could respond. I had to stop myself from throwing the phone against the wall. "He's in the city. Cheshire analyze the call for any noises we can place. Hatter, get in touch with your contacts. Find out if anyone knows anything about Dnais Umbrell."

"How do you know his real name? Why haven't you mentioned this sooner?" Hatter was glaring at me, but I didn't have the time to care.

"It's personal. I've got things to attend to. Meet back here in one hour." I dismissed them, storming out of the apartment.

I paced the alleyway, trying to ignore the stench wafting from garbage piled around the metal door. I had turned my phone off before coming here, praying that I was correct about my theory. I heard the door creak open, so I jumped grabbing the tiny man whose head peaked out. Slamming him into the brick wall, feet dangling above the ground.

"Where is Jabberwocky?" I growled at him.

"Caterpillar. I wasn't expecting you." Jubjub hadn't changed a bit, his beady eyes darting anywhere, but my face.

"Answer the question." I shook him slightly, trying to get my point across.

"I-I-I haven't seen Jabberwocky since your woman took over the city. He's disappeared along with all of my Red Party contacts." He was clearly panicking now.

"We both know that isn't true. I've had you followed for months. You've been doing some very interesting runs to the boonies." I smirked when his face dropped. I had left him alone, hoping that our tails would catch bigger fish. I'd never worried about Jubjub, he played both sides, for his own safety.

He started to struggle against my hold. Which was completely useless but admirable, nonetheless. Eventually he gave up, "Why don't we go inside and discuss this, civilized-like."

I sat him down, hoping he wouldn't run off. I wasn't really in the mood for a chase today. Instead, he swung the door open, leading me down a dimly lit hallway. He pushed another door open, pointing me toward a ratty chair. I raised an eyebrow, "Sit. I'll have to get my papers together."

I paced for a minute refusing to rest while Alice was in the hands of Jabberwocky. I knew exactly what Dnais Umbrell was capable of. I'd been surprised he hadn't recognized me that night in the alley when Alice tried to seduce him. We'd gone to school together and even played rugby. I'd always known something was off about him. He enjoyed violence at a young age. When we had reached puberty, rumors began swirling about the girls he took out. I'd been too wrapped up in my parents' death to really deal with it. When we graduated and he'd entered the Suits training, rising to the top so quickly I hadn't been surprised. Until one night when

I was twenty-one. I witnessed him snap the neck of the girl he'd been fucking in an alley behind the Hearts Club. I hadn't realized how deeply he was fucked up. Now he had the woman I loved, a woman he'd already threatened. I knew Alice was capable, I just didn't understand how she'd even ended up with him.

"Here's everything I have about what Jabberwocky has been getting from me. I swear I have nothing else to do with them. I don't want any trouble." Jubjub was shaking when he handed me the stack of papers.

"You shouldn't have been helping anyone in the Red Party if you didn't want a visit."

"Jabberwocky has been threatening my wife. He'll kill us both when he realizes I gave you this information." The man snapped.

I suddenly felt guilty. I grabbed a pen and paper off the desk and jotted down Cheshire's number. "Call this number. He'll help you both get to safety. We really aren't monsters."

Tears welled in his eyes, "Jabberwocky grabbed Alice in the sixth district. I saw her entering."

My eyes widened. I couldn't be angry that he hadn't told me immediately, I'd terrified him. "Thank you. Pack up and call that number. We'll do everything we can."

I exited the building, flipping through the papers he'd given me. Most of the orders were for food and other basic necessities. An order for some rifles was concerning. I'd hand the papers to Hatter, to see if he recognized any of the names. He'd grown a decent network throughout the city and boonies. He was far more likely to know who people were. Without thought I turned my body toward sector six. I hadn't planned to walk there really, but I couldn't stop myself. I had no idea why Alice would've been picking through the old remains. It was dangerous, buildings still occasionally collapsed. The debris and dust made it unsafe. What did she know that the rest of us didn't? We'd had so many conversations about not hiding our plans from each other. Especially after her stunt with the boonies. The walk was long, and I found myself staring up at the sky, squinting to see if I could see the dome that Hatter's father had described. Nothing about the grey sky gave any hints. Alice was the expert on all things magick, we needed her to figure out all the information we'd gained from Joshua. I felt nauseous when I was standing on the sidewalk leading into the ruined sector. I inspected the closest building; it could have been a storefront or an apartment. It was impossible to tell. My parents had passed down what information they'd known that had led to the creation of Wonderland. All they'd know was that this sector of the city had been destroyed before the destruction of the city had been stopped. Something crunched under my boot, and I looked down, finding human bones crushed beneath me. I continued slowly picking my way further into the area, careful to avoid areas that were clearly unstable. Eventually, I stood at what I expected was the center of the destroyed maze of ruined buildings. I glanced around; the silence was eerie. I sat down on the edge of a large stone, running my hand over my head. If Alice was here, it mattered, but I had yet to see anything that was useful.

"You know she's not here." The raspy female voice had me reaching for my gun, turning toward the sound. When I swung around and found the grey head of an older woman I relaxed slightly. Her blue eyes glimmered at me, and recognition sparked. "You! Who the hell are you?"

The woman chuckled, "You aren't ready for those answers yet. Alice is getting close though. Coming here was her first step."

I sighed, "Do you have to be so cryptic?" Mischief shined in her eyes, causing my heart to squeeze. I'd seen the exact same look on Alice's face many times. "Just tell me what you know."

Her face became very serious, "Roman Ainsworth there are many things that I know. The least of which is that you are wasting precious time."

"I came here to figure out why Alice was taken from here. Clearly you know something about it." I snapped.

"Dnais Umbrell ambushed her, while she was investigating this area. He'd been following her for weeks." She explained.

"If you knew that, why not warn her?" I asked.

"There's only so much I can interfere with. Things will always happen the way they are meant to regardless of how we fight it. It is best to follow the flow of the universe." Her words were profound, but more cryptic messages I didn't have time to decode. "There will come a time where you understand. Right now, you need to get Alice to safety."

Frustration grew. Of course, I wanted to get her away from Jabberwocky. It was the only thing that mattered to me right now. I needed to get back to the guys to figure out what our plan was. Without any idea where he could hold her, we were stalled out. "Can you tell me anything useful?"

Several moments of silence passed, it was clear the woman was contemplating something. I tried to give her the space to do it, if she could give us anything it could make a huge difference. "I will tell you two things. Use the information wisely." She took a deep breath, "Alice is not in the city, but she isn't outside the boundaries. I don't know any specifics past that." It wasn't a lot to go on, but it was definitely helpful. In my haste, I started to walk away, but her next words stopped me in my tracks. "What you are contending with will change everything. Soon Alice and I will talk, but there are more things that must happen." Chills ran down my spine, I turned to speak, only to find the woman's eyes glowing. I stumbled away. "Go Roman. Do not return here without the girl."

I nearly ran out of the sector. I didn't stop moving until I was climbing the stairs to our apartment. When I opened the door, I found Cheshire, Hatter, and March staring at me. Papers, food containers, and computers filled the space around them. Exhaustion was etched on all of their faces.

"We have a lot to talk about," I demanded.

Chapter 8

Alice

I was freezing. I had decided I had to be in some kind of walk-in freezer. I could see the breath puffing out of my lungs. They burned with every inhale, but that wasn't even my biggest concern. The blood I could feel dripping from my nose and wrists certainly was more worrisome. Yet somehow still not as concerning as Jabberwocky standing before me, a table of sharp objects before him. I forced my breathing to remain even, letting him see the panic I felt was not an option. Jabberwocky loved reaction, so he'd get none from me. He had muttered to himself for several minutes staring down at the tools, before finally turning toward me. I reached for my magic, but it was slumbering, locked away from my use.

"I've given your little harem time to get together what I requested. I just don't think I can stop myself from having a little fun with you." Jabberwocky gripped my hair, forcing me to look into his black eyes. "If I have any regrets, it's not taking you in that alleyway. It would have saved everyone so much trouble."

I said nothing, any hint of emotion would only encourage his insanity. "I can't harm you beyond repair until they fail their little mission." He tapped the knife he was holding against his chin, the grip on my hair easing slightly.

"I can understand why Roman is so obsessed with a young little lioness like you. So pretty, ripe for taking." I wanted to cringe; my mind raced for ways to distract him from where his mind was heading. When his phone began ringing, I sent a silent thanks to the Creator. His growl of frustration as he answered wasn't comforting. Without any warning, he slapped me so hard my ears rang. My face pounded, and I felt the swelling begin along my jawline. "It's done... You know I can't get her out until.... Fucks sake, woman. Leave me be." I was catching snippets of his conversation, "You'll have what you want in time." He slammed his phone down on a rickety table and turned back to me. The anger simmering in his eyes caused terror to rise in me. "Now where were we?"

He picked up his knife, it was seconds before the sting of a cut sliced down the cheek that was already pounding. I felt the warm blood begin running down my face. I bit down on the scream that desperately wanted to escape me. He growled when my only reaction was a slight jump. "You'll give me what I want, obviously I'm being far too gentle." With those words his fist connected with my sternum, causing all the breath to leave my lungs. He gripped my hair, forcing me to meet his eyes, "I don't know that I'll ever give you to the Queen." I couldn't stop my eyes from widening. "Ah, you didn't know. I've always worked for the Queen of Hearts, Penthea Rose is pathetic trash by comparison. Don't get me wrong, without her hard work, we never would have managed to destabilize the government in Wonderland. All you did was fall right into her plans. Your friends will never beat her, especially when you're out of their reach."

I had to stop a smile from splitting across my face. I had figured out Jabberwocky was following me the day before our second failed ceremony. I had hoped he'd reveal himself there, but instead he stood back and waited. When I'd gone to the sixth sector hoping to find answers on how Wonderland's barrier was erected, I'd known the moment he'd caught my trail. I hadn't expected him to grab me. Instinctually I reached for my magic, only to remember it had been neutralized. I expected it had something to do with the metal cuffs on my wrists. A few of the magick users that I'd rescued after the Red Party had been removed from power had mentioned similar things being used on them. I'd never come into contact with anything like it until now.

Jabberwocky regained my attention when his knife sliced my shirt open. He caressed it over the swell of my breasts, not putting enough pressure to cut. When he moved down toward my abdomen I had only a moment to prepare for the first of what would become many cuts.

I cracked my eyes open when the room was completely silent. I moved as much as I could while tied to the chair. My hips and legs had gone numb hours before, losing circulation. Moving caused the cuts that riddled my stomach and chest to pull, a tear leaked down my swollen face. I had no idea how long Jabberwocky had spent cutting me until I finally began to cry. That had been enough to end his torment. I knew it wouldn't last for long. I was slightly dizzy from blood loss, but I wouldn't let that stop me from trying to escape. I couldn't let Jabberwocky take me to the Queen of Hearts. While I had considered it, hoping it would give me insight into where she was hiding, I had no doubt she would end me quickly. If she was so much more powerful than the Red Queen, I'd seen no evidence of it, but I wasn't willing to risk it.

I couldn't wait for the guys to figure out where he was holding me. There was a chance they wouldn't be able to figure it out. I twisted my wrists hoping I could wiggle the cuffs off. When that plan failed, I start to rock back and forth, causing the chair to rattle. It was weak, and if I could create enough force, I could probably break it. Once it was rocking hard, I threw myself backward, the pressure of my weight on my shoulders caused a cracking sound. Pain ran down my arm, but I didn't stop moving. The legs had broken under me, giving me some freedom of movement. I used my free legs to stand, kicking the remnants of the rope and chair pieces away.

I half walked; half hopped toward the table with various sharp objects. I picked up the smallest item and used my unharmed left hand to find the lock. Then I inserted the tiny tip into the lock and jiggled and maneuvered it until the handcuffs fell away. I would have to thank Cheshire when I saw him. He'd sat with me until I could quickly pick any lock. I felt my magick flood back into my body, but I didn't have a moment to breathe a sigh of relief as I grabbed my left shoulder, forcing it back into place. I bit my lip to stop myself from making any noise.

I heard footsteps approaching the door, so I moved behind it. As it opened Jabberwocky cursed. Once his head was in sight I reached out, gripping either side. His face sizzled slightly as I fed electricity into his body. He didn't immediately collapse, but I jumped away hoping he was incapacitated enough that he wouldn't follow me. I tried to run but found I didn't have the energy to do much more than jog. The halls in this building were identical and pitch black, making it difficult to find any exit.

"You're very smart little lioness. I wouldn't have thought you'd even be able to move after everything I did to you. I won't make that mistake again. Once I have you back, I'll make sure you can't walk to get away from me." Jabberwocky's voice echoed down the halls, forcing me to walk faster. I felt blood trickling down my body, dizziness was setting in. I found a door with sunlight leaking in and threw it open. My eyes burned as I squinted down the alley. I made sure the door didn't slam as I exited the building. I stumbled toward the street, praying someone would pass by. I glanced back toward the building behind me, cataloging it in hopes I could make it back here. I continued to drag myself further away from it. The streets were eerily empty, I could hear sounds in the distance, but my vision was starting to go black. The last thing I heard before passing out was a bird's song overhead.

Caterpillar

"There are only three places she could be. Hatter, you are taking Sammy and his guard into sector five. One of the buildings there is abandoned, but some citizens have been complaining about strange noises in the night. I've sent you the details in a text." He nodded and immediately left the meeting room. "Cheshire, you're heading to the boonies with Lily, Idalia, and their team. It's the least likely place, but Lily seems to believe it still needs to be investigated."

Cheshire saluted, causing me to roll my eyes. "Heading out now boss. Bring our girl home is a go."

March coughed once he'd left the room, looking at me, "Are you l-leaving me here?"

"No, you're with me. We're going to the place I think is most likely for Jabberwocky to be frequenting... sector twelve." Something like surprise lit March's eyes, but he didn't comment further. "Do you have your gear? We need to leave asap."

"I'm ready." I stared at him for a moment, fire was burning in his honey-brown eyes. I could tell he was wound tight, I only hoped that would be a good thing for what we were about to do.

I had chosen to not bring a team with March and I. It had been a gut feeling, that either we wouldn't need the team, or they'd get in our way. I didn't want Wonderland to be stretched thin. So here we were, standing in front of another metal door, barely on its hinges, alone.

"Look," March pointed down, and I noticed the dots of blood leading away from the door. "It better not be hers," I growled back.

I pushed the door open, squinting into the darkness. When nothing immediately jumped out, I entered. March flipped on the heavy metal flashlight he was holding. I glanced toward the ground, the blood trail leading further into the building. As we followed it, a sinking feeling settled inside of me. There was not a single sound in the entire building. If that was Alice's blood there was a good chance, she was severely injured. After weaving through the maze of halls for Creator only knows how long I heard the muffled sounds of an argument.

"I didn't lose the girl. She got away," I knew Jabberwocky's voice instantly.

I tried to process what he was saying, but when an unfamiliar woman's voice responded. "It's your incompetence that caused it. I won't be the one telling the Queen about this."

"I'm not afraid of the Queen, but we need to find the girl. The trail just disappears. If her harem had been the one to find her, they would have already knocked the door down." I smirked, pushing the door open.

"You're right about at least one thing you've said Dnais." Jabberwocky and a black-haired woman turned toward my voice. The woman drew a gun, aiming it right at my chest. She was unfamiliar to me, so I made sure to catalog everything about her that I could. Her black, glossy hair fell straight down her back. Her dark brown eyes glared at me. Her skin was darker than my own by a couple of shades.

"Ahhh Ainsworth, I wondered when you would make an appearance. It's unfortunate that what you're looking for isn't here." Jabberwocky mocked me. How he'd known we didn't have Alice I couldn't be sure. "I wonder who did pick up the wounded lioness."

I didn't let my fear show on my face. Wherever Alice was, at least she wasn't still in Jabberwocky's clutches. Before I could open my mouth to say another word, March flew past me. With lightning speed, he snatched the woman's gun from her, slamming his fist into her nose. Jabberwocky stumbled back as March went to grab him. I tried to grab the woman before she could flee, but March's grunt of pain stopped me. I turned back toward him to find Jabberwocky with a knife to March's throat. "He's good, but far too predictable. I would expect you to train your men better,"

I stared at March, trying to come up with a plan. I could reach for my gun, but Jabberwocky could easily slit March's throat before I could shoot him. Not to mention that he was using March as a human shield. I didn't speak, running through every possible scenario. "I'll tell you what Roman, this one time I'll let you both walk away. I have bigger fish to fry." He pushed March toward me, but didn't account for March's fast reflexes. March caught himself, grabbed the daggers attached to his belt, and sunk both into Jabberwocky's fleeing back. He missed slightly, sinking one into his right shoulder. The man groaned in pain but reached back yanking one of them out, before turning on March. I leaped in, landing a punch before Jabberwocky could react. He hurled the knife he was holding at me, and I felt the moment it sank into my stomach. I fell against the table, gripping the knife. March reacted, grabbing the dagger stuck in Jabberwocky's shoulder, and forcing it through until the tip of the dagger protruded from the other side. I watched in a mix of amazement and horror as March put all of his weight into pushing down, severing Jabberwocky's arm from his shoulder. The dismembered limb fell to the ground with a sickening thud. Jabberwocky's scream was unlike anything I'd ever heard before. March didn't spend another moment on him, rushing to me, "We need to get you to H-H-H...." March couldn't speak. I could see his hands shaking.

I held up a hand to stop him, "I'm okay. I'm okay, we just need to keep the knife in until we can get to Hatter or Alcinda." He nodded in agreement before pulling my arm over one of his shoulders. He glanced down at Jabberwocky who was laying on the floor screaming as he bled.

"That's for Ali." He looked at me after a moment, once again inclining his head before we began the trek out of the building.

"You c-can't ride the bike out of here. I'm calling R-Rab to pick us up." I couldn't speak through the blinding pain that had begun in my stomach. "You're gonna be f-fine. Alice would never forgive me if I let you die."

I wheezed a laugh, "Do you want to talk about it?" I knew changing the subject was for the best, "You just cut off a man's arm. Are you okay?"

"I d-did what n-n-needed to be done." He was staring down at his phone, ignoring my gaze.

"You reacted before thinking," He opened his mouth to argue, but I stopped him, "You're angry. I understand that better than anyone, but you attacked them before we could coordinate."

"You're blaming me for that?" He motioned to the blade in my stomach. I had been trying to not think about it; the reminder forced me to consider the pain I was in, blinding me for a moment.

"No... We'll discuss it later." I closed my eyes, leaning against the dingy wall of the building we'd just exited. I didn't know how long passed before I heard the rumble of an engine, but I was thankful when my uncle jumped out of the truck and rushed toward me.

"What the hell happened?" He asked as he helped me into the truck. Once I was settled in, March stepped away, going to ride one of our bikes back to the apartment.

"Jabberwocky was here. He had Alice, but I think she escaped." I explained between harsh breaths.

"Hatter is waiting at the apartment with Alcinda. We'll get you taken care of quickly." I could see the panic in Rab's face when he met my eyes. Ever since Mary Anne died, any injury we came across terrified him. I grasped his shoulder, trying to comfort him.

I felt the blood slowly leaking out around the knife still sticking into my stomach. I knew I couldn't remove it without risking my life, but I desperately wanted to. The wound was beginning to itch and burn. "We're not far, Roman. Just hold on. It would be easier if you could stay awake. Talk to me."

I sighed, "Have you noticed anything about March?"

He was quiet for a moment, "He's certainly changed a lot in the last year. I'm proud of the progress he's clearly made since learning about his magick, but.... He's clearly dealing with some things it doesn't seem like anyone can help with."

I considered his response for a moment. I didn't have anything to say, so I stared out the window. The city rushed past. A few citizens were milling the streets, but it seemed most people were staying inside. I'd noticed it a couple days before, less children running around the town square. The energy in the city was strange, and I couldn't figure it out. Joshua's announcement had certainly shaken a few people, but this seemed like more. When Rab pulled up in front of our apartment, I was surprised to see March and Hatter come running up to the truck. "I'm going to try to heal you here." Hatter said, "I have to pull the knife out, take a deep breath." He didn't give me any time to react before he yanked it out. He laid his hands over the wound, and I felt like I was on fire. I must have made some noise because he looked up at me. He pushed my shirt up, staring at the stab wound. The panic in his eyes caused me to gulp. "March, go get Alcinda."

"What's going on?" I gritted out around the burning sensation in my chest.

"I just poured every ounce of power I had into you, and you didn't heal at all." He pulled his shirt over his head, pressing into my stomach to stop the blood flow.

My head was swimming, and I couldn't form words. I heard running steps before a blurry Alcinda appeared before me. "Roman, what are you feeling right now?"

I choked out the only word I could find, "Fire."

She cursed, and I felt her cold hands on my abdomen, "Hatter, I want you to try to heal with me. I've never seen anything like this."

Rough hands joined the ice-cold fingers on my middle, and moments later fire spread through my body. I felt my body bow, I could hear cursing, but nothing mattered. "S-stop! It's clearly not working." March's voice cut through the pain I was feeling. "Hatter give me your shirt. We've got to stop the bleeding. J-Jonah, get Cheshire, Sammy, and Patrick. We're going to need to carry him—" I didn't hear any more words as my entire world went black.

Chapter 9

Alice

I awoke to the humming of a song I'd heard many times before. I stretched slightly, but pain shot through my midsection causing me to hiss.

"Good, you're awake." I sat up when I didn't immediately recognize the voice that spoke. I met crystal blue eyes and realized I knew exactly who this was. "You recognize me. That'll make this conversation easier. I'm sure you have questions." I didn't speak at first, staring at the old woman. I had thought about her many times, had wondered who she might have been. She was exactly as I remembered, down to the brown frock she wore. "You've been through a lot. Take your time. We can speak when you're ready."

I just nodded; my mind couldn't process anything at the moment. I glanced around the room we were in. I was sitting on a large, comfortable bed. A small makeshift kitchen was directly next to me. Two large chairs took up the rest of the very small room. The walls were painted blue and decorated with birds and other animals I didn't recognize. It was clear the old woman had lived here for a long time. She had busied herself with making a pot of tea, that was currently whistling loudly, causing me to flinch. "I promise I'm not going to hurt you. I am sorry I didn't prevent Jabberwocky from taking you."

"Prevent it?" I asked, staring at her.

"Do you know why the people called this city Wonderland?" I knew she was changing the subject. Could see some kind of strange emotion in her wrinkled face. I shook my head, unable to conjure words. The woman had me entranced as she fluttered around her small home. When I remained silent. She turned toward me, and stared for a moment, before saying, "Do you know about Alice's Adventures in Wonderland?"

I nodded, my mother had named me after the main character of the story, of course, I was familiar with it. "I am. Written by Lewis Carroll in the eighteenth century."

"Correct. Do you know what he was inspired by?" She pressed, forcing my mind to slow down and consider.

"I read somewhere that he was inspired by drugs or some kind of medical condition he had," I responded, unsure of the point of this line of questioning.

"Those are some of the stories that were spun at the time, yes..." She trailed off.

"But they aren't true?" Something about the way she said it, "They're just stories after all."

I didn't like the look in her eyes as she began to speak, "The fabric of our entire world is stories, Alice Young. In the end, we can only hope that we become pages in someone's book." Her answer was so confusing I couldn't respond. Thankfully she continued, "Our little city hasn't always been the only place to exist. When I was a young girl, the story of Lewis Carroll was legend. He was an aide to the savior of my homeland."

"Your...homeland?" I scooted toward the end of the bed. Clearly, this woman was absolutely insane.

She sighed, "I know you aren't going to believe me. I didn't intend to ever have to lay things out like this... There's no easy way to explain it."

"Oh, don't worry about it. I need to be going anyway." I attempted to stand, only to be overcome with pain. My butt met the bed hard, stars crossing my vision.

"I guess I should have started this off more simply. It's been a very long time since I had a full conversation with another person." She chuckled as she helped me sit back. She shoved a cup of tea in my hand, "This will help. I promise I didn't go through all the trouble of getting you here just to poison you." I nodded, taking a sip. The hot liquid slid down my throat, leaving a pleasant warmth in its wake. After a few moments, I felt better, shifting slightly to feel more comfortable. "Let me start by introducing myself. I am Eumonia Lyon."

I quirked an eyebrow, "Obviously, I don't need to make an introduction."

Her smile became sad, "I've known who you are for a very long time."

"That's not creepy at all."

"At least you're in joking spirits." She became more serious, "I cannot keep you here for long, there are many players involved. You have to be very careful who you trust, I cannot give you all the information you need now. Too many unknowns are outside my control."

Her rambling made me realize something, "You are a seer."

She nodded, "I am." Tears welled in her eyes, "I have seen many things at my age. I've rarely been able to prevent anything. Today, I made the choice to save you from any further pain."

"Thank you." I drained my teacup, gently setting it to the side. "Wait, you're a magick user... but you said something about your homeland?"

"I did. You see magick users weren't native to Earth. A few of our people intermingled with people on Earth. Occasionally magick would make its way here, but when I was young it was nearly unheard of. Now, the magick users in Wonderland are the most that have ever resided on Earth."

"Wait. Where are you originally from? Can we go there?" The thought of seeing a place where magick users thrive would be amazing.

"That's a very long story, that we don't currently have time for. But magick users come from Undraland. It doesn't exist on this plane, and has been inaccessible for a very, very long while now."

"Undraland." I repeated, feeling ridiculous, "You're saying… Listen, lady… Eumonia, whatever. Shit in Wonderland is bad enough. I don't need a senile old lady telling me fairy tales." I snapped.

"I can't make you believe me, but Undraland is where all the magick users in Wonderland hail from. It's been enough generations now for everyone to forget. That may have been for the best." The sigh Eumonia released was full of grief.

"Look. I'm sorry. I've clearly had a rough few days. I was supposed to be married and settling into a life that doesn't include Queens and nonsense." How the hell else could I explain the Queen of Hearts to anyone?

"No need to apologize, dearheart. It's just the ramblings of a very old woman. Why don't you rest? When you wake again, I will escort you back to the city proper." Just the suggestion of rest had my eyes feeling heavy. I was asleep before I could utter another word.

When I awoke, silence filled the space, and I sat up. I felt surprisingly better, I was able to stand and stretch slightly. My left arm was held in a sling now. When I went to remove it, my shoulder revolted, and I chose to leave it in place. I paced around the small room for a few moments, searching for an exit. When none were immediately available, I flopped back down on the bed. I was surprised by how little the cuts on my body hurt. I maneuvered my shirt open enough to look down at it. I let out an audible gasp when I saw that all the cuts were closed. Some of them were deep enough that tissue had been showing.

"My husband was the healer, but I've learned some tricks over the years." Eumonia's voice startled me.

"How many days have I been here?" I asked, concerned, wounds that deep didn't close in a day.

"Three days, the tea I gave you promoted sleep and healing. I apologize for not forewarning you, but I didn't think you'd take it if I explained."

I was silent for a moment, considering her response, before I nodded, "Thank you."

"It is my pleasure to help you." Her eyes were misty as she watched my face. The loneliness wafted off of her, and it broke my heart.

"Why do you stay here? Well, where is here?" I asked. I wanted desperately to know more about her.

"I've made my home here for many years. The animals keep me company. This is for the best." Everything Eumonia said was so cryptic, that I nearly rolled my eyes.

"I need to go home. My... my family has to be worried." I never knew what to call my men. In my heart they were my husbands, but with two failed marriage ceremonies that wasn't yet accurate. "But you have so much to tell me, how can I get in touch with you?"

A sad smile flitted across her face, "When you need me, I will be there. Until then, you won't remember where I live."

"How—" Before I could finish my question, Eumonia's warm hands landed on my cheeks. A quiet roar filled my ears just before I passed out.

"Alice! Oh my god, Alice!" The feeling of hands shaking me woke me from my slumber. "Why are you on my doorstep like some kind of abandoned orphan?" I cracked my eyes open to find Dina leaned over me. Her eyes were puffy, "You've been missing for days..." She trailed off, something dark passing in her eyes. "I'm going to go get Hatter, he's the only one home right now." I didn't try to stop her, simply pushed myself up and stared down the hallway after her.

My memories returned quickly. At least Eumonia's little trick hadn't been entirely effective. I might not know where she lived, but I remembered everything she'd told me. Unfortunately, I also remembered every moment of Jabberwocky's torture. Chills ran down my spine, I'd never felt weaker. If Eumonia hadn't saved me, I'd be dead... or much worse. Running footsteps brought my attention back to the present. Hatter's stricken face was in front of mine within seconds. His green eyes were rimmed with red, the white streaks in his hair were more stark than before causing my eyebrows to furrow. "Who was hurt?"

"Oh, sweetheart..." He trailed off, and I watched a tear run down his cheek.

"Who, Hayden?" I demanded.

"Caterpillar." He responded, nearly choking on the name.

"Take me to him." I insisted, forcing my body to stand.

"Alice... I... Roman is gone."

"Gone? What do you mean gone?" Panic was bubbling in my chest.

"March and Caterpillar came to save you from Jabberwocky. In... in the tussle Caterpillar was stabbed. Your mom and I did everything we could. Healing magick wouldn't work. March and my dad tried to stitch and save him but.... He's dead, Ali." I collapsed back to the floor, my mind completely blank. Roman couldn't be dead, not because he was trying to save me. He couldn't be gone. My world began to crumble, my vision darkened, my heartbeat in my chest so hard I thought I might be dying as well. Arms wrapped around me. I couldn't hear any voices over the strange keening sound that must have been leaving my own throat, "I'm so sorry, Alice. I'm so sorry. I'm here. I'm here." Hatter's words did nothing to ease the pain I was feeling.

"He can't be dead. Take me to him." I insisted once I was capable of thought.

"Jonah is preparing him for their family's traditional funeral..." Hatter looked away from me. "The Ainsworths do a pyre ceremony. Something about returning to the ashes they came from. It didn't make sense to me. We're going to do it in your wildflower field tomorrow."

"I need to see him," My voice broke halfway through my sentence.

"Let her see him, Hatter. It won't be real until she sees for herself." Dina spoke up for the first time.

I tried to smile at her but failed miserably. Hatter sighed, but conceded, grabbing my hand, and leading me down to the basement of our building. It was cold and dark as we approached a single metal door. I'd never been to this part of the basement, only the gym. Hatter knocked but opened the door immediately after. I took a deep breath before I followed him in. It was dimly lit, but I could clearly see Jonah leaning over Caterpillar. His hands were braced on the table. As we approached I saw the tears running down his face as he cried over his nephew silently. I stared at those tears as they rolled down his cheek, dripping onto the table. I couldn't bring myself to actually look down at Caterpillar's body. Hatter clasped Jonah's shoulder comfortingly, but the room remained silent. Finally, Jonah lifted his eyes to mine. We stared at each other. I couldn't be certain what he saw in mine, but I knew exactly what he was feeling.

"You destroy them all, Alice. Anything else is too good for them. There should be no mercy." Before I could respond he turned on his heel and left.

I stared after him, contemplating those words for a long time. Hatter stood beside me silently, intertwining our fingers. Eventually, I decided it was time to look at Caterpillar. He looked like he was sleeping peacefully, his brow was smooth. I snorted; Caterpillar never looked so peaceful. I choked on the sound realizing he was really gone. I couldn't stop myself from laying my head against his chest, listening for his strong heartbeat. When silence answered my plea to the Creator, tears began to leak out of my eyes. I straightened as I cried, smoothing his hair back, and patting the tie Jonah had dressed him in. I realized they'd put him in the beautiful suit he'd bought for our wedding. Something about that realization crippled me, my knees weakened. I would have hit the ground if Hatter hadn't been there to catch me.

"It's my fault, Hayden. I did this." I was nearly screaming as I spoke.

"No, sweetheart. The only person to blame for this is Jabberwocky and the Queen of Hearts." He squeezed me gently.

"I love you for believing that, but I knew Jabberwocky was following me. If I had told someone... If I had made different choices he'd still be here." I was hysterical, barely able to think as I babbled.

Hatter didn't respond, so I continued, "It should have been me. It should have been me. He had me, Hatter. He was going to give me to her, if I hadn't tried to escape Caterpillar would be alive."

"Do you really believe he would have been willing to let them take you?" Hatter snapped. I was shocked at his tone, "He loved you more than anything in this world. He'd be happy you made it out alive. Don't disrespect him by blaming yourself."

I had no words, so I simply nodded. Hatter led me away from Caterpillar's body, and back up the stairs. I was spaced out, barely able to think as he led me into our apartment. It was eerily silent. Hatter forced me to sit on our bed before disappearing into the bathroom. I heard the water turn on. I didn't know how much time had passed before he returned, lifting me from the bed and carrying me into the bathroom. He stood me in front of the shower, slowly stripping my clothes off, careful to avoid the sling on my arm. Once I was naked, he took me in, seeing the mostly healed cuts and bruises. It was obvious some of the cuts would scar, more evidence of all the pain Wonderland had caused me. I couldn't find my vanity to be concerned about new scars right now. I'd take a thousand more scars if Caterpillar walked through the door alive.

"March removed Jabberwocky's arm before he got Caterpillar out of there." I could tell he was trying to be comforting, but something about the image that filled my mind caused me to laugh. It wasn't long before my laughter turned to sobs. "Cheshire and March should be back soon. They went with your mom to represent you and Caterpillar. We've been careful not to release any information to the citizens..." He trailed off as he slowly removed the sling holding my arm still. I was careful to hold it to my chest as he helped me into the shower. I was surprised when he stripped and joined me. When he looked at my face he shook his head, "I'm just going to help you wash off. To be honest, you smell awful."

I gave him a watery smile before I closed my eyes. He was gentle as he washed every inch of me. I was thankful for the love he was showing me, even though I could feel the waves of grief coming off of him. "Thank you." I croaked.

He grunted a response before stepping out of the shower to help me climb out. He wrapped a white fluffy towel around me before grabbing a brush to get the knots out of my hair. Once I was dry and my hair detangled, he pulled me back into the bedroom. He picked out one of

Caterpillar's shirts and pulled it over my head, helping me into a pair of my workout pants. "Rest." He ordered.

"Hayden..." I couldn't figure out what I wanted to say, but he understood. He sat next to me, pulling me close.

We spoke no words, simply laying there soaking in each other's warmth. I felt something wet hit my cheek and looked up to find him crying. It triggered my own tears and so we held each other while we cried.

Chapter 10

January 30th, 2159

"We have to tell the people that Caterpillar is gone." Jonah was growling at all of us. My head was pounding. We had been going in circles for an hour.

"I agree with you, and I know you are grieving, but we have to think strategically Rab." I know what my mother was saying was reasonable, but I agreed with Rab. We needed to grieve and plan privately. We also had to decide what the story was before we revealed Caterpillar's death to the citizens of Wonderland. I was numb to it all. I felt like nothing truly mattered now that he was gone. We should have been married and living our dreams. Instead, he was dead, and I was stuck in another war dealing with a bunch of dumbass politics.

"Alcinda, the day Mary Anne died I was quiet. I handled it... I won't do it again. They've taken the last of my family from me. It's time to activate the citizens of Wonderland. They should be fighting for their freedom as hard as we have. Maybe they need to lose people they love to take things seriously." My eyes widened at his words.

"You don't mean that, it's just—"

"Just nothing! My nephew is dead! Stop being the cold-hearted White Queen for a millisecond Cindy." He deflated after he was done, sinking back into his seat.

I could see my mother's jaw working, the pain and hurt I'd seen cross her face almost brought me out of silence. "I'm sorry. You are right. I'm just concerned we cannot handle the mass panic of every citizen." I knew she was being reasonable. I made eye contact with Rab and saw the same defeat in his eyes that I felt.

March, Cheshire, Hatter, and I were sitting in silence as they argued. When Rab gave up his fight, Hatter finally spoke, "Right now we need to allow ourselves to focus on grieving. We can at least let Rab complete the funeral rites before we make a decision. We aren't currently capable of handling mass panic. Tillie, Cahir, and Jackson haven't been able to find any signs of Jabberwocky. He must have survived."

My vision turned red with rage at the mention of Caterpillar's murderer, "Our focus needs to be finding him."

"We cannot get wrapped up in vengeance. We have enough problems." My mother snapped at me.

"Would you have ignored vengeance if someone had killed Dad?" I growled at her.

She went still, staring into my eyes. I don't know how long we stared at each other before she said, "Yes. I would have let the world burn around me unless it was you or Lily."

Silence stretched across the room. "Dad would have deserved to be avenged and so does Roman."

I turned on my heel and walked out of the room without another thought. I heard chairs scrap and footsteps, but I didn't look back until I opened the door of my apartment. I was tired of these meetings; I wasn't made for politics. My skin was itching as I flopped down onto the couch. Cheshire and March mirrored me, falling onto our furniture. None of us spoke, all lost in our own thoughts and pain.

"It's my f-fault he's gone..." March's whisper was heavy in the room. I looked at him, unsure what to say. I felt the same way, "I know you're going to argue with me, but if I hadn't f-flown off the handle it wouldn't have happened. He wouldn't have gotten hurt." Tears were leaking from his eyes at his admission, "I can't I-live like this. I hate myself."

"Blame and revenge aren't going to bring him back." Cheshire's words surprised me, I turned toward him, but he held up his hand, "We're all grieving, we're all angry. Trust me, I want to end anyone affiliated with the Queen of Hearts and Jabberwocky, but it isn't worth the rest of us losing our lives as well. That isn't what Roman would want."

I knew he was right, but I couldn't bring myself to verbalize that. All I felt was a vast emptiness in my soul. As if the Creator had ripped a piece of me away. I stared at the wall behind Cheshire, the misery in the room was palpable when Hatter walked in. He was the only one of us still trying to act normal. Some part of me was proud of him and deeply ashamed of myself. Hatter must have read my mind, because he said, "Caterpillar would be ashamed of all of us. Now, we're all going to sit down for a full meal. Alice you are going to tell us where the hell you've been for days. Then we're going to crawl into bed together and find what comfort we can. Is that understood?"

Cheshire smiled, standing, "I was just trying to explain that to these two." I glared at him, but he just stuck his tongue out at me.

"I'm not hungry, but if you'll sit. I will tell you about.... everything." I turned to March, "If you think you hate yourself... well it's a club with good company."

So, I told them everything, every cut Jabberwocky put on me. Every detail I could remember about Eumonia. When I was done no one was breathing, simply staring at me. "We have to find her." Cheshire finally said, "Clearly she knows things that we need to know as well."

"I don't think that's worth focusing on. She's obviously a powerful magick user. If she doesn't want to be found, I doubt she will be." I responded.

"Could it have been an illusion?" Hatter asked.

I thought for a moment, "I don't think so. Illusion magick... it's complicated but there's always something slightly off about it. It's not extremely strong, that is why I don't use it often."

"I wish I'd killed him." March said, something in his eyes sent a chill down my spine, "He hurt you. He killed Caterpillar. He's s-s-signed his own death warrant."

I nodded, "I don't blame you, Max. I know you were just concerned about me. I don't think Roman would blame you either. You just need to work on your self-control. We don't send you into the field often enough, that needs to change." I felt a bit better after talking, it was easier to breathe.

"No one ever blamed you, March. Or you Ali. We all know the risks." Hatter said.

March didn't respond, staring off, a look in his eyes haunted enough to cause a squeeze in my chest. I walked over to him, laying a hand on his shoulder, "I love you. Roman loved you. There's nothing you could do that we wouldn't love you."

A tear rolled down his cheek, his voice cracked as he said, "I love you too."

Hatter clapped his hands, drawing our attention to him, "Now it's time to eat."

I was too hot. I tried to turn over, but when I couldn't move, I cracked my eyes open. It was dark, but I could make out Hatter and Cheshire on either side of me. Their arms touching where they were thrown over my midsection. I was careful to slide out from under them without waking anyone. I glanced back, finding March was curled into Hatter's back. Something about the peaceful sight of them all sound asleep brought a smile to my face. It felt wrong, Caterpillar should have been taking up half of our huge bed. I left the bedroom, wandering toward the kitchen. I picked my phone off the counter, finding it was just after four am. I decided to go to the gym, I wasn't going to be able to get back to sleep. I closed our front door as quietly as possible, ensuring my steps were silent as I passed Dina's door as well. I was shocked to find Jonah running on one of the machines when I entered the room. I nodded to him before making my way to the hanging, weighted bags. I pulled the sling off, I needed to feel something, and staying incapable wasn't going to work. I didn't waste time putting gloves or bandages over my knuckles before I was throwing all of my weight through my fists into the bag. I ignored the way my shoulder twinged. I could feel the muscles and ligaments struggling. I took deep breaths through my nose, releasing all the pain, rage, and fear I felt into my punches. I only stopped when electricity crackled up the bag, causing the chain that held it to spark. I stepped away, my hands on my knees, forcing my breaths to remain calm. I opened my eyes and saw blood on my knuckles, causing me to curse.

"It doesn't work." I glanced to Rab as he approached, first aid in hands. When I raised an eyebrow at him, "The working out. No amount of punching is going to make those feelings go away." He grabbed my hand, spraying some stinging liquid on it before wrapping it. We didn't speak as he cleaned my hands. "When Mary Anne died, the first thing I wanted to do was crawl into her grave with her. By the time I was angry enough to find a punching bag, nothing helped. Even time hasn't eased the pain. Roman helped... you helped. The people that I loved saved me."

Rab's words brought tears to my eyes, "I'm so sorry... I can't even imagine what you're going through." I flung my arms around his neck. Ignoring the sweat dripping off both of us. "You've been like a father to me, Jonah. I can't tell you how much I love and appreciate everything you've done for me. I know he felt the same way."

"Go talk to your mother about that shoulder. I could tell from across the room that it was not healed properly. She's in the conference room." He dismissed me without another word, but I didn't take offense. Losing Caterpillar was hard for me and the guys, but it was unimaginable for him. I made my way up the stairs, into the conference room where I found my mother looking over some papers.

She looked up when I walked into the room, and I could see the exhaustion in her face, "When was the last time you slept well?"

She gave me a sad smile, "When you were about two months old."

I snorted, "Fair enough. Better question, when was the last time you slept at all."

"I got a few hours last night, but I needed to go over some of Caterpillar's notes on his dealings with the merchants in sector eleven." She explained.

"And that couldn't wait until daylight?" I shot back.

"I needed to do something." She looked away from me, before asking, "What did you need?"

"Jonah said I should have you look at my shoulder." I explained, "I'm not going to keep wearing that damn contraption."

She rolled her eyes, but stood next to me, laying warm hands on the bare skin of my shoulder. I felt the tingle of her magick against my own before warmth ran down my arm. I rolled my arm when she moved away, relieved that it felt normal again. "Thank you."

She just nodded, "Go back to sleep, Alice. Tomorrow, we send Caterpillar back to the Creator."

I cringed at her words but left the room without argument. I couldn't shake the feeling that something was off, but I ignored it quietly opening the apartment door. I walked toward the bedroom, no one had moved, so I carefully crawled back in between Hatter and Cheshire. My mind wouldn't stop, but I did my best to rest.

Chapter 11

January 31st, 2159

No one had spoken or eaten this morning. We dressed in silence, occasionally brushing against each other in comfort. All of the men were wearing black, I had opted to wear a pale green floor-length gown that Caterpillar had bought me. I'd never had the chance to wear it for him, it felt appropriate to at least wear it to send him off. We'd discussed bringing weapons and ultimately decided Wonderland wasn't safe enough to go anywhere unarmed. A knock on the door interrupted our silent morning. I finished strapping my daggers to my thigh, while Cheshire opened the door. Dina and Griffin stood in the doorway, both in all black. I wished everyone had chosen to wear colors, Caterpillar deserved a colorful send-off.

"You look beautiful. Cater would have loved it." Dina said as she wrapped her arms around me.

I sniffed in response, before changing the subject, "Who has Elsie?"

"Ilaria offered to stay behind and watch her and Lewis." I loved Dina, she had always known when not to push me. "Your mom and Jonah have already left. Everyone else is supposed to meet us there."

"Let's go." I motioned for everyone to join me. We were a somber procession as we made our way to the underground garage. Griffin had scoured through the city before Elsie was born and found an ugly, rusted blue van that could seat eight people. We all piled in, I sat in the back with

Hatter and March on either side of me. Our fingers were entwined. Hatter would squeeze my hand every now and then, giving me a meaningful look.

I was numb as we drove out of the city, I watched the buildings slowly disappear. The road became bumpy as we approached my field. The sky was grey, the flowers unbloomed. It looked exactly as awful as I felt. We trekked to the middle of the field where someone had erected a wooden altar. Caterpillar's body was lying atop it, Rab was laying sticks and some kind of plants around him. I could see his mouth moving but couldn't hear his words. I kept my distance knowing that whatever he was saying was private.

I turned away watching as Tillie and her husbands approached. She jogged up to me, throwing her arms around me. I felt her tears fall onto my chest, I patted her back until she sniffled and pulled away, "I am so sorry, Ali. I can't imagine how you're feeling. Roman was such a wonderful man."

"He was. Thanks for coming Til.'" I stepped away from her. I greeted Duchess as she approached with Lily and Idalia. "Are you doing okay? I am sorry I haven't come to see you since... everything happened?"

She rolled her eyes, "Alice, stop being a martyr. You just lost one of your men after being tortured. I think I can survive a few days alone."

Her dismissal put a smile on my face, "I can always rely on you to be yourself at least."

"Love me or hate me, it'll be for who I am." She nodded. In a way, I admired Duchess for her lack of giving a damn. She had survived her mother, and it was clear in her mind that nothing else could harm her now. In reality, I was jealous, some part of me felt like my life was over with Caterpillar gone. I knew that wasn't fair to Cheshire, Hatter, and March, but I could tell they felt the same way. We all needed each other, and one of us being gone was like missing a limb.

Slowly, everyone arrived, circling Caterpillar's body, and chatting quietly. I looked at the faces of the people who had become closest to me.

Lily caught my eye and approached me, "Rab says he's going to start soon. Are you ready for this? We've never seen a funeral like this before. It could be shocking."

"It's what he wanted. Apparently, his parents weren't able to have the traditional burial because they were killed by the Suits. This type of thing hasn't been done in so many years. I'm glad we're able to honor what he would have wanted." I knew I sounded robotic as I repeated what Jonah had said to me.

"I know none of this is easy. What happened with Jabberwocky... you haven't had a chance to process that. Mom told me he tortured you... I'm here if you need me. Idalia too. You're not alone, Ali." Lily stared into my eyes, imploring me to open up.

"I'll be okay. I always am." I said back, holding the tears at bay.

Lily opened her mouth to continue speaking, but thankfully Rab interrupted. "Thank you all for coming. Roman cared for all of you, and I know he would be touched by your presence here. I wanted to explain the ceremony and give everyone a chance to speak before we finish. I'll begin," He cleared his throat. "The Ainsworth family has many traditions. Some have been lost as the years have passed, but when my brother and I were young our grandfather died. My father took us to the boonies and introduced us to the Ainsworth funeral rites. Our family believes that only fire can send us to the Creator." I nodded. He'd prepared me for this, "Today we will honor Roman, and our ancestors by sending him to the Creator in the proper way. My nephew brought me so much joy. Mary Anne and I were never able to have children... Roman was a son to me. His loss isn't just mine, all of Wonderland will suffer for what will be returned to dust today."

A tear rolled down my cheek as he stopped. My mother stepped forward, laying a gentle hand on Rab's shoulder, "I've known Caterpillar most of his life. I was fortunate enough to see the child he was and the man he grew to be. I was blessed that my daughter chose to share her life with him. The time was far too short. He will be greatly missed." I watched as Rab and my mother stared at each other, something passing between them.

Hatter joined them next, "Caterpillar was a brother to me from the moment we met. I was sixteen, bullheaded, and looking for a fight. He showed me how to use my skills, my aggression for the better. Without him, I wouldn't be the man I am today. There just aren't words..." He stopped, turning toward Caterpillar's body. "Some part of all of us is going to burn with him today."

March rushed to Hatter's side as tears began sliding down his cheeks, "I-I'm not much of a p-public speaker. For good reason. But Roman deserves every kind word he's receiving. He supported us in the darkest of times. He never asked for anything in return..." March stopped, wrapping arms around Hatter, hiding his face from the rest of us. A sound left my lips, but I wasn't ready to speak.

Cheshire reached down, squeezing my hand before he too joined them. "I lived to irritate Roman. He was so easy to get a rise out of, but he was never truly angry with me. When my parents passed, I couldn't have dreamed of a better person to help me grieve. Like Hatter, he was my older brother in every way that mattered. I know he would want us to move on, and be happy without him. Every day I hope I can honor his memory."

Everyone looked at me, waiting with bated breath for me to speak some profound words about the love I had for Caterpillar. I was stumped, I couldn't express the emotions that swirled like a vortex in my stomach. "Roman is the reason I have everything I have today." I stepped toward my family. All huddled together, welcoming me with open arms as I cried. "Without his work, his sacrifices nothing we've accomplished would have been possible. To lose him.... I still can't imagine how we will all continue forward."

"Together." Hatter said, before pressing a kiss into my hair, "We will do it together like we always have."

We all stood embracing. I could feel the shaking and tears from everyone, the heat of our bodies comforting. Finally, Rab pulled away, pulling a pack of matches from his suit pocket. "I release you to the Creator, Roman Ainsworth. May we meet again." I watched as three matches were lit and flew from his hand. In slow motion the fire began, smoke at first, before growing, dancing from red and orange to hot blue. I was entranced by the flames, but unable to look as his body was consumed by them.

A loud commotion forced my eyes toward our vehicles. Smoke filled the air, but the unmistakable figure of the Queen of Hearts walked toward us. She had an air of arrogance that I could feel even twenty feet away. "This really was so touching to watch. Clearly, Roman Ainsworth was a well-loved man."

I could feel the vibrations of growls coming from the men around me. Electricity crackled around my fingertips without me calling for it. "Today isn't the day."

"Oh, Alice dear. It's the perfect day. I have so much to celebrate. After all, I've killed one of the leaders of the Resistance who so cruelly took my brother out of power. The news is breaking across Wonderland now. I'm sure the citizens who have already been losing confidence in their new government will be shocked that they've hidden such a crucial detail from their people."

"Fuck…" My mother inhaled. Rab had been right. We should have told our people what happened. What I wasn't prepared for was my mother and Rab flying past us, weapons already drawn, pointing at the men who had begun flanking our group on all sides.

"You all have had so many opportunities to do the right thing. We all know none of you know how to lead a city. I mean look at you, the White Queen, letting her headstrong daughter lead an entire city. Why even begin a Resistance if you're too weak to lead it?"

I saw my mother pause as she landed a punch on a woman who was circling, "You could never begin to understand my reasons."

"That's what I would say too." The Queen of Hearts laughed, "Always so secretive. Wonderland should be called the City of Secrets."

I was frozen as I watched the people I love fight. Shots rang throughout my wildflower field, smoke hung heavy in the air. The Queen of Hearts kept talking, but I had stopped hearing, buzzing filled my ears. The Queen of Hearts kept approaching me, even with the chaos around her, her steps never faltered. She was almost nose-to-nose with me before I reacted. I took several steps back, "Why?" was the only word I was able to choke out.

"Now you're finally asking the right questions." She smiled at me, peaceful. She wasn't deranged like my aunt; sanity was clear in her eyes. "I told you; you've interrupted my plans. I don't want to do all of this. I could stop all of this if you'd just cooperate. Haven't you lost enough?"

"What do you want?" I couldn't believe I was even asking. I should have fought. She was close enough that I could use my daggers or my magick, but I just stood...talking.

"You have a handy power, Alice. I saw your little trick with Penthea. We could come to an arrangement. You offer me your services, strip a few choice people of their abilities. Share some of that power with me. It would be so easy. No one else would have to get hurt." Her posture was so relaxed as she spoke.

"I'm not a battery for you to use," I snapped at her. She'd pulled me from my inaction. I dug into the well of my magick, finding a warm, soft place to land as I spiraled into it. I felt my hair fall from its braids, felt the air thicken with my power. I looked into her dark eyes, and saw a hint of fear as I stood straighter. "You've taken something precious from me." A huge arc of electricity flew from my hand, headed straight for her chest. How she managed to just step out of the way of it stumped me, but it didn't stop me from sending another and another. I hoped I could overwhelm her. She was agile, jumping and weaving away from me.

"This could have been so easy." She sighed, and I watched as time seemed once again to slow, and stretch, "You can't imagine the powers that I hold."

She was standing before me, a dainty hand wrapped around my throat, walking me backward toward the fire that burned away. "Why don't I send you to join your man." My eyes widened; I felt the heat at my back. I couldn't swallow with her hand wrapped around my throat. I forced my hand up, forced my body to obey as I slapped her across the face magick wrapped around my hand. I could see the glow of my skin as it met hers. She hissed as the slap broke her hold on me and apparently whatever she'd done to time. I could hear Hatter shouting commands, bodies littered the ground. Idalia was surrounded by six men. I met her eyes, and saw the slight panic she felt. I nodded, hoping she understood what I wanted her to do. I returned my attention back to the Queen of Hearts. I grabbed two of the daggers strapped to my thighs, letting both fly into the backs of two of the men surrounding Idalia. I grabbed another, rushing the Queen of Hearts, grabbing her hair in one of my fists.

"You calculated incorrectly. Caterpillar's death didn't cripple me. I am full of rage. I will destroy you, wipe you and all of the Red Party from memory. Nothing will stop me now." I held the knife to her throat, prepared to slit it. I didn't have the chance as she disappeared from my grip. I whirled around searching for her. A hit from behind had me stumbling toward the fire, falling to my knees on the ground. I felt my dress tear, but I didn't stop, propelling myself back to my feet, closer to the fire than I would have preferred.

"I really do admire your confidence, young lady. I wish it didn't have to be this way." Once again, she landed a blow. I smelled burnt hair, heat burning my back. I tried to stumble away from her, toward safety. Just before she landed another punch, a blackened hand reached out of the fire grabbing her. I blinked, rubbed my eyes, tried desperately to make sense of what I was seeing.

Caterpillar stood, covered in black soot, gripping the slim wrist of the Queen of Hearts. She looked at him in horror, and he simply stared back.

His grey eyes filled with rage I had never seen. I watched the scene, noticing every inch of Caterpillar was exposed, perfectly alive.

"Void." The Queen of Hearts whispered before she yanked hard away. Fleeing several feet away. I stood, flying after her, but a hand around my middle stopped me. Caterpillar's hand was on my stomach as he pulled me against his body. He was vibrating. I glanced down, seeing his soot-covered hand leaving a print on the dress he'd picked out. It stood out against the pale green. I could feel the heat of him through my clothes, so hot it nearly burned me.

"I believe it's time that you leave. We both know you aren't prepared for this fight." His voice filled the clearing, and everyone stopped, turning. Staring. I couldn't think as I pressed back against him. Nothing was real. Caterpillar was dead and this was some sick trick someone was playing on me. I still stood, his hand gripping me tighter as my body tensed.

In the blink of an eye, the Queen of Hearts and all of her men disappeared. No words spoken, no great threat or promise of future fights. They simply vanished into thin air. The clearing was silent. Only the air blowing through the surrounding trees could be heard. Rab was the first person to approach, with a slight limp in his walk. "How?" His whispered words carried over the clearing, jarring us all.

"It was never Rise and Fall." I furrowed my eyebrows at Caterpillar's response.

Rab's eyes filled with understanding, "Fall to Rise... Does that mean?"

"Yes." The pain in his voice set me on edge. I was reading between the lines of their conversation. Understanding dawned on me moments after it hit Rab. Caterpillar's father likely would have been able to resurrect if he'd been given the proper Ainsworth funeral. Instead, the Red Party disposed of his body the way they disposed of all executed people. Throwing them outside the boundaries of Wonderland for predators to feast on.

"Is Caterpillar a zombie?" Cheshire spoke up.

A slap rang out, "You watch too much fucking TV." Hatter growled.

"It's a valid question. He was dead twenty minutes ago. Body burning, off to join the Creator. Now he's standing there completely fine. Clearly a zombie." Cheshire shot back. "Do you have a craving for brains? If so, I recommend eating Tillie. I'm sure she'll be filling enough."

"Shut up, Cheshire," Caterpillar growled behind me.

"Do I take orders from a zombie, Alice?" He looked toward me. It was clear he was trying to ease the strange tension that had filled all of us.

"If you don't want to be eaten, yes." I joked, turning in Caterpillar's arms, taking in his face. The breath in his chest. I dropped my voice to a whisper, "Care to explain?"

He just looked down at me, studying my face. I couldn't imagine what he was seeing, but I was self-conscious now. "Magick." He responded, shrugging his shoulders. "I have some guesses."

"She called you a void…" I prodded.

"Electrify me." His words shook me.

"What? No. I don't want to hurt you." I tried to step away.

He pulled me closer to him, reminding me just how naked he was. Only my body protected him from everyone's view, "Do it."

I sighed, calling a small amount of electricity to the tips of my fingers I sent it into his shoulder. He didn't even flinch as it made contact, so I called more. Nothing I did seemed to have an effect, "A void… magick can't affect you."

"That's why we couldn't heal you." My mother's voice broke our private moment.

"Yes." He confirmed, "Could we move this conversation somewhere with pants?"

Hatter snorted, "No one wants to see all that anyway."

"I would," I grumbled quietly, causing Caterpillar to chuckle against me.

"Later princess. We have a lot of catching up to do." He whispered into my ear.

Chapter 12

We stood in our apartment, waiting for Caterpillar to get out of the shower. None of us spoke, waiting with bated breath on how this was possible. Only Rab had joined us. My mother and Tillie had rushed to the town square to begin undoing whatever damage the Queen of Hearts had done. What little I'd heard from them since we separated wasn't good news. Caterpillar and I would need to make an appearance soon, but we had far more important things to worry about at the moment. I couldn't even process all that had happened since the Hummer had been wrecked. Hatter's father's announcement about the dome around the city. March's fear of Dodo and his mother were so far in the past. I knew those problems still existed. They had to be handled, but Caterpillar's death and subsequent resurrection were the most pressing matters at the moment. When he stepped into the living room, hair dripping, but clean and fresh faced I began to cry. He rushed to me, wrapping arms around me, "It's okay. I'm back. We're all here. Alive."

"What the hell happened?" I begged. Any answer might relieve the pain warring inside me.

"All I remember was Hatter and your mom trying to heal me. I felt like I was on fire. When I woke up, I was surrounded by flames that weren't burning me. I started putting the pieces together before I saw you fighting the Queen of Hearts." Caterpillar explained.

"And you being a void is why you came back to life?" Hatter asked.

"No, I don't think they're connected. I had no idea about being a void until she called me that. It makes sense though. Magick has always affected me less than others. With my body fully rested I guess my void magick has actually activated." He responded.

"And the whole Fall to Rise thing?" I asked, looking between Caterpillar and Rab.

"We always thought the family's motto was rise and fall. It's been passed down for generations, long before Wonderland existed. Until today, Fall to Rise... we can resurrect when we die. I'm not sure if there are specific conditions." Rab answered.

"We aren't testing it." I insisted.

"Of course, not..." Caterpillar trailed off, clearly deep in thought. "I think we can assume it has to do with the funeral rites. There are far more questions than answers, but today I don't want to worry about it. I want to spend time with my fiancé."

Rab nodded, "I understand... I am glad to see you alive and breathing. Regardless of how that happened, you are a son to me Roman. Losing you is one of the hardest things I've ever experienced."

"You've been a father to me as well. I'm sorry you had to grieve my death." They embraced for a long moment before Rab left.

"So do we need to leave since you want to spend time with your fiancé?" Cheshire asked, "We're just chopped liver, huh? I'll remember that next time you decide to die."

Caterpillar rolled his eyes, but pulled Cheshire into a tight hug, "You're stupid. I missed you too, Cat."

They embraced for a long moment, before Cheshire pulled away, misty-eyed, "Alright. Does anyone else have any secret powers they'd like to reveal now? It's getting a little out of hand people."

"It's not our fault the Red Party tried to suppress regular citizens magick." Hatter defended, "Dad has no idea where any magick would have come from on his side. He assumes it would have been from Mom."

"I hope my mother doesn't have any magick." March spoke suddenly, his words causing my stomach to drop, "If it's anything like mine...." He trailed off, a strange look in his eyes.

"If she did, she would have learned to use it by now." Hatter squeezed March's shoulder, "You don't need to worry about her or Dodo. They have no power in Wonderland."

"But they d-do have some power over me." March shot back.

"Only what you allow them to," Caterpillar chimed in, "You decide what you give to other people. If you don't want them to have power over you, then don't give it to them. You are stronger than this Maxton."

I was impressed by Caterpillar's words. I hadn't really noticed the relationship between them before now, but it was clear from the look in March's eyes that he was touched. It warmed my heart that my men were close. I knew they all had relationships before we met, but they've grown even closer as our relationship has blossomed. Cheshire noticed the beginning of tears in my eyes and pulled me to his side.

"I don't know about you guys, but it's been an awfully long week. I desperately need to blow off some steam." Cheshire wiggled his eyebrows at the other three men.

Caterpillar grunted, but his long legs ate up the ground that separated us. His mouth crashed down on mine. Devouring me to my very soul as he stripped me out of my filthy dress. None of the rest of us had considered a shower after his miraculous resurrection. I stood in the middle of my four men completely bare other than the heeled boots I'd worn with my dress. "Can't believe I died and almost didn't get to taste you again," Caterpillar growled as he lifted me. He pressed me against the closest wall, my legs thrown over his shoulders. In seconds he was lapping at my core, bringing me to the brink of release.

"You can't hog her just because you died, boss." Cheshire saddled up to us, interrupting Caterpillar's work. I growled, reaching down to grip Cheshire's hair. He grinned up at me, "What, little lioness, were you close?" I froze, debating how I felt about the nickname. I'd heard Jabberwocky use it, but when Cheshire said it... it sent a thrill down my spine.

"Why don't we move this to the couch? I know everyone wants a piece of the princess." Caterpillar whispered into my ear. I slid down the wall until I could wrap my legs around his waist. I felt his cock bobbing against my ass, straining to get out of his loose pants. He dropped me unceremoniously onto the couch, kicking my legs apart. I rest my chin on the back of the couch, glancing to March who was standing in Hatter's arms. When he caught my stare he walked over, dropping his pants, showing his perfectly curved cock. I grunted as I extended my neck to capture it in my lips. He moved closer, pressing his cock against my tongue. The groan he let out as he slid into my mouth sent a wave to heat to my pussy. I felt someone tease my entrance. I pushed back desperate to be filled. "Oh no, princess. This all happens at my pace. But you're such a good girl for being so desperate for me."

March picked up his pace, causing spit to drip down my chin. I felt fingers prod my ass as Caterpillar fully seated himself inside me, "She is so needy. I think she needs to be completely filled." Cheshire's lilting voice with such dirty words always turned me on. We'd done some ass play, but we'd never tried double penetration. I was nervous but forced my body to relax.

"She's so wet on my cock, Ches. So eager for her little ass to be taken." Caterpillar teased me, pulling out completely. Cold liquid shocked me as it was drizzled over my hole. I watched as it sailed through the air, Hatter catching it as he stepped behind March. He'd slowed his pace down, obviously forcing himself not to cum. I watched as Hatter coated his fingers in lube, pressing his lips into March's neck as he slid his fingers inside him. March moaned, pressing his cock deeper down my throat. I forced myself not to gag, taking every inch of him until his hips were pressed against my nose.

"Are you ready for me, baby?" Hatter asked after several minutes. March strangled out a yes. As Hatter began to press into him, I felt the head of Cheshire's cock press against my ass. I tensed, completely overwhelmed.

He slapped my ass, "Relax. You need to take all of us." I moaned as he continued to press into me.

Caterpillar reached down, teasing my clit. "That's such a good girl. Look at you, connected to all of us. Our perfect girl. Are you going to cum with all your holes filled?" At his words I pressed back, forcing Cheshire to fully seat inside of me. Hatter pounding into March, forced me to sputter around his cock. I was so overwhelmed with sensation, a vessel for my men's pleasure. I always wanted to be this deeply connected to all of them. Tears leaked down my face as March grunted, I felt his cum fill my mouth. I swallowed every drop, kissing the head of his cock as he pulled away. Hatter still pounded into him, but reached down, gripping my hair, forcing me to look into his eyes. "Did you like the taste of his cum ?" I nodded unable to speak as Cheshire and Caterpillar found a rhythm that was wreaking havoc on my body.

"Please," I choked out.

"Fuck," Cheshire groaned as he found his release, filling me with more cum. "Such a perfect ass. All ours." He collapsed to my side but was quick to take one of my nipples in his mouth, sucking diligently.

March was moaning, quietly begging Hatter to finish. It didn't take much longer for him to find that release. When he'd recovered, he gathered up a sweaty and depleted-looking March, sitting them both down on the couch cuddled together as they watched. Caterpillar pulled away, picking me up, turning me around until my legs were wrapped around him. His cock drilled into me from a different angle. "Touch yourself for me, princess. Cum all over my cock." I did as he said, frantically playing with my clit, seeking my orgasm. As the wave began to crest, he slammed into me, and I felt his warm cum fill me at last intensifying my own orgasm. He stood holding me as we panted together. Eventually, he sat on the couch, adjusting me to comfortably sit in his lap. I could feel all the cum leaking from me onto his lap. He chuckled, "I guess we're all going to need showers now."

No one moved as we basked in the afterglow. My skin was as bright as it had ever been, anytime we all were able to be together it seemed to strengthen. My magick was quiet but purred under my skin. My mind floated back to my conversations with Eumonia. Something had been niggling in the back of my head about the old woman since she'd appeared on the sidewalk just before Mary Anne was killed, but I still was no closer to puzzling it out.

"What is running around in that head, princess?" Caterpillar's voice startled me out of my thoughts.

"I guess we should probably catch up on everything that's happened... You know that I managed to escape Jabberwocky before you got there." He nodded, some regret in his eyes, "Well I didn't get far before I passed out. When I came to, I was with an old woman—"

"Did she have blue eyes? White and silver hair? Super cryptic?" Caterpillar cut me off, grilling me.

"Yes, but how do you know that?" I asked, sitting up.

"When I came to get you from the boonies. She appeared out of nowhere." He revealed, "Who the hell is this woman?"

"I know she's a magick user. She's clearly got some kind of mental magick. She knocked me out and dropped me in front of Dina's apartment without being seen." I said, standing.

"Is she in league with the Queen of Hearts?" Hatter asked, untangling himself from March to stand as well.

"I don't think so... Honestly it seemed like she was on our side." I thought for a moment, "But if any of us see her, we need to tread carefully. We don't know anything about this mysterious old woman."

"Should I send people to check for her?" Hatter asked, motioning for all of us to follow him into the bedroom.

"No, I don't want to spook her. She hasn't done anything to harm any of us. In fact, she likely saved Alice's life." Caterpillar said. "Now we're not worrying about anything else until tomorrow. Tonight, we're going to focus on each other."

No one argued.

Chapter 13

February 1st, 2159

"You need to make an appearance today. Certain citizens are close to rioting if we don't produce Caterpillar now." Rab looked almost happy as he spoke the words. "I understand you all want to spend time together. To take a breather from everything that has been happening, but Wonderland needs you."

"When are we allowed to tell these people to go fuck themselves?" Cheshire was hissing. The way his hair was standing up made him look like an angry cat. I couldn't stop the chuckle that left me as I imagined a purple and pink cat hissing at an old rabbit.

"I know it isn't easy to lead, but you've been chosen by the people to do this." Mom jumped in, clearly trying to prevent a confrontation.

"I never agreed to any such thing." He snapped. I could see the bags under his eyes, watched him stifle a yawn. Cheshire was always the most jovial of us, even when things were hard. If he was acting this way, there was something wrong. I needed to talk to him privately.

"Caterpillar and I will go to the town square in two hours. Let everyone know." I dismissed them as nicely as I was able to. "Cheshire, I need your help in the conference room. Meet me there in ten." He didn't argue but I could see the annoyance in his eyes.

"You up for some sparring, Roman? See if death affected your skills at all?" Rab asked. Caterpillar nodded, kissing my forehead before he left.

"I'm going to meet my dad. I ran out on him the day Alice was kidnapped. I haven't hardly spoken to him since." Hatter glanced to March, "Do you want to go with me? I know he'd like to see you." March hesitated but eventually nodded. Both of them disappeared into the bedroom, leaving Cheshire and I standing alone in the living room. Neither of us spoke, but I could feel the tension coming off of him. After a few minutes of silence had passed I padded out of our apartment to the conference room. I could feel him following me. I walked straight to the table, turning to sit on it, watching as he closed the door behind us.

"What's wrong?" I asked the moment I heard the door click closed.

"Nothing." He rolled his eyes as he spoke, "I'm not a child Alice. I don't need to be taken to the principal's office over a little spat."

"We both know how much you love Rab. I care about how you feel, Ches. If something is wrong, I want to be here for you." I said, ignoring his attitude.

"Al, what isn't going wrong right now? Caterpillar literally fucking died. I think my little petty feelings aren't on the top of our priority list." He snapped back at me.

I stood, moving toward him. Once we were eye to eye I grabbed his hand, "Nothing about your feelings are petty. Please talk to me."

"It isn't fair of me to complain…" He trailed off looking away from me, "It's just… everyone else has so much happening. Hatter's Dad turned up randomly, March is out of sorts in so many ways. You were kidnapped and tortured. Caterpillar died… It's selfish."

He stopped when I forced him to look at me again. "I can't support you if you don't tell me how you're feeling. There is a lot going on. The people that you love are dealing with very traumatic things right now. It's okay if you are also overwhelmed."

Suddenly he started laughing, a guttural laugh that completely threw me off. I stepped back when he doubled over, gripping his knees. He was wheezing when he finally started to speak, "Can you imagine? If… If I really said to you... Alice, I'm hurting because everyone is all wrapped up in their trauma and lives that I'm being left out. That Wonderland has taken over our lives." Hurt filled his eyes, "I always thought after we beat the Red Queen it would be over. The constant fighting, the never-ending stress... It's worse now that it was when Penthea was still in power. At least then we made sure to enjoy the moments we had because we all knew it might be our last.... But I would never say that because it wouldn't be fair to you. Or anyone else."

"At least you'd be being honest." I whispered, still processing his words.

"Maybe. Or maybe I'm just being a jackass." We looked away from each other, clearly unsure where to go from everything he'd just let out. I understood how he felt, there were moments I felt the same way. I never wanted to be a leader in Wonderland, but at least we all had the best interests of the citizens in mind, "I'm sorry, Al. I shouldn't have said anything." Cheshire speaking broke me from my thoughts, "I haven't felt right since the wreck. I'm just trying to hold it together for everyone else."

"Please don't apologize. I'm not upset with you. I want you to tell me how you feel... I'm just processing. There's more going on than any of us can really keep up with."

"Well at least there's five of us to split all of this up with. We have each other." He pulled me into a hug as he spoke.

"I know we've all been neglecting you Ches. I know it isn't easy to watch all the people you care about fall apart. Is there anything I can do for you? You should have my mother check you out in case the wreck caused a concussion or something." I was worried about him. Guilt ate at me for not noticing he was struggling sooner. My kidnapping and Caterpillar's death had been the center of everyone's attention for days, but that didn't mean everyone else didn't matter. We were all alive and fine now. Remembering that Caterpillar was actually alive sent warmth through me. I couldn't imagine having to actually live my life without any of my men.

"I just needed to vent. Thank you for listening. Now how are we are going to kill the next hour and a half before you have to go be the big bad boss again." Cheshire asked, holding me at arm's length.

I wiggled my eyebrows, "I have a few ideas."

"I knew I loved you Al." He laughed before he turned pressing me into the conference room wall.

I smoothed my hair down after removing the helmet Caterpillar had forced on my head before we left the house. I found his mother henning adorable now, even though we both knew I almost never wore a helmet when riding. Apparently, Rab had elected to get all of us bikes while we'd been indisposed since we no longer had a vehicle that would fit us all. Hatter had been reluctant but had messaged me earlier admitting that he loved the feeling of the wind in his hair. He'd spent the rest of the time texting me updates on his plans to force March to ride on his own. Apparently, March had insisted he'd be riding bitch forever. I snorted aloud as I reflected on that text message.

"Get your game face on, princess. I don't think this is going to go smoothly." Caterpillar whispered in my ear as we approached Wonderland's Founder's statue. I nodded, taking a deep breath.

The town square was bustling but as people began to notice us voices were raised. It was impossible to understand what they were saying, though

I caught a few words here and there. It was clear the Queen of Hearts little announcement had quite the effect on people. We stood in silence as people gathered as close as they could to us. I saw a couple of familiar faces in the crowd, a few of Sammy's men nodded toward me. I could tell they were here to support us if things got out of hand. The noise began to crescendo, voices rising, demanding answers for what they'd been told.

Caterpillar raised his hand, signaling for silence. Within moments the noise had died down. I admired the respect he commanded from others. I stood a bit behind him, allowing him to lead this situation. I was only here for support. "Thank you all for coming today. I know some rumors have been circulating, a lie spread by the Queen of Hearts. I hope you can all see that I am alive and well."

"But doesn't little miss magick there have the ability to fool us?" The male voice was hard to pinpoint, but I scoffed at the comment.

"Roman Ainsworth." I raised my voice over the crowd that had begun talking again, "That's his true name. Illusions are broken by them."

People began nodding at each other, seeming to accept my answer to the challenge that had been presented. Caterpillar continued speaking as everyone stared at us expectantly. "I know these are uncertain times. The Red Queen's reign is in recent memory, but I want to assure all the citizens of Wonderland of one thing." He paused for dramatic effect, "There is nothing we will not do to prevent the Queen of Hearts from taking this city. All we ask is for your cooperation and trust."

"How can we trust you? You haven't managed to rid Wonderland of its issues since you took over." I could tell the voice was the same as the one before. I gave a small nod to Patrick who had appeared at the front of the gathering. He turned, moving through the crowd.

"Have your lives not improved since the Red Queen was taken out of power?" Caterpillar asked firmly, I could see him making eye contact with people in the crowd. I saw shame on some people's faces as they knew things were better than before. "If you agree with the Queen of Hearts, you are more than welcome to join her cause. Remember that she will not take this city from me. From us." Caterpillar grabbed my hand as he spoke, pulling me next to him. This was a show of power, not for our citizens, but for the sympathizers. I had no doubt the Queens of Hearts had people in this crowd. I let my electricity spark in the air around me. I had always been careful not to have someone so close to me when I did this, but I glanced toward Caterpillar, toward the sparks racing down my arm toward him. As they reached him they guttered out completely. I raised my eyes to his, felt something welling in my chest. The sounds in the crowd faded completely. His grey eyes bore into me, I heard a dark whisper rumble between us, "You are mine." Heat flooded me, I could still feel the electricity snapping around me. However his void power worked, as soon as my electricity made contact with his skin I felt the magick fade away as if it had never existed.

"This is my-our- city. The Queen of Hearts will answer for the damage she has caused, but know this..." I locked eyes with Patrick who had a familiar face in his grip. "Anyone who tries to hurt the people I love answers to me." I hadn't raised my voice, but the words boomed across the town square, silence followed for several moments. Claps and cheers eventually crescendo. I heard a few shouted praises, but I didn't care as I locked eyes with Dodo.

"Meet us at her place." I spat at Patrick, refusing to make any acknowledgement of March's grandfather.

I let Caterpillar climb on the bike first. He grunted at me when I tried to climb on without the helmet. I rolled my eyes, but acquiesced. Our speech was going to have consequences, but we'd discussed that before we'd left home. It was time we found a way to get ahead of whatever the Queen of Hearts plan was, but first I had more important fish to fry. March deserved peace, and I would get it for him today.

Chapter 14

Maddie: I'm keeping him busy, but you'll need to be quick.

Alice: You don't have that much stamina. Better start thinking of other ways.

Maddie: You are such a dirty girl. I'll remember that little comment next time I get my hands on you.

I grinned down at the text exchanged, ignoring Dodo's heavy breathing across from me. Caterpillar had taped his mouth shut as soon as we'd walked in the door. I had my leather boots resting on the table we sat at, forcing myself to be as relaxed as possible. Caterpillar leaned against the wall behind me, glaring. We hadn't spoken a word, letting the tension in the room build. This was part of the power play I knew I had to play with Dodo. He needed to be too afraid of us to fuck with March. The thought nearly caused me to drop my relaxed demeanor. I wanted nothing more than to see him suffer the way I'd watched March suffer. He still came awake, sweating and crying some nights. It came in waves; he would have a few good months and then spend weeks sleepless. Barely functioning. We had to force food down his throat sometimes. I couldn't see how Hatter handled it on his own before, but according to him this was new. I felt guilty that I hadn't paid for more attention.

"Princess, we do have other things to do today." Caterpillar's voice invaded my thoughts.

I cleared my throat, "Is this really worth our time?"

"Of course not, but you know how I feel about hecklers." He shot back.

I let a grin spread across my face as I stood, circling the desk. I stood behind Dodo, watching as he tried to turn his head to see me. I laid my hand on his shoulder, my grip was deceptively light. "Now, I don't believe for a moment the Queen of Hearts sent you of all people to upset us. It's simply too low brow of her. What I think is you wanted our attention, well you have it, Gavin." I emphasized his name. I watched the glee in Caterpillar's eyes as Dodo reacted to us knowing something about him. "What do you have to say for yourself?" He let out a series of muffled noises, and I laughed, "Oops, my apologies." I reached around and ripped the tape off of his mouth.

He hissed a bit before he began speaking. "Is this how you are going to treat citizens when they have complaints about how you run this city? Just you wait until I tell my friends about this. I'll have you know that I know all of the large business owners in—"

"Is there a point to this rant?" I spoke over the top of him, circling back to my seat. "We both know you've lost a lot of your power since we forced the closure of your shop due to safety concerns after you were found selling guns to known Red Party members."

"No one will work with you anymore." Caterpillar's smile was menacing as he moved closer to me. "So, what was that little stunt? You could sow discontentment silently."

Dodo was too stunned to speak as his brown eyes bounced back and forth between us. He sighed and his shoulders deflated slightly. "Claudia has insisted this was the only way to get an audience with you. I am out of options."

If I didn't know how vile this man truly was, I would have felt bad for him. "You raised her, so if you're having problems with her that's your fault. You could have left her to rot in the institution."

"She's my only family." I growled at the words, "We both know my grandson wants nothing to do with me so you can't seriously expect me to count him." I nodded, seeing his point. "I would like a ceasefire, some kind of agreement where I can exist peacefully within the city. I know Maxton is... involved with you. Despite my daughter's ridiculous belief that she can become close to her son again... I simply want to spend the rest of my life quietly."

I glanced up at Caterpillar who wore a deep frown, "You certainly won't find it this way. I don't want you or your daughter in my city. All of us know exactly what she allowed to happen to her son. If you think for a moment, we have any leniency for that you're mistaking."

"Well, I didn't do it!" Dodo exclaiming, standing from his chair, "I couldn't care less about that boy or his deadbeat father. I told Claudia to let the poet have the boy when he was born but she wouldn't do it. I didn't see her for years until she came crying to me about that man she'd shacked up with. I pleaded with the King of Hearts for help, my daughter.... She isn't right."

Caterpillar and I both sat in silence absorbing all that we'd learned, "Get out." I whispered.

"What?" Dodo looked stunned.

"Leave and pray you never cross us again. Find a way to control Claudia or I'll find a way to expel you both from the city. March will not live in my city in fear for the rest of his life." I turned my back dismissing him completely. He didn't hesitate to jump up and leave. I listened to his footsteps clicking down the ornate hallway.

Once I was certain he was gone, "I hate this place, but everyone is so terrified of it, it seemed like the right move."

Caterpillar pulled me into a hug, forcing a heavy breath from me, "We need to eventually take this house back. Your mother started her life in these walls."

"Just because I know you're right, doesn't mean I'm ready." I sighed. Just being here made my skin crawl.

"You don't have to be yet. Today we can go back to our apartment and enjoy a hot meal with the people we love." Caterpillar pulled away to look me in the eyes, "Are you okay with what just happened?"

"I have so many questions. Not just about everything Dodo just said, but everything that's been going on. It's just information overload." I admitted, running a hand through my hair.

"I know, princess. Let's go home, you need a hot bath. We can spoil you for the night."

"Have I mentioned how much I love you?" I said, grinning.

"I could stand to hear it more." He chucked, kissing me. I let him lead me out of the Red Party's former headquarters, forcing all the thoughts from my mind. Some problems could be dealt with later.

"Why the f-fuck did you not tell me what happened today?" A headache was forming behind my eyes, but I tried to ignore it. My hot bath had been cut short when Hatter and March had come into the apartment screaming at each other. Well March was doing most of the screaming, "I-I am not some f-fragile child. I can't believe you would disrespect me like this, Alice."

"Don't speak to her like that." Cheshire snapped, causing my eyebrows to raise, "That is my future wife you're talking to." I watched as Cheshire stood, arms crossed in front of March. March was taller, but a bit thinner.

I could see rage nearly seething around both of them. I didn't believe they would come to blows, but I looked toward Caterpillar and Hatter who stood off to the side. They mirrored each other, arms crossed, brows furrowed.

"I knew as well, Maxton. If you want to be mad at anyone, I was the one distracting you." Hatter spoke trying to dispel the tension that was building in the room.

"Ches, it's okay. He's allowed to be angry with me." I spoke softly, trying to assist Hatter. "I'm not offended."

"He can be as angry as he likes and not yell or curse you. That is unacceptable toward a woman you claim to love." March deflated at those words. I saw the guilt and self-hatred fill him. I knew March was struggling, I just couldn't entirely understand why.

"I'm sorry that I chose to deal with Dodo without consulting you. I hope you can understand why I was trying to protect you from him." I stepped around Cheshire, getting between the two of them. "I know where you're at. You can't handle any more on your plate right now. Please forgive me for trying to protect you."

He looked at me. I saw a war behind his eyes, "I know you meant well, b-but..." He paused, the muscle in his jaw clenching, "I'm trying to get better. I can't do that if you all continue to take away my power in situations like this. I just want support."

A knot formed in my throat. He was right, we all treated him with gentleness, but March was still a man. A man who had survived horrors the rest of us couldn't comprehend. I definitely considered him fragile. I wanted to wrap him up and protect him from the world. Reality began to set in, our protection of March was part of why he couldn't move forward. I took a deep breath, considering the best way to approach this situation. I glanced toward Caterpillar and Hatter trying to tell them what I'd realized with my eyes, but both of them looked on tight lipped. I huffed slightly, I'd have to discuss it with them in private later, but right now I had to address

March. "I will keep in mind that you want to be involved with decisions like this in the future. I think we are all guilty of trying to spare you from stress." I paused trying to think of how to continue, "But I will not accept the way you've spoken to me today. I didn't deserve to be screamed at." I saw fear in his eyes, so I rushed to continue, "I think we've all noticed something going on with you and chosen to ignore it. I'm not ignoring it anymore. It's time to talk to us."

"I-I-I," His face was red, and he glanced toward Hatter for refuge. I was proud of him for a slight shake of his head. I grabbed March's chin gently, forcing him to look me in the eye. I didn't speak waiting for him to process, "I already t-told you all I hate myself." He collapsed onto the couch, and I went to my knees in front of him. No one else moved, "I'm so angry... I hate my magick, I hate everyone related to me. The only light in my life is in this room, and everyone is s-suffering.... I can't live like this forever." A single tear fell down his face, "I killed Caterpillar."

I looked toward Caterpillar, who immediately began speaking, "I don't blame you. You were reckless, but I understand why. Alice was missing, and... you're dealing with a lot..." He stopped clearly considering. "But if you ever put any of us in danger like that again. I cannot let it slide Maxton. There will be consequences." I raised my eyebrows, wondering exactly what he meant. The images flashing through my mind weren't innocent, so I shook them away. March seemed a little shocked as well, but Caterpillar continued. "And you still owe Alice an apology for speaking to her like that. And frankly the rest of us as well. This is supposed to be a safe place for all of us. Leading this city is stressful, and we all play a role in that. Even you."

Hatter walked toward us, but reached suddenly, grabbing March by the neck. "I love you, Maxton, but I told you last year I was done coddling you. Your emotional state is serious, and we all care, but I won't accept you taking it out on us. If you can't control yourself, I will have Alcinda put you in an apartment alone." I felt a bit sick at the look of horror on

March's face. Hatter's words were almost cruel. "I don't want you to feel lesser than, and I had better not hear any further talk of you hating yourself. I am going to speak to my father and see if we can get you someone to talk to about those feelings. If you ever hurt yourself...." Hatter stopped, shaking his head. "I won't even think about it.

Tears were flowing steadily down March's face as he met my eyes again, "I'm sorry, Ali. I will be better... for you."

"I need you to do better for you. I want you to love yourself as much as we all love you." I sat up, pulling him into a hug. He nodded but was clearly too emotional to speak.

"Now, March go in and run Alice another hot bath. It was rude to interrupt a moment she needed." Caterpillar ordered. I furrowed my eyebrows but said nothing. Once March had stood and walked out of the room Caterpillar spoke again. "He needs discipline and self-control. These things he's feeling. I don't think it just his emotions. I have a feeling some of this has to be with his magick."

"We still need to care for him." I argued, "He needs a soft place to land."

"He'll have it when that's what he needs, but if he can scream like that. If he can cut Jabberwocky's arm off, then he can go in and run his future wife a hot bath as apology for his behavior. And he can cook dinner tonight."

"Aren't you punishing him like a child?" I didn't mean to argue with him, but I was concerned with taking it too far.

"You think I'm punishing him?" Caterpillar snorted, "Creator, Alice. I'm holding him to the same standards I'd hold any of us to. When we fuck up, we apologize. He chose to come into our home screaming while you were trying to relax. He didn't give us a chance to even talk to him about what actually happened for fucks sake. All he knows right now is that we detained Dodo today. He'll get the information once you've had a chance to relax. I can nearly see the electricity buzzing under your skin, has been since we entered that place."

I gulped. I hadn't considered anyone else would notice how on edge I was. My nerves were frayed. My magick was thrashing against my skin. My instincts screaming that something was wrong. I just couldn't narrow down specifically what that was. "I know you're right."

"Of course I am, princess." I rolled my eyes, causing him to grin, "Now go, strip your clothes off right in front of him. Let him have a good look and then kick him back out to us. I will tell everyone the details of our day while you rest."

"Yes bossman." I saluted him as I began walking toward the bedroom.

March was sitting on the edge of the tub, long fingers skimming the water, testing the temperature. His dirty blond locks falling into his face. He hadn't noticed my entrance, so I continued to watch him. He was a beautiful man; poems could have been written about his strong but delicate features. "You know it's creepy to stand there in silence." He turned toward me, but his eyes were downcast.

"Thank you for running the bath." I stripped out my clothes before stepping all the way into the room. "And I accept your apology." I pressed my lips to his cheek. I could feel his eyes on me as I stepped into the hot water, slowly, methodically submerging myself.

"Your scars are beautiful." He blurted the words out, eyes widening when he realized what he'd said, "I m-mean… you've been through a lot Alice. I don't want you to think that I d-don't see all of you. You're one of the only lights in my life. A flame keeping me entranced."

My resolve to follow Caterpillar's instructions wavered slightly, but I forced myself to only smile. "I see you. And I will be here whenever you need to be warmed."

He stood staring at me, clearly wanting more, but ultimately realizing he wasn't getting it. "Enjoy your bath."

I watched as he turned and walked away. I pushed myself under water, letting the water soak all of the stress from me. Somehow, I was going to carve peace out of the chaos I lived in. Even if it took every ounce of me to do so.

Chapter 15

February 5th, 2159

A few days passed in relative quiet. Hatter had been the most active, leaving at least once a day to handle something that Caterpillar had insisted, I didn't need to worry about. Of course that didn't stop me from being curious. I just decided not to push it; I had bigger concerns.

"I'm going to speak to my mother. I need to discuss this Eumonia woman with her. I'm certain she might know something." I announced.

"You should give yourself another day or two. It can wait. The Queen of Hearts is clearly reeling from Caterpillar's resurrection. Why can't you let this go?" Cheshire was typing away on his laptop, not entirely paying attention to me.

"Because I know it's important." I crossed my arms staring him down.

"Fine, but I'm going with you." He sighed, closing his computer. "But you owe me later."

I winked at him as I skipped toward the front door. "I'm sure Dina will be happy to see that I'm alive since you've had me locked up in here for days."

"She lives six feet away, I'm sure she knows exactly what you've been up to." I turned on him, flailing to slap his chest. He skirted my hands, managed to press a kiss to my cheek before he took off down the hall. I rounded the corner, and he'd completely disappeared. I stepped carefully, knowing he was playing a game, stretching his magick muscles. It was good to see him use his magick, in many ways Cheshire had been the most hesitant to test his abilities. I found that surprising, when we'd met he'd had the most obvious talent. His magick was potent even if he wasn't training or resting enough. I'd always assumed Caterpillar would be the most against magick. Which would make sense considering his recently revealed ability. He didn't like for us to try to rely on magick, even for healing. He'd insisted that March learn more first aid skills after Cheshire almost died when we took over the city. I needed to discuss his magick with my mother. If there would be a way to train his void abilities like the rest of us trained. I was so consumed in my thoughts I forgot that Cheshire had disappeared, until he appeared suddenly beside me, arm resting on my shoulder. I couldn't prevent that scream that ripped from my throat.

"Creator woman, is one of your abilities sonic booms?" He rubbed his ears as he glared at me.

"It's your own fault for startling me." I chuckled as I pushed the conference room door open with my foot. "Oh shit." I grabbed the door and closed it immediately, my eyes wide from what I'd seen.

"Was that?" I nodded at Cheshire question, "With?"

"Yeah..." I hadn't been prepared to see my mother and Jonah embracing passionately.

"I can't even be mad, weren't we doing the same thing a few days ago." The twinkle in his eyes sent warmth through my body.

"I had no idea." I whispered, trying to creep away from the door. With any luck they hadn't noticed our intrusion.

We didn't make it very far before my mother's voice rang out, "Ali, what can I do for you this morning?"

Cheshire coughed, clearly feeling the awkwardness that hung in the air. "Well... I..." I couldn't remember what I'd come to discuss with her now.

My mother grinned, "I am still alive, Alice. I would think you of all people could understand wanting to have companionship in this life."

"Of course," I rushed to speak so she wouldn't go into any further detail, "I just didn't expect." I motioned toward Jonah who had appeared in the doorway behind her. "Ah but I am happy for you both." I felt my face getting hot.

"I'd like to keep this just between us. I don't expect you not to tell my nephew, but…" I knew what he was saying, and I nodded.

"I came to speak to you more about Eumonia." I changed the subject.

"Come on in and take a seat. I agree that we need to investigate this woman further." She ushered us into the room. I hesitated to sit, struggling to look either of them in the eye. I'd never considered my mother with anyone other than my father, or Rab with anyone other than Mary Anne for that matter. The more I considered it; the more sense it made for them to find comfort in one another. "Alice, let's go over the details again." My mother's voice brought me out of my thoughts.

"Well, we know that somehow, she knew Jabberwocky had me. She was the one who rescued me when I managed to escape." I started.

"You were in sector six when he took you. Why were you there?" Rab stopped me from continuing.

I hesitated, "Well I knew he'd been following me, but I also… When Joshua brought up concerns about the dome over the city the first place to come to mind was sector six. I can't really explain to you why." It was just a gut feeling I'd been having. Something I'd felt.

"Have you been there before?" My mother's tone was full of question.

"No never," I defended. "It's almost like…" I trailed off trying to explain how I'd felt that day, "Like my magick was calling me there."

"We need to go back," Cheshire spoke, surprising me, "If you're saying magick was calling you there. You have to go back and find out why. We need more answers and less questions."

"I'm not sure that's safe." Rab interjected, before I could respond. "Wonderland has been dangerous for all of us, is venturing into a sector we know is unsafe the best idea?"

"If we want Wonderland to be safer than we need to take risks. If Alice's magick is calling her to this place, then I think we'd be stupid to ignore it." Cheshire argued.

I looked to my mother who was staring at the wall, unblinking. When she remained that way for several more moments, I realized what was happening. I raised my hand, halting the back and forth between Cheshire and Rab. I didn't speak, just nodded toward my mother. A very slight golden shimmer had started to appear just around her head. I didn't often see her have visions. I'd always been under the impression she only had them while she slept, but it was clear something magick was happening to her. Rab sat down next to her, when he reached out to touch her, I laid my hand over his. A slight shake to my head was the only explanation I gave. I didn't want to interrupt whatever she was seeing. We all sat with bated breath for what felt like an eternity. Until she gasped, knuckles turning white against the table before she stood, knocking her chair back. I jumped out of my seat, reaching for her. Her entire body was shaking, her breaths shaky as she tried to begin speaking, "My father... my father."

I glanced toward Cheshire in confusion, "Mom, mom. Slow down."

"Get me a pen!" She was shouting as she pulled away from me, "Hurry, before I lose it." Rab scrambled across the room, nearly throwing paper and a pen at her in an attempt to calm her frantic words. I tried to glance over her shoulder at what she was writing, but she was hunched over it, muttering to herself. "Alice, you're going to go to sector six. It's... well I don't know much more than you're going. Jonah, we're going to... my father's home."

"What did you see Mom?" I asked, confused.

"I can't explain until I go. I need to go." She brushed me off, heading toward the door. I'd rarely ever seen my mother have visions. If this is what it was like all the time, I couldn't imagine how she'd managed to run the Resistance.

I started to speak up, but Rab stopped me, "I'll go with her. Are you going to sector six now?"

My head was spinning, but I nodded, "I will, but please keep me updated. I've never seen her like this before."

"I'll watch out for her." He responded, giving me a small smile, before he rushed out of the room after her.

"Well, that was weird." Cheshire said, after they'd both disappeared down the hallway.

"Extremely. You ready for an adventure?" I responded.

"We should get with everyone else before we leave." He hesitated.

"What are you a scaredy cat?" I taunted.

"Fine, but you answer to Caterpillar later." Cheshire sighed, following me out of the room.

"You're still afraid of big, bad Caterpillar, Chessie baby?" I shot back.

"When it comes to your safety? Hell yeah, I am." He laughed, throwing an arm over my shoulders.

I looked at Cheshire's profile, taking in his grin, underneath I could see the slight tense in his shoulders. I paused, "If you want me to go grab the other guys that's fine with me."

He stopped, grabbing the back of my arm, "And give up my alone time with you? I don't think so. You had me at adventure, Alice."

I parked the bike, quickly throwing the helmet off my head. Cheshire was right behind me, his pink and purple hair perfectly tousled as he hung his helmet on one of his handlebars. "Woman, has anyone ever told you that you drive like you have a death wish."

"Coming from you I'm taking that as a compliment. You're lucky they even gave you something to ride." I shot back.

"I'll give you something to ride." He wiggled his eyebrows at me suggestively. I grinned, but a sudden pull in my chest forced me to turn away. I stared at the crumbling building closest to the entrance of sector six. Vines curled around it; tiny pink flowers were struggling to survive the colder weather. I stepped forward, my skin buzzing incessantly. I needed to go. "Al, wait." Cheshire's voice barely registered, "What are you feeling?"

"A call." Were the only words I could find, as I continued my march forward. I forced myself to take in my surroundings, careful to step over slabs that had once been stores and homes. I had no idea what this area had been before it had been destroyed, but I imagined it was much like the rest of the city. How many people had died because they'd been unable to escape as nature ripped their homes down around them? The ground seemed to shake as if it could hear my thoughts, was remembering how it felt that day.

"Woah." I looked back to find Cheshire, catching himself from tripping over a root in the ground. "Slow down, Al. I can't keep up with you."

I forced myself to stop, letting him catch up to me. He grabbed my hand, entwining our fingers. "Do you feel anything?" I asked.

He closed his eyes, seeming lost in thought for a moment, "It does seem… different here."

I nodded, I couldn't put my finger on it either, but I decided to continue forward. I glanced back toward the bikes realizing I could no longer see them. We were quickly approaching the center of this sector. The buzzing under my skin was nearly unbearable the further we went. We rounded a corner, and I stopped in my tracks. I ripped my hand away from Cheshire's as sparks began to burst from my skin. His muttered curse as he stumbled back didn't stop my feet from carrying me to the center of a large, scorched circle. The magick that radiated from it made it hard for me to breath. I fell to my knees, laying my hands flat on the circle. Vibrations ran up my arms, I felt a pull at the center of my magick. I started to pull away, but I couldn't. I was held in place, my magick pooling in my hands as they glowed a bright silver. I tried and failed not to panic. My breathing was labored, a pain took root in my chest. I managed to call out for Cheshire before my entire world went black.

Chapter 16

❧❧❧❧❧ ❦❦❦❦❦

Cheshire

I ran toward Alice the moment I saw her fall to her knees, but I ran into some invisible barrier. I slammed my hands against it, trying to force my way to her. I watched in horror as her skin lit up brighter than I'd ever seen it before. I was helpless when I heard her call for me. Rage bubbled in my chest, my woman needed me, and I couldn't get to her. She'd been through the last few weeks, and I was once again helpless to do anything for her. I paced around the perimeter of the barrier, occasionally trying to press through it.

"Use your magick." A woman's voice had me spinning around, pulling one of the guns from the holster on my back.

When I saw the grey, old woman with bright blue eyes standing before me, I knew exactly who she was, "Eumonia."

Her eyebrows raised, "I must be slipping if Alice remembered my name."

"Did you do this?" I snapped, annoyed. I turned back to check on her, only to find her so bright I could barely make out her form.

"I wouldn't do anything to harm her." Her vague response didn't help my agitation, "Sinclair, just use your magick. It will let you through." I cringed at the use of my real name. I had no idea how she even knew it, but

I hated hearing it. Only my mother had ever called me by my full name. Anytime I heard it I felt a twinge of pain in my chest. I shook my head, forcing the thoughts of being an orphan away. It had been too long since I'd lost my parents to still focus on it. I had a family and right now the center of my world needed me. I hesitated before I closed my eyes, reaching into the back of my mind, finding the twisting power that hid there. Alcinda had tried to work with me after the Red Queen had been defeated, but I didn't have any desire to learn more about my powers. I'd flex them occasionally just to make sure this was all real. I grabbed onto the magick in my mind, forced it down my arm. I didn't open my eyes as I laid my hand against the invisible barrier. I could feel the resistance at first, but within seconds I stumbled. I opened my eyes, finding myself just a few feet short of Alice. I rushed to grab her, and found that her body was hot, nearly burning with the amount of electricity that had come from her. I didn't hesitate to gather her into my arms even as little spikes of electricity zapped against my skin. The feel of her against me caused me to immediately begin sweating, but I ignored it, pushing my away back out of the barrier, toward Eumonia. She beamed at me, "Very good. Follow me. She'll need to be cooled off before she'll be able to awaken."

I stopped, unwilling to follow this strange woman anywhere. "I need some answers before I go anywhere with you."

"I'm a seer. That's as much as I'll tell you now." She was stern, motioning for me to follow her without any further explanation. I considered my options, staring down at Alice's red face I cursed. I had to jog to catch up with her. She weaved in between the crumbling structures and trees that had grown tall since the destruction of this sector. The further I followed her the more nervous I became, but I knew she might be able to provide answers we were in desperate need of. Whatever vision Alcinda had led us here. Led us back to Eumonia. When she stopped in front a tiny tree I questioned my decision. She laid her hand against, I could see a very slight glow light around her hand, before a door appeared in its place.

She opened it, motioning me inside. The room was exactly as Alice had described it. The walls were covered in fantastical murals, bright yellow grass, teal skies, animals I couldn't even begin to identify. "Sit her in here." Eumonia directed me to a large metal tub. She was pouring water into it. "I don't have a way to make ice, but it's cool enough outside this water should help with her overheating. Take her clothes off, I don't have anything for her to wear." I nodded, carefully following her instructions. Undressing an unconscious person was harder than I expected, but I managed. I sat her into the water carefully, holding her head so it wouldn't go under the water. Eumonia took a cloth and dabbed some water onto her face. I watched the woman's face as she carefully wiped dust away from Alice's face. Her eyes were misty with unshed tears, if I didn't know better, I'd say her eyes were filled with motherly concern.

Without thought I blurted, "Who are you, really?"

She met my eyes, blinking away whatever emotions she'd been feeling. With a sigh she began to speak, "I know that it's time to explain, but... I'm a very old woman Sinclair Malone. Telling my story won't be easy. Let us wait until Alice is awake."

I cringed again at her use of my name, but I couldn't bring myself to ask her how she knew it. I stared down at Alice, admiring her smooth skin, an undertone of the silver glow still shining through. She had always been strikingly beautiful, and I loved that she knew it. Confidence was one the sexiest thing she'd ever worn.

"Cheshire, Ches." Alice's voice brought me out of the fitful sleep I'd fallen into. I had no idea how long I'd sat holding her head, hoping that she'd wake up.

"Looks like you're waking me up for once." I smiled, pulling her down into my lap. She had obviously been awake for a while. The end of her hair were still dripping wet, but she'd clearly dried off and redressed.

"At least you know I'm not crazy." She gestured to the room, ignoring my comment.

"I've never thought you were anything but completely sane. Now the rest of us are hopeless. We all lost our minds a long time ago." I meant every word; without Alice the world didn't make any sense to me. We'd only been together about eighteen months, and yet the moment I'd laid eyes on her she had changed everything.

"As beautiful as this moment is, I believe I have some explaining to do." Eumonia spoke, starling me.

Alice nodded, "I need some answers."

She motioned for us to join her at the small table that was pushed into the only free corner of the room. I sat Alice on her feet, stepping around her to pull out a chair, ensuring she was comfortable before I sat down. I knew I was feeling nervous energy. Whatever we were about to learn was going to change our lives. They both looked at me when I didn't immediately sit down, so I flung myself into the chair next to Alice. No one spoke at first, the room seemed to hold its breath as if even the air felt the tension in the room.

"When I was a young girl, I loved to play outside." I glanced to Alice in confusion, what did this old woman's childhood have to do with what was happening now? "I had a passion for animals, but especially birds. It was no shock to my parents when my first magick to present was my ability to see through an animal's eyes. My father never felt it would be useful to my position-"

"What position was that?" I blurted, impatient.

She chuckled, "Well I was a princess." She stopped, watching us both react, "See, you need to hear the whole story for any of it to be believable. I wasn't born in this city. I was born in a place called Undraland—"

Alice started laughing, near hysterical, "You—You're still trying to tell me Lewis Carroll's story was true." I saw anger flash in Eumonia's eyes, and I laid a hand on Alice's thigh, trying to reign in her sass. I had a gut feeling we needed to hear what she had to say. Alice took a deep breath, "I'm sorry. Please continue."

"Alice isn't far off. Lewis Carroll was from Undraland. He was the Undralandian who led Alice Liddell safely to the Red King's castle. He stood by her side while the child slayed a grown man with the vorpal sword. The same man who wiped her memories and escorted her back to Earth. He stayed, spinning his tales to ensure reality never made it to the people of this realm. His sacrifices saved my realm, allowed nearly two centuries of peace in Undraland." Her impassioned speech made it clear that she believed every word of what she was saying. I found myself believing it to.

"So, you're the princess of Undraland?" I asked, unable to stop myself.

"I became the Queen of Undraland at thirteen. Both of my parents died of a mysterious illness. I was unprepared, but I had advisors and close friends who helped me. Unfortunately, the illness that killed my parents began to take more and more citizens. A strange haze began to fill the air, the sky became a sickly green color. It was a slow progression, we didn't realize until it was far too late." A tear ran down her face as she spoke. I watched Alice reach across the table to comfort her. I saw she had her own tears falling. I threw my arm over her shoulders, trying to support her. "Lewis Carroll couldn't return to Undraland because he was not a portaler. The gift was extremely rare, mostly running in the Red King's line, which had been completely wiped out by that point. I was blessed to have a good friend, Rhosyn, who was able to assist me in escorting fifty of my staff and council to Earth. My goal was to see if a cure could be found here. Rhosyn was able to hold the portal for all of us to get through. What I didn't foresee was her death immediately after my husband stepped through. I watched in horror as she fell backward through that portal, locking all the rest of us here. Permanently."

"I'm so sorry." I couldn't find any other words. Eumonia's story was hard to believe, but some part of me knew she was being honest.

"Where are the other fifty people? Wonderland doesn't have many people near your age." Alice asked.

Eumonia laughed bitterly, "There is no one in either realm as old as I am."

"How old are you?" Alice asked, seeming confused.

"By my last calculation, I turned one hundred and sixty-eight years old last month." She responded without hesitation.

My mouth dropped open in shock, and I couldn't stop the words that left my mouth next, "You look great for your age. I wouldn't have guessed a day over seventy-five."

Alice and Eumonia snorted at the same moment, but Eumonia continued. "What we arrived to on Earth was almost worse than what our homeland was going through. It seemed the Creator had long since given up on this realm. Natural disasters were ramping up, killing millions. We landed at a spot not far from where we sit now. I didn't allow myself to even consider what we had lost. The people of Earth were suffering. My people and I did everything we could to save anyone we found. Eventually I made it here, watched as children were crushed by falling buildings. It was clear that a mass extinction was the only goal. I made a decision in a moment of desperation. You see I was blessed with three abilities. Of course I'd already mentioned my connection to animals, as I've mentioned I'm also a seer, but I'm also an extremely powerful shielder. What happened today, it was a refresh. The magick that has been holding the barrier for so long is weakening. I don't know why, but Alice was called here because she is the most powerful magick user in the city. The barrier is an almost living thing now. It needed magick to survive." Alice looked panicked, but closed her eyes, and I watched as electricity crackled at her finger tips. After a deep sigh from Alice, Eumonia continued. "I've gained more abilities as I've aged, not long after this I became able to manipulate memories. I believe this was an extension of my seeing abilities. Magick is an ever-evolving thing. Especially in those of us who have been blessed by the Creator with more power."

"So, Joshua's concerns about the shield around Wonderland were valid?" I confirmed, my mind overflowing with information.

"Of course, they were." Alice rolled her eyes, "But if you've been alive this entire time. Why would you save this city, the people here, just to allow the Red Queen to rule."

Eumonia cringed at the question. "I know it may seem callous of me, but as a seer it is my responsibility to only interfere where I am allowed." Alice went to speak but she held a hand up to stop her, "It's important you allow me to continue. It took me months to recover from that much magick use, but slowly the people left alive in the city and the Undralandian's began to work together to rebuild. My people knew what I had done, what we were now faced with. They integrated with the people of Earth. Everyone looked to me to lead us. I did what I could, all of my people had abilities that made life is easier. My shield seemed to allow the city to mostly function as it had before Earth's destruction had begun. My only problem began when I did not age as I should have."

"Are all magick users' immortal?" I was brimming with questions. Would all of us live forever? My heart beat faster at the idea of a life with Alice that would never end.

"No, very few are. So, I grew my ability to alter memories, until I was able to cast a web over all of Wonderland. And one night, long after my husband had passed, and my children were grown I removed myself from existence. I'd began planning it years before, I'd already created this place. And here I've been, watching, waiting until I was needed."

"You're needed now." Alice said firmly. "Clearly, I know nothing about this city. We shouldn't even be running it!" She slammed away from the table, running hands through her hair.

"I am, but not for what you are thinking." Eumonia stood as well, walking to Alice. The old woman, grabbed her, pulling her into a tight hung, "You see, Alice. I did have children, most all of the Undralandian's did. Our magick has lived on long after my friends and family have died. My line lives on in you. You are a Lyon Queen. You are meant to rule Undraland."

I stared at Alice, but I didn't see the woman I loved. In her place I saw what Eumonia described. A queen without her throne.

Chapter 17

Alice

I couldn't breathe, couldn't think as Eumonia's words sank in. "You—You're my grandmother?"

"There's quite a few grandmothers between me and Lillian, but you are of my blood." She confirmed.

My head was spinning, I fell back onto the wooden chair closest to me, "I can't be a queen. I hate leading. I don't believe any of this. It can't be real."

A warm hand landed on my shoulder, and I glanced up through blurry eyes at Cheshire, "I believe her." He whispered, before kneeling in front of me, a hand on my calf, "It's the first time anything about this city has made sense."

"I cannot be a queen." I murmured to him.

"You always have been." He said, tilting my chin to force me to look at him. His dark blue eyes held so much emotion, so much pride I felt my chest constrict even further. "I've known since the moment I met you, Al. You are going to change our entire world."

"I don't know how." I whispered back.

"That's what we're here for. Me, Caterpillar, Hatter, and March. We're going to stand by and support you while you electrify the entire world." The reverence in his voice brought me down.

Slowly I began to calm, to think clearly. I glanced to Eumonia who stood off the to the side, staring at one of her art covered walls. I took them in again, seeing them for what they must have been. She painted these, images of her home. Of Undraland. A place that she would never see again. My heart ached for her. I couldn't imagine being ripped away from my home, being forgotten by everyone who might have loved me. "I am sorry for how I've acted toward you."

Eumonia turned to me, a small smile on her face, "I would do the same in your situation. It's smart not to trust people just because they've asked you to." She stopped, our eyes meeting. I finally realized that her eyes reminded me of my own. As long as it had been a part of her lived on in me. "I am happy that I have finally been able to share my story with someone."

"It's an honor to know you." I pulled her into a hug, enjoying her warm embrace. I'd never had a grandmother. A part of me desperately wanted to sit down and hear anything and everything she would be willing to share about her life. She knew far more about magick than anyone I'd ever met. In just the short time I'd been here, I had learned so much of our history that my head was overflowing.

"The honor is mine. I am glad to see my legacy live on." Her smile was sad, her weathered hand resting gently against my face. "I would like to meet your sister, I've heard she inherited my power. I am still surprised she was not called here. Her shielding magick seems to match mine."

"How do you know so much about all of us?" Cheshire asked. I'd almost forgotten he was there. His power was growing stronger.

Eumonia whistled loudly, a sudden flapping of wings caused me to duck. A huge white bird landed on her shoulder, "This is Azura. She is my eyes through the city. I could have many, but she is most special to me. She's a descendant of the bird I came here with. Earth had a similar creature in doves, so my sweet Sybil was able to breed. Several of her offspring have given me a look into the outside world."

I nodded, pushing away the slight terror I felt as the bird's black eyes stared into mine. It cocked its head, flapping its wings slowly. I didn't expect for it to gently lift itself from Eumonia's shoulders and land on mine. I was stiff as it rubbed it's head against my cheek. I slowly reached my hand up, running my fingers gently over one of it's pure white wings. When it didn't immediately begin pecking my eyes out, I relaxed. A quiet ding brought me back to reality, I turned toward Cheshire, causing Azura to fly away from me. Cheshire was typing fast, glancing up at me, "I really don't want to cut this short."

"But?" I pushed, knowing something was wrong.

"Your mom fainted at the Red Party's base. Rab is asking us to come help him, she's back awake, but frantic. Hatter also says Duchess is at the apartment with Dina asking for you."

I sighed, "How can I get in touch with you?"

Eumonia smiled, "I'll be around when you need me. At this moment, all I will leave you with is this, be careful who you reveal the information I've shared with you to. Not everyone in Wonderland is what they seem."

I nodded, understanding exactly what she meant. I'd have to be very careful, but I was used to it at this point. I only trusted a very small group of people, and unfortunately, I had a feeling someone close to me was involved with the Queen of Hearts. I'd been thinking about it ever since Caterpillar's funeral, no one knew he was gone. Very few people ventured all the way out to the wildflowers, mostly out of fear. Someone had told her where we would be or she had a power similar to Eumonia's which I found far less likely. Cheshire grabbed my hand, escorting me toward the door.

"Oh, Alice." Eumonia stopped us, "Stop referring to that place as the Red Party's base. I built that home for my family, it belongs to you now."

I gave her a small acknowledgement, unsure if I could truly ever think of that mansion as a home to anyone but my aunt and the horrors she'd committed.

Cheshire and I argued the entire drive about him staying with me. I insisted that he go home to see what was happening with Duchess. I had decided Duchess could wait. I knew the state my mother had been in hours before when she'd rushed out, but I didn't want to completely leave Duchess hanging. I was thankful that Rab was with her, but I knew she needed me. I was weaving my bike around pedestrians as I approached the Red Party's base at top speed. My tires squealed as I came to a stop just mere feet away from the double doors that led into the foyer. I took a deep breath before I pushed them open, unsure what I would find. The house was silent as I looked around, taking it in with fresh eyes. If Eumonia had originally built this for her family, it had once been a home just like her small alcove. I tried to imagine it covered in similar murals; some part of me wanted to rip the garish wallpaper down to reveal the secrets that lay underneath. I couldn't today, but soon I would do just that. My boots scuffed against the floor loudly as I made my way toward the stairs.

"Jonah?" I called out as I stepped onto the next landing. Only an eerie silence responded, causing goosebumps to break out across my arms. "It's not like Penthea is going to jump out and grab me." I muttered to myself in frustration. I wandered down the winding hallway, careful to listen for any sound of them. I came to the end of the hallway, finding two white double doors standing open. I approached slowly, peaking my head in to check out the room. When no immediate threats jumped out at me, I entered. The smell of stale air and must struck me, as I began to explore I realized this room had been untouched for a very long time. Thick layers of dust coated almost every surface. I could see an indent on the bed where someone had clearly sat, so I ventured toward the next open door in the room. I peaked in finding an opulent but not garish bathroom. I chose not to investigate it any further, venturing toward the large windows on the far side of the room. I looked out, shocked at the view, I could see a perfect view of Wonderland from here. I could almost see the shaky boundaries of each sector. The citizens milling around outside were completely unaware of me watching them. I pressed my cheek against the cool glass, taking a deep breath, feeling a sense of peace for a moment. As I turned my head slightly I noticed another door, that was cracked slightly. I walked toward it, pushing it open with my foot revealing a brightly lit stair case. I didn't hesitate to take the first step when I heard murmured voices from below. I took the stairs two at a time, worry for my mother driving my steps. "Mom?" I shouted out, as I stepped into a dim room.

"Alice? Over here!" Rab shouted out.

I rushed toward them, my mother was passed out on the ground, sweat pouring off of her. The room was freezing so something was definitely wrong. "We need to get her to Hatter."

"I know, but right before she passed out... I don't even know how to explain this. She said you needed to go into the vault." He explained.

"That isn't nearly as important as getting her to someone who can help her." I snapped at him.

"It was to her," He snapped back, "She was making no sense, she brought us down here almost in a trance. Whatever she wants you to find it needs to happen. Now."

I gritted my teeth wanting to argue with him, "If I stay here and look around will you take her to Hatter?"

"Of course." He stopped, looking down at her, before looking to me again, "I care about her. I know what you saw earlier. I hope you can under—"

I held up my hand to stop him, "I don't want details. I love you both. You're adults it's none of my business what you do."

He smiled softly before carefully lifting her into his arms, "I'll call if anything changes."

"Tell the guys what's going on." I instructed.

He nodded, before slowly climbing the stairs. My mother's mop of curly, golden hair hung over his arm. I watched him until he disappeared into the room above. I stood, staring around the dimly lit room. Nothing stood out, it seemed like a perfectly normal basement, dusty and unused aside from a couple of boxes. I stared at them, my eyes unfocused as my mind raced with everything that had already happened today. My heart pounded in my chest, learning the truth of Wonderland wasn't a small thing. I had to tell everyone, had to decide if I should tell all of the citizens of the city. Eumonia deserved recognition for all that she had sacrificed. The boxes in the corner began to mock me. I was too terrified to even begin digging into whatever my mother had wanted me to find down here. I forced myself to shake those feelings away, walking purposefully to throw open the top of the first cardboard box. I wasn't prepared for the entire box to disintegrate the moment I touched it. I had to bend to catch the papers that tumbled out. I sat down as they fell over my lap. I squinted at the slanted writing of the closest page, my eyes widened as I took in the words.

Alcinda smiled at me for the first time today. Lillian was overjoyed when I told her. It's the first time I've seen her happy in weeks. Penthea cannot get adjusted to her new home. It doesn't *help that her bastard father ran himself into a tree just weeks after they moved in. I can smell the magick growing in her, and something about it brings me great terror.*

These papers were about my mother, I began reading faster, taking in more and more information. These seemed to document my mother's childhood. The writer described her as a bright, happy child. I smiled at a paragraph describing her losing her first tooth. I sat hunched over there until I'd read every page in the first box. I didn't hesitate to move to the first one, finding even more pages of the same writing. Eventually, I came across a letter that had been signed.

Oran Molyneux or better known to you The White King.

I paused, letting it sink in that these were all the words of my grandfather. The man that Penthea killed, who cursed her with his dying breath. I'd never talked to my mother about what she had told me that day. It made more sense to me now. The White King described my aunt as a moody child with anger issues. Over time it seemed that my grandparents became terrified of her. Once her powers developed, she'd been locked away from the rest of the family. The White King had tried to bring in other magick users to help her learn control, but she did everything she was capable of to run each person screaming away. I hated the feeling of pity that coursed through me. Her childhood didn't excuse the monster she became, but it was clear to me that she was shown very little love. As I opened the last box I was surprised to find only three pages in it. I lifted them out carefully, my eyes devouring the words on the page.

I've had another vision of the strange girl, the green light emanating from her. Alcinda has inherited my seeing ability, but I've done all I can to prevent this vision from getting to her. It haunts my dreams each night. Even in my waking hours I can smell the strange magick coming from it. Whatever is coming will surely destroy us all. Penthea has moved out, I could see Lillian's relief, felt it reflected in my own heart. I have hope that Frederick will keep her occupied. His love for her is unconditional. He's been a loyal friend for many years, I can only hope she doesn't harm him.

I wondered for a moment why neither Lily nor I had inherited a seeing ability. It was clear that the ability came from Eumonia, if our grandfather and mother had it why hadn't one of us manifested it. Magick was strange, some abilities seem to run in families, while others seemed to manifest based on the person. Clearly March and Penthea had powers that were based more around their childhood experiences. Lily had Eumonia's shielding ability. From what I'd read here my abilities of power manipulation may have something to do with the White King's ability to smell magick on someone. An idea began to form, and I yanked my phone out, typing a text to Caterpillar. It didn't take long before he responded.

Bossman: Where the hell are you? Rab just brought your Mom in. You need to get back here now. Dina and Duchess need to speak with you ASAP.

I rolled my eyes, before looking around the small room. I wanted to take all of these papers with me, but I needed a way to transport them. I grumbled when I realized there was no easy way for me to take them. I stuffed the last couple pages I'd been unable to finish into my jacket, and raced up the stairs. Whatever was going on at home needed my attention more than the letters of a man long dead.

I could hear the voices from the hallway, no one was truly shouting, but it sounded like half the city was shoved into our tiny apartment. When I opened the door, I was bombarded by Dina who was near hysterics.

"It's Griffin, you've got to go... now."

"Alice, where the fuck have you been?"

"I think my parents might know something about the Queen of Hearts."

I held my free hand up, stopping everyone from speaking. Dina was crying on my shoulder, "Is Elsie okay?" I tried to keep the panic out my voice, but my goddaughter's safety was my first priority.

"She's with Lily and Idalia." She sniffed, "I got a call from a man, claiming they have Griffin. They want us to meet them at the outskirts of Wonderland, out past the boonies." She was tripping over her words as tried to get them out quickly.

"Did they give you a time? How long has he been missing?" I grilled her.

"I haven't seen him since this morning when he left to go paint. It was his day to get out of the house." She collapsed into the chair I led her to, "They said tonight at midnight."

"The guys and I will go. We will get him back, Dina. I promise."

"I'm going too." She insisted, "He's my husband, Ali."

"It's not safe." She started to argue so I continued, "Don't put Elsie's only other parent in danger. I will take care of it."

I saw her consider my words, before she nodded, taking a deep breath. I looked toward Duchess next, "What's going on with you?"

"I received a letter. I think you need to read it." She handed me a small, folded page.

I skimmed over the words, realizing quickly it was from her father. "How did he get this to you?" Who would have helped him get this out of the hospital they were being held in.

She held her hands out, "I have no clue, as soon as I realized what it was, I came straight here. It was taped to my door this morning."

"They were in the building." I glanced to Cheshire, "Don't we have cameras?"

"I've already tried to look, somehow nothing showed up. One second her door is clear, the next the letter is there." He seemed frustrated, someone had been able to manipulate his technology.

"He's apologizing?" I asked.

"I guess so. My father was always... kind to me." Duchess looked away. I could see the feelings that warred inside of her.

"You should go see him." I suggested. I saw the look on Caterpillar's face but chose to ignore it. "Maybe he'll tell you something about the Queen of Hearts."

"I have no desire to see either of them." She snapped at me.

"Okay... will you at least think about it?" She nodded at my question, but stormed out of the apartment, slamming the door.

Hatter stood, "Dina, why don't we take you back to your apartment. You should lay down for a bit, and I'm sure Elsie is worried with how long you've been away."

She was staring off into space, barely acknowledging she'd been spoken to other than standing to take Hatter's arm. I watched them leave; eyebrows furrowed in concern for my friend.

"Al, I hate to add anything to your plate," Tillie had been so quiet since I'd walked in. I hadn't noticed she was here. "The Queen of Hearts has been spotted by some citizens on the outskirts of the sixth quarter over the last few days. I wasn't certain it was important until Cheshire told me what was going on."

I sighed, "I'm not at all surprised. For now, hold off on doing anything. I have a feeling she's going to come to us."

"I also wanted to mention since it's just us," She worried her lip. "I'm sorry to bring this up again, but there's no way the Queen of Hearts just guessed where Caterpillar's funeral was going to be held. We have an information leak."

"I've had some ideas on that, Til. No offense but only the five of us can know how I'm going to handle that." Caterpillar piped in saving me from having to respond.

"None taken. I don't think I want to know how you're going to deal with whoever has betrayed you." Tillie admitted with a shiver, before standing to leave, "If there's anything I can do to help..."

"We'll call you." I responded, sending her a small smile before she left. "Does anyone else have some huge problem for me to fix." I grumbled once I'd thrown myself down on the couch.

"We all need to rest up for whatever we're going to find when we go to get Griffin tonight." Caterpillar said.

"Alice and I need to discuss what happened in sector six today." Cheshire insisted, looking toward me. I shook my head, unable to vocalize a fraction of what had happened today. "Okay, well. The short and sweet. Alice is descended from royalty. All of us with magick aren't actually from Earth... originally. Eumonia is Alice's immortal grandmother." He took a breath before saying, "Does that about cover it?"

I nodded, "Good enough for now. I need to go check on my mother before I try to rest."

"She's asleep, I healed the cut of her head where she fell. I don't expect she'll wake until tomorrow." Hatter said, just as he returned, "Dina is being watched over by Lily. Idalia is on her way to figure out where Griffin was taken from, she's meeting up with Patrick."

"I caught my mother and Rab together this morning," I blurted out.

"Together... like?" Caterpillar made a slight move with his hips unable to speak the words.

"Pretty much." I chuckled.

"As long as they're happy." He shrugged. "Anyway, it sounds like you've had quite a busy day. Let's rest up."

I had no arguments as he picked me up from the couch and took me toward the bedroom.

Chapter 18

February 6th, 2159

It was almost pitch black on the edge of the boonies. Whatever light emanated from the city didn't reach out this far. Only the lights from our bikes allowed us to see. Patrick was speaking quietly with Caterpillar, giving him any information we might need as we made the journey to the meet up spot. We'd decided to go on foot in hopes of catching them off guard. I glanced over to March who looked uncomfortable in his black vest and cargo pants. We'd all dressed the same, ensuring we could all carry as many weapons and supplies as possible. I had six knives strapped to each thigh, a pistol on each hip, and a small gun tucked into my boot. Other than March who mostly had medical supplies in his vest, I was the least armed. Magick was always my primary defense.

"Patrick says it's about three miles from here. There's a large metal building, he thinks that's where they'd be holding him."

"Oh yay, a hike." Cheshire rolled his eyes before adding, "In the dark."

"I know you're an inside cat—" I didn't get a chance to finish my sentence over Hatter's laughter. Cheshire glared at me, but I continued, "Just pretend you're after a mouse."

I could see the slight smile on Cheshire's face as he tried to scold me, "We've got a Griffin-napper to deal with, Alice. Try to be serious."

"Serious? When you just said the words, Griffin-napper?" I shot back.

"I'm sure Dina and Griffin would appreciate your levity in this face of this, but let's get walking. Three miles is a long way to go in an hour." Caterpillar called out, already walking away from us. I jogged slightly to catch up with him. We all walked in silence for a while, I reached for Caterpillar's hand, needing to feel the warmth of him. I prayed they hadn't hurt Griffin. Dina would never forgive me if anything happened to him. I glanced around, squinting into the darkness. I could only make out the shape of trees. Caterpillar's flashlight was the only reason we weren't tripping over roots as we walked.

"So, Ali. You really are a princess." March said, breaking the silence, "How're you feeling about it?"

"Honestly, along with everything else I haven't had a chance to think about it. You know it's not even been a month since the Hummer was wrecked? I'm just surviving at this point. Someday I'll have time to actually process all the shit that's happened." I ranted a bit, "You know Caterpillar was dead like a week ago. I was lightly tortured—"

"Lightly tortured is not a thing, and we aren't making it a thing." Hatter interrupted, "He cut you up. I've seen the scars."

"They glow differently when she's lit up." Cheshire pointed out, "Like the light has found a way to start escaping. They're brighter than the rest of her."

"I've noticed too." Caterpillar spoke up, "I hate that we weren't there to protect you from him, but your scars are beautiful, princess."

"If it m-makes y'all feel better I did cut his arm off." March pointed out.

I chuckled, "I hope he died from blood loss."

"Do you really think we're that lucky?" March shot back.

"Creator, no." Hatter responded, "Seriously, sweetheart. It's okay if you're not okay right now. You only had a couple of days to breathe. I wish we could have given you more, but we've got to find a way to defeat the Queen of Hearts now. Her influence is spreading."

"It is?" I asked. I knew Hatter had been out gathering intel, but I hadn't had a chance to ask more about it.

"I don't know much, but it does seem like more and more citizens are starting to support her. I've broken up a couple of secret gatherings." He explained.

"It makes no sense for anyone to want her in power." I mused, "They have no clue who she is. No one does."

"Maybe they think the grass will be greener on the other s-side." March offered. I considered that. Things had improved since I took the Red Queen out of power, but maybe not enough to make people feel we were taking care of them. I couldn't please each and every citizen. My goal in removing the Red Party from power had been to give everyone equal opportunities. I didn't want anyone being used or abused by people in power. However, many of the citizens benefitted from the few that were being abused. Leveling the playing field hadn't appeased anyone. I sighed, unable to come up with a solution that would please the entire city.

"It's not all on your shoulders." Hatter spoke as he bumped my hip, "You've got us, and we have people that care about the city as much as we do. As long as we're together..."

Bright lights cut off Hatter's reassurances. We all jumped out of the way as a huge truck plowed through the grass we'd been trekking through. It didn't slow at all, as if the driver hadn't even noticed us in the path. "Well, I guess we're going in the right direction." Cheshire said, breathing hard.

"Guess so." I mumbled, taking the lead this time. We walked in silence, no doubt all lost in thought. My feet were sore when we came to the building that Patrick had described. I saw no sign of the vehicle that had nearly run over us. It was eerily silent as we approached the cyclical metal building. It was covered in vines and rust. A slight buzz under my skin stopped me from trying the door that was hanging off its hinges. "We're early."

"By five minutes, Al." Cheshire said, looking up to the top of the building, "Whoever we're meeting is already here. Waiting."

"This is all feeling very... trappy." Hatter said.

"Don't say that." Cheshire snapped at him, "That's basically begging to get trapped."

"Let's just go inside." Caterpillar sighed, ripping the door off its hinges, "Oops."

I chuckled as he helped me inside. March and Cheshire followed, Hatter taking the rear. Inside was just a long hallway, no doors or windows to be seen. I looked up, not finding anything strange. "This is just a random abandoned building."

"We need to go back to the city." Cheshire said, "Maybe this was just a distraction."

"Oh, it was." The Queen of Hearts voice rang all around us. We immediately fell into a circle, backs facing each other, searching for her. Loud clanging was the only warning we got before we were plunged into complete darkness. "Don't fret, Alice. Your sweet, painter friend is perfectly safe. I'll take very good care of him until some more reasonable members of your group agree to my terms."

"What the hell do you want from us. You crazy bitch." I shouted, trying to feel my way along the wall.

"Tut-tut, that is no way to speak to your betters. I've given you every opportunity to see reason. Now... well you'll be out of my way now." Her voice was echoing, starting to sound far away, "At least I've given you all your final moments together."

Silence followed. I hit a wall, and banged on it, hoping I could find whatever door would lead us out of here. "Ali, we've g-g-got a problem." March's voice was further away than I expected.

I turned, unable to see, "What's wrong."

"Can't you all s-smell that?" March sounded slightly panicked.

"Smell wh-what." I could barely get the words out because I started to feel lightheaded.

"We're being druggggg." Cheshire's words floated away, and I heard the sound of someone collapsing to the floor.

"Guys? Where the hell are you?" Caterpillar sounded normal, but I couldn't force my mouth to speak. I couldn't stop myself from sitting down, my head spinning.

"Have I ever told y'all how much I love you." Hatter's voice was higher than usual. I decided to try to crawl toward it. I bumped my head against a warm body, "Oh, sweetheart. You're here." Strong arms wrapped around me, trying to lift me up. I was dead weight, unable to hold my own body up. "My pretty, pretty little magick girl."

I snorted, my words slurring as I spoke, "You're maaagick too."

"Only when y'all almost die. Never let me practice." Hatter grumbled.

"I really think we have bigger concerns right now." Caterpillar voice was close now.

"Cater baby..." I couldn't remember what I was going to say, so I just clapped my hands. Fascinated by the sound.

"March are you still conscious? I've got Cheshire." Caterpillar called out.

"I-I am. Everyone use your undershirts to wrap around your f-face." March instructed.

I tried to unzip the vest I was wearing, but I couldn't figure out the zipper. Rough hands grabbed me, pulling at my clothes, "Nooo," I struggled slightly.

"Hush, you like it when we take your clothes off." Caterpillar snarled. "What the fuck is wrong with all of you?"

"They can't help it." March was close now. I heard clothes shuffling more. "I've read about reactions like this b-before."

"Why am I not being affected?" Caterpillar asked. I could barely follow the conversation, but I was doing my best.

"N-no idea." March responded. I heard the sounds of skin slapping, "Hayden, leave it alone." When I could think more quickly, I'd realize how well March was handling this situation, but right now. My head was spinning while my vision was a kaleidoscope of color despite the pitch-black room.

"Ches is out. Alice, how are you feeling?" Caterpillar asked. I was seeing bubbles pop in my mind, so I only giggled in response. "Fuck."

"There's no way out of here," Hatter's panicked voice drew my attention. "No one knows where we are."

"Patrick and Tillie have the coordinates. They'll come looking." March's assuring words would have worked better without Caterpillar's whispered, "Eventually."

Hatter's breathing was heavy next to me. I fumbled around until I found his clammy hand. "Be okay." I managed to say. The dizziness reached a fever pitch, causing me to lay down suddenly. My hearing started to fade away, but not before I heard Caterpillar and Hatter arguing about gas being lethal.

Bright lights invaded my hazy mind, forcing my eyes open. I hissed as my eyes took in sunlight. "Are you all alright?" I couldn't respond because of the dryness in my throat.

"Is Griffin in there too?" Dina's voice forced me to sit up, tears pricking my eyes. Griffin hadn't even been here. We knew there was a chance it was a trap, but we'd been extremely stupid to all pile into one room. If one of us had just stayed outside maybe we could have still gotten some information on where the Queen of Hearts was holding him. Jackson and Cahir's matching faces appeared through the doorway. They motioned for me to crawl to them. I followed the instruction, letting them lift me down onto the ground. In the light of day, the area didn't look so scary. Overgrown was an understatement. It would be too dangerous for most citizens to come this far from the city.

Jackson put a hand on my shoulder, forcing me to sit on the ground as they pulling an unconscious Cheshire out. March followed, looking groggy but overall unphased. Caterpillar and Hatter came together. Hatter was pale and shaking, clearly still dealing with the effects of whatever had been in the gas that poured into the room. March immediately went for Hatter, pulling him into a hug, silently comforting him. "Griffin?" Dina called out behind Cahir, who turned to push her away with a silent shake of his head.

"No. No." She backed away, shaking her head. She turned on us, tears shining in her dark eyes, "Was he here?" I couldn't find the words, but she saw the answer on my face, "We have to find him. Look at what Jabberwocky was able to do to you. To Caterpillar!"

"I'll find him, Di. I promise. Have some trust in me. I got you and Lily out." I raised my hands. I knew I shouldn't be feeling defensive, but I couldn't take the look in her eyes.

She swallowed whatever else she wanted to say, staring me down, "Okay." She turned without another word, climbing into a van I didn't recognize. Tillie waved at me sadly from the driver's seat.

"Let's get you guys home." Cahir helped me to my feet.

I climbed past Dina, into the very rear of the van. The leather seats were ripped and worn, but it was roomy enough to fit all of us. Cheshire was carefully secured into a seat. I looked over him. He was pale, blue veins stark on his face. He was breathing, but it was extremely shallow. A warm hand, fell to my knee. I raised my eyes to meet the wide, green gaze of Hatter as he too looked over Cheshire. "He'll be okay. I can heal him soon."

"You need to rest first," March interjected, "Ches will b-be okay. He just needs some time."

I tried to relax into my seat, but the ride was bumpy as Jackson maneuvered over the grass and dirt that led back toward the main road. My head pounded; my thoughts formless as I watched the green scenery fly by. We came to a stop just outside where Sammy made his home, the same dingy building I'd spent time in with him over a year ago. I'd given him money to begin fixing it up, and I could tell he'd started to make improvements. The outside still left much to be desired, but overall it seemed like the people I saw milling around were cleaner and happier. "Patrick is going to drive you back into the city. We have things to handle here." Jackson, Cahir, and Tillie all climbed out of the vehicle. "Rab called a meeting for tomorrow morning. We'll see y'all then." Tillie explained. I watched as they made their way inside the building. The car was silent aside from our breathing. I searched for something to say, but the waves from emotions coming from Dina made it impossible. I couldn't blame her, if I was in her shoes I'd be furious. I was angry with myself. We should have prepared to handle a situation like that better.

"Dina, I'm sorry." Caterpillar spoke, relieving some of the tension. "We should have known exactly what would happen, but I'd hoped he'd actually be there. It was extremely shortsighted." She turned in her seat, her long hair swinging around her, but she didn't respond. Her dark eyes bored into him, "There's no excuses for him not coming home with us today. It's understandable to be angry with us. You know exactly what these people are capable of. When Alice was taken by Jabberwocky, I was terrified."

"They'll torture him for information." She whispered, a tear falling down her face, "He's a sweet soul, Roman. He can't take it."

"Give him more credit than that, Di." I jumped in, "Griffin may be a pacifist, but he adores you and Elsie. He'll do anything to protect you both."

"They aren't going to t-torture him." March said, surprising us all.

"How do you figure that?" Dina asked.

"They already have someone giving them information. We've discussed it several times, but this situation confirms it. How would they have known where Griffin's liked to paint? Someone has given them this information." He explained.

I looked at Caterpillar, who was clearly impressed by March's steady explanation. We didn't give him nearly enough credit. While he didn't like being overly involved in the politics, March had been paying attention to our little group.

"Find out who it is." Dina snapped, "Maybe they'll know where he is."

"I've already got a plan. You'll just have to trust us." Caterpillar nodded at her, giving me a look I couldn't decipher. We hadn't discussed what he was going to do, but I knew it was going to have to be drastic now.

Chapter 19

February 7th, 2159

Cheshire had slept well into the night, but he'd woken up chipper as if we hadn't all just been drugged the night before. Luckily, Hatter had calmed down without my mother's help because she was still out of commission. She'd woken up just long enough to assure Rab that it was just her magick being depleted. I had a feeling that wasn't the whole truth, but I didn't have time to worry about that right now. My mother was a grown woman. I had to trust her judgement, even when I might want to question it. I sat at the head of the conference room table, twiddling my thumb as we waited for Duchess to arrive. I began studying the rest of the people in the room. Someone I cared about was betraying us, feeding the Queen of Hearts information. Had gotten Griffin kidnapped, but I had no idea who it could be. Lily cut her eyes to me, trying to communicate something silently, but I shook my head. Ilaria and Idalia were speaking quietly, their identical heads leaned close. It was almost impossible to tell them apart. Tillie was sitting on the edge of her seat, typing extremely fast. Jackson and Cahir weren't joining us today, apparently another secret meeting had been planned and they were taking point on it. Rab was pacing by the window, I swear I could hear him muttering to himself. Patrick and Sammy were standing chatting with Hatter and March. I didn't expect the two men of betraying us. They'd been our biggest supporters, but their presence here was comforting. Duchess stormed in suddenly, crossing her arms when she came to a stop across from me, "What the hell is this about?"

Caterpillar stood, matching her stance. "We failed to retrieve Griffin from the Queen of Hearts. We needed to get everyone together to coordinate our next steps. Alice also wants to try something..."

I took a deep breath, "I've learned some information that I am not going to share yet, but it's had me thinking about magick. I'd like to test all of you. I'm just going to be searching for a small kernel of power. I won't take anything, but I'd like no more surprises about magick."

Rab approached me, holding his hand out. I took it, reaching into myself to access the power I'd used the least. I hadn't even touched it since I'd taken Penthea's power. I called it to the surface, directing it from my chest, down my arm and into Rab. A black hole was my response, I'd considered this outcome, so I pulled away, stepping toward Caterpillar. When I repeated the effort with him, I was pushed away. His dark power refusing my request. I looked back toward Rab, shaking my head. He gave me a small smile, "I expected not."

I moved to Cheshire who leaned against a wall, "We already know you have magick, but I want to just feel it." He pulled me to his chest, placing his hands under my shirt on my lower back. I chuckled, directing my power down my spine to where they rested. His magick immediately responded to me, stretching toward me lazily. I imagined blowing it a kiss before I pulled away. Cheshire didn't release me immediately, pressing a light kiss to my cheek.

I skipped over March and Hatter, leaving them for later. I clasped Sammy and Patrick's shoulders at the same time, once again a black hole was my response. I nodded, and they smiled. "I knew I wasn't going to ever be as cool as you." Patrick joked.

Tillie laid her palm on the table for me. Idalia and Ilaria were next, all three women were unsurprised that they did not have any traces of magick.

Hatter grabbed my hand, pressing his lips to my palm. His magick swirled in my mind's eye, white and glowing, warm much like the man himself. March was hesitant as I reached for him, "You don't have to be afraid." I tried to encourage him.

"Can you take it?" He responded.

I froze, surprised at the question, "I could... I don't know what kind of affect it'll have on you."

He clearly considered my words, "I'll think on it."

I nodded, as I pressed my lips to his cheek, reaching for his magick. It was a twisted ball, shying away as I reached for it. I sent a tiny thread of my magick toward it, the moment our magicks touched, I couldn't stop the gasp that left my lips. His magick unraveled, reaching out for mine. It wrapped around me, refused to let me leave the bridge that connected us. It was aggressive as my own magick tried to calm it. I hissed aloud, "You need to help."

March cringed, but slowly his magick pulled away. I could see the slight pain in his eyes, but I didn't want to address it right now. Instead, I gave his hand a squeeze and moved toward Duchess.

"Absolutely not." She snapped, "I don't have magick. Much to the disappointment of my mother."

"I'd like to just check." I offered.

"No." She crossed her arms. "There's no point wasting either of our time. What good does this do in handling the Queen of Hearts?"

I furrowed my eyebrows at her defensiveness, "I understand you may be nervous to find out—"

"You clearly don't understand. Don't come near me with that freaky magick of yours, Alice Young." She crossed her arms, sneering at me.

I held my hands up in defeat, "Okay, okay. I'll respect that."

I considered her for a moment, dark circles lined her brown eyes. Her skin was pale. Her short blonde her that she usually kept carefully sculpted was a halo of curls around her head. Duchess was clearly not doing well. I thought after her move things would improve for her. All of us had come to care for her, even if she was prickly. "I need to talk to you. Privately." She insisted.

"Later," I said, turning away from her, "We've come up with a new plan. In two weeks, Hatter's father is going to exit Wonderland temporarily. We may have found a fix for whatever issue he saw. Everyone will need to assist us. The Queen of Hearts cannot learn about this plan. If she isn't already aware of the issues with the barrier, we don't need her to find out. We've already seen the panic in a few citizens, the entire city could fall if this information gets out." I looked to everyone in the room, hoping I wasn't overselling this idea. Someone here was betraying us. Someone I trusted with my life had been feeding the Queen of Hearts information since before our first wedding ceremony. I already knew from Eumonia that my magick had repaired the barrier for now. Cheshire and Caterpillar had made plans on how to track everyone as the day approached.

"Why isn't he here?" Tillie asked, "I haven't seen much of Joshua."

"He's been helping me," Hatter offered. "Most people in the city don't remember him, so he has some ability to fly under the radar. He's helped me gather quite a bit of information."

Even I was surprised by that. I hadn't seen his father hardly at all, assuming he was off living his own life away from us considering his disdain for our relationship. I felt guilty for not asking Hatter more about what was going on with his dad. I had been neglecting everyone in my life. It may not have been my fault, but I should know that life was too short to take anyone for granted. The Creator blessed me when Caterpillar's magick was revealed, but that wouldn't always be the case. Any of us could be hurt or killed protecting Wonderland. The Queen of Hearts was clearly a powerful magick user. I couldn't figure out exactly what her powers were. That was far more dangerous than any political power she could gain. I didn't listen as Caterpillar went over various plans and complaints from some of the working citizens. I looked around the room wondering why any of my friends would even consider helping someone take Wonderland from us after everything we'd done. A tiny spark of rage twisted in my gut, when I found out who it was, I was going to find a way to make them pay for hurting us.

"If any of you have any questions you can direct them to me." Caterpillar said, dismissing everyone. Tillie was the first out the room, rushing out without a word to any of us. Rab not far behind her, nodding to me. My mother still hadn't woken up, reminding me of the letters sitting in my bedside table. I needed to figure out what those letters meant, why I had needed to find them.

I stood to leave, but Duchess stopped me, hissing behind clinched teeth, "I got another letter."

The guys were in a deep conversation, so I motioned for her to follow me. I walked with purpose into our apartment, motioning for her to take a seat. I walked into the bedroom and grabbed those letters. The looping words warming my heart. My grandfather had loved my mother, he would have loved us. If only Penthea hadn't killed him, cursing herself and by extension the entire city. I walked back into the room, tucking the letters into my pocket, unsure if I should share them with Duchess. I sat across from her, waiting for her to speak.

She stared down at her hands, "My father is requesting that I visit him. He's claiming that I am in danger."

My eyebrows shot into my hairline, "Why?"

"If I knew I wouldn't be here," She snapped, but looked guilty, "Sorry. It's been a very stressful month. I don't know anything, but I will not go there alone."

I took a deep breath, understanding, "You want me to go with you?"

She nodded, but didn't speak. We sat in silence for several long moments, and I watched her. She was twitchy, glancing around the room, but never meeting my eyes. "I didn't want to ask, but.... I have no one else."

"I'll go." I said immediately, "Is tomorrow, okay?"

"Yeah..." She clearly wanted to say something else, but shook her head, standing. "I'll meet you here in the morning."

I couldn't get another word out before she had run out the door. I sat in confusion for a long moment, unsure what to make of Duchess' behavior. Ultimately, I decided it was a problem to deal with tomorrow when we were together. I leaned back, pulling the last couple letters the White King had written to my chest. I stared at the ceiling, my heart beating fast, unsure why I felt unsettled. My magick was buzzing against my skin. I rolled my eyes, it was two letters. I took a deep breath and began reading. The letter was nothing special, though the writing seemed more rushed than the ones I'd read before. I tossed it to the side, unfolding the final page. It was short and sweet, but I had no doubt it was exactly what my mother expected me to find.

```
I've foreseen my end. I know it's only a matter
  of time before she comes. I haven't had the
heart to warn Lilian or Alcinda, but I did show
her where I kept our riches. She'd looked at me
oddly, as if she had some idea what I've learned.
 I pray to the Creator that Penthea will spare
Cindy her wrath. I've made many mistakes in my
life, steering Wonderland away from magick is my
biggest crime. If I had listened to the council
 of my friends, I would have used my abilities
 to find the other magick users in this city.
But I was afraid. I've had the same vision for
  twelve years; it has made me afraid of what
magick is truly capable of. I should have done
my family the service of learning more. The few
families that tend to Wonderland's running are
sworn to secrecy about their powers. Secrets are
```

```
often the downfall of the most powerful people.
Myself included. My daughter is young, but I see
in her my fire. She will survive my end, and I
know she will make Wonderland a better place.
                    Penthea knows
```

The letter cut off abruptly, leaving me confused. What did my aunt know? Dark brown spots on the paper hinted toward blood. I wondered what had happened to stop him from finishing this letter. I know Penthea killed him and he'd cursed her to suffer. I'd thought over that information often. I had no idea how anyone would be able to curse someone long after their death. Maybe the Creator heard his pleas and granted his wish. It had never made sense to me, but obviously there was much about magick that I didn't know. Apparently, no one knew. I whispered to myself, "Eumonia would." I needed to find her again soon. She had more knowledge than anyone about magick. I don't know how long I sat there staring at the ceiling. It was the first time I'd been alone with my thoughts in weeks. I decided not to waste my chance, I stood, rushing into the kitchen. I hadn't baked in months. I yanked ingredients down from the cabinets entirely unsure what I was planning. I mixed and kneaded without thought, letting my mind drift blissfully unconcerned about anything but the pastry in front of me.

An arm wrapping around my middle caused a scream and electricity to rip out of me. "Oops." Caterpillar chuckled darkly, pressing his lips to my neck, "Good thing I'm magick proof."

I rolled my eyes, "I wouldn't trust that ability completely. What happened to magick isn't always the answer?"

I turned in his arms, watching his brows furrow, "It still isn't... but you have to admit with everything we now know. Magick is a lot more important in Wonderland than I originally thought. And if we all come from... what's it called?"

"Undraland." I offered.

"Right, there. Then we need to learn more about it." He finished; his grey eyes boring into me. As always, he knew something was wrong before I could even open my mouth, "What happened with Duchess?"

"She got another letter from her father, claiming she's in danger. I'm going to go with her to see him tomorrow." I explained.

"Absolutely not." Caterpillar growled, "Putting you anywhere near the Red Queen isn't an option."

"She doesn't have any power anymore." I shot back, pushing away from him to check on my pastries.

"Maybe so, but she still has influence over others. She could hurt you in other ways." His voice was full of concern.

"I don't even think we'll see her. We're just going to see the King of Hearts. Y'know I've learned a lot about him from the White King's letters. He betrayed my grandfather, maybe I can find out why." I was thinking out loud, but I realized the answer to that question did matter to me.

"One of us is going with you." He insisted, giving up on convincing me not to go.

"Where are we going?" Cheshire asked, appearing from nowhere.

"Alice is going with Duchess to see her father tomorrow." Caterpillar explained, "One of us needs to go with her. I already have a meeting with Rab planned."

"March is the only one of us available." Cheshire offered. "Hatter and I are sitting down with his dad so I can get more information about what exactly he saw outside of the city."

My ears perked up, "Why?"

"In case we ever need to leave." It was a short response, and I could tell Cheshire had other motives, but I decided not to push.

"I'll be fine alone. March doesn't need to go there. It's just going to bring up bad memories." I said, bending to take my pastries out of the oven. They were golden brown, the lemon center slightly caramelized. They smelled amazing. Pride filled me as Caterpillar and Cheshire both moved to grab one, completely ignoring how hot they were. They were completely distracted from the conversation. Low moans left both of their lips as the tasted my food. "Are they good?"

"This is why I married you." Cheshire moaned, reaching for a second one.

I slapped his hand away, "You still haven't married me."

"I've tried." He defended himself, "We should try again soon."

"Not until after we catch whoever is feeding the Queen of Hearts information. I don't want our wedding to be interrupted again." I said.

"Well, it was Hatter's dad that showed up last time. I don't think we can blame her for that." Caterpillar pointed out.

"I'm going to." I shot back, sticking my tongue out. "Do you have any ideas who it could be?"

Caterpillar looked at Cheshire meaningfully, "Don't worry about theories princess. Whoever it is will be caught soon enough."

"Tell me." I insisted, crossing my arms.

"He thinks it's Duchess." Cheshire said before Caterpillar could respond, "So does March. Hatter and I agree she's the most likely, which makes her the least likely. If that makes sense."

I went cold at that accusation. Duchess and I weren't super close, but I considered her family. If she was the one betraying us... I shook my head, banishing the thought. "She hates the Red Party more than we do."

"So, she says, but we've never been able to find out who left her the dead rabbit or the letter from her father." Caterpillar said, "We can't rule anyone out."

"I know that." I sighed, realizing he had a point. We couldn't trust anyone but the five of us. I trusted my mother and Rab, but we also hadn't provided them all the information we'd learned. "I'll see what I can glean tomorrow. I just want to get Griffin home."

"We will." Cheshire spoke around a mouth full of pastry, causing me to chuckle, "Stop worrying, Al. We have a good plan. It's going to work."

I nodded my head, smiling in hopes that they would drop the subject. Some part of me doubted this was going to be as easy as everyone else seemed to think. If someone close to us had been able to get away with helping the Queen of Hearts for this long... They were smart and fooling everyone around us. Myself included. I shook my head, forcing myself to let it go for tonight. March and Hatter had rounded the corner, darting for pastries, grinning and chatting as if everything was okay. So, I forced myself to join them, to laugh and eat, but my magick was a knife under my skin. Whatever happened next, it was going to change our entire world.

Chapter 20

February 8th, 2159

I was leaning against my bike, waiting for Duchess outside the mental hospital turned prison. We'd agreed over text that meeting there was for the best since neither of us had a car. I heard the click of her heels long before I saw Duchess. Her curly hair framed a perfectly made face, her bright red lips should have been set in her dazzling smile. Instead, they were pursed as she approached me. "Thanks for coming."

"Don't thank me until it's over." I said.

She gave a tight nod, leading the way into the building. I inspected her outfit; a soft pink dress hugged her waist before falling to her knees. "My name is Vivica Rose, I'm here to see Frederick Rose." She spoke with confidence to the front desk woman. I smiled over her shoulder, waving. It was the same woman who had been here when I'd met March's mother.

Denise smiled back at me, but no recognition shown in her eyes. "Alice Young." I offered when she glanced to me. She handed us two small stickers, insisting that we place them on our shirts, "Do either of you have any weapons? We cannot allow any in the building."

Duchess glanced at me with a raised brow. I shrugged before grabbing the gun tucked into my worn leather boot and the two daggers strapped to my waist. I dropped them into the bucket that Denise offered. She motioned for us to follow a guard that had appeared to her right. He grunted, walking us to the elevator. I gulped but followed him on, it lurched hard before we began descending. I gripped one of the bars on the wall, not making eye contact with Duchess who was looking at my white knuckles. I shook my head, signaling her not to worry about me. I could finally breathe again when the elevator creaked its old metal doors open, letting us out into a brightly lit hallway. The guard still didn't speak as he ushered us into a small room with four chairs. Duchess took a seat, folding her hands into her lap without another word. I looked around the room, pacing behind her.

"Sit down." She hissed through her teeth, "Pacing shows nervousness which shows weakness. This is your first meeting with my father, he'll expect you—" Her words her cut off as the door opened, revealing the King of Hearts.

He'd lost weight, his belly no longer hanging over his pants. His wrists were cuffed, but he didn't hesitate to try to open his arms for his daughter. She stood, pressing a kiss to his cheek, "Hello daddy."

"Hello, Vivi. Thank you for coming to see me." His voice was soft as he inspected his daughter, "You look well. You're being treated well?"

She nodded, "I'm...good."

He sighed, "I'm glad. I'm so sorry Vivi. If I had known, we would have hidden."

I felt awkward listening to their private conversation, knowing I was intruding on a private moment between them, "It's okay. This was for the best."

I was as shocked as the King of Hearts at her words. "Viv, I know you may think this girl is powerful enough to protect you, but..." He looked to me, assessing. "There's many things you don't know."

"Like what?" I asked before I could stop myself. Duchess glared at me, but didn't respond looking to her father pointedly.

He looked between us, sighing, "Let's sit down." Duchess helped him into his seat before taking the one across from him. I pulled a chair around to the end of the table and waited for him to begin to speak. He continued to study his daughters face, "I want you to know that I truly loved your mother. I know she wasn't always kind..." I scoffed, earning a cringe from him, "Her methods of showing love were...warped. It wasn't her fault, she was failed by everyone in her life. Even me."

"Is that an excuse for her abusing me?" Duchess snapped at him.

He looked stunned at her words, "I-I... she's not why I called you here."

"You always excused her behavior. Was it okay when she locked me in a closet for a week because I'd cried in front of the Knave?"

"I never said that was okay!" He defended, but deflated, "I failed you both. We didn't expect to have children. Running the Red Party took me away from you both too often. It was my job to protect you."

Tears shined in both of their eyes as they sat staring at one another. I shifted in my seat, knowing I was intruding. Frederick cut his eyes to me, "I'm sure Alice here knows exactly what I'm talking about. The pressures of running an entire city."

"She doesn't matter," Duchess snapped, "Why am I in danger?"

I breathed a sigh of relief at her pulling his attention away from me. I didn't want to admit to either of them at I couldn't imagine raising a child while running this city. Not that I'd be the monster Penthea was. What she had done to her own daughter had no excuse. "The Queen of Hearts will take the city. It's just a matter of time." He announced.

"Not if I can do anything about it." I snapped.

"Do what you can. Pray to the Creator, but I promise you that she will take Wonderland from you one way or another." His voice was steady, his brown eyes boring into me.

"Can you tell me how to stop her?" I asked.

"You can't. She is the most powerful woman in the city. Penthea, as much as I'd never tell her, pales in comparison to what the Queen is capable of." He shivered, "I beg you, please get my daughter out of this city. Fighting her is useless. She takes what she wants."

"I've already defeated one crazy aunt. I can do it again." I responded.

He laughed, "She isn't Vivica's aunt. Or mine. I admire your confidence girl. I really should thank you for taking us out of power. What she has planned... I'm glad I won't be in her way."

"I thought she was your sister." Duchess said, looking confused.

"It was an easy way to explain our relationship when you were a child..." He trailed off, lost in thought. "But that doesn't matter. All you need to know is that you need to get out of Wonderland. Away from her."

Silence lapsed over the room. Duchess and her father stared at each other, some unspoken conversation that I didn't understand. She stood suddenly, "Come on, this was a waste of my time. As if leaving Wonderland is actually an option."

"We all know it is. You think I haven't heard about the man who came back?" I had to hide the surprise on my face at his words. I shouldn't be shocked that he was still being fed information. "We live in the city of secrets; don't believe for a moment you know all of them."

"Why did you betray my grandfather?" The words came out of my mouth before I could stop them.

He went pale, his adams apple bobbing in his throat, "Oran was my best friend. I worshipped the ground he walked on. He was almost like a father to me."

"That doesn't answer my question." I rolled my eyes.

"Isn't it obvious, girl. If anyone should understand I'd think you would," He sighed at my confused expression, "Love. It's the only thing that can make a man betray everything he holds dear."

"Was it worth it?" Duchess quiet question held so much emotion I was smothered by it.

The King of Hearts brown eyes searched his daughter's face. "It was—" Whatever else he was going to say was cut off as the ground began to rumble underneath our feet, dust fell from the ceiling causing me to cough. The door flung open, and a guard motioned for us. I grabbed Duchess, dragging her behind me as I ran. The King of Hearts trailed behind, seemingly unconcerned about the quake. They weren't terribly uncommon in Wonderland, but something about this one sent my magick buzzing under my skin. Duchess tripped, causing us both to tumble to the ground. My head bounced against the floor. My ears rang with the force of the impact. Strong hands pulled me up, the guard setting me back on my feet without a second look. I shook my head, trying to get my bearing again. We were standing in front of the elevator, I glanced back, "We need to take the stairs."

"This is faster," The guard barked at me.

I didn't respond, motioning for Duchess to follow me. I struggled to keep my balance as the tremors became more intense. It didn't take long for me to find the stairwell entry. I noticed the guard and the King of Hearts hadn't followed us. "This is really taking a fear of elevators to an extreme, Alice." Duchess' voice was strained.

I ignored her and began climbing the stairs. An explosion followed by another tremor tossed me into the wall. My magick was near painful. "Something is wrong."

"No shit." She muttered back to me. I ignored her attitude, continuing our journey up the stairs. She had every right to be emotional. She obviously loved her father, and she'd gotten no real answers from coming to see him. We finally found a door to exit the stairwell, but as I tried to push it open it didn't budge. I huffed, leaning against it. The ground trembled under our feet again, mocking me. "Let's try together." Duchess said, knocking her shoulder against mine. With our shoulders touching we both pushed against the door. When it didn't give way, Duchess slid down the door, sitting on the ground. I stepped away, pacing the small landing trying to come up with a plan.

"We can't just stay in here." I hissed as two more tremors cause debris to fall around us, "The building is going to come down at this rate."

"You're the one who refused to get on the elevator." Duchess rolled her eyes.

"Move over so I can try again." I said, ignoring her.

I took a deep breath, take several steps back. I rushed the door, throwing my weight into it. My shoulder screamed as the door gave away underneath it. I stumbled over the doorway, narrowly avoiding being run over by several men running by. What I didn't expect was to turn and find the Red Queen standing in thin, white linen clothes. A blank look on her face until her red eyes met mine. A strange mix of fear and anger stared back at me from those eerie colored eyes. I wondered if they'd always been red, or if her magick had somehow changed the color. I didn't know how long we stood there, staring at each other before Duchess grabbed my arm, and whispered. "We need to get out of here."

I nodded absently, letting her drag me away. I never took my eyes off of Penthea, something in her pale face entrancing me. I watched her mouth move, heard her words float to me over the sounds of chaos. "I wasn't the only one." The words made no sense, held no deeper meaning that I understood. I shook my head, paying more attention to Duchess' tight grip on my bicep her perfectly done nails digging into me.

"Stop." I breathed, forcing my feet to stop moving. Her nails dug in deeper before she released me, "We can't leave any people in the building."

She sighed, "You and your bleeding heart." Without any further argument we ran back inside, escorting people out. The building had at least a hundred people living there under guard for many reasons. When we'd converted it partially to a prison, we'd kept all the staff and patients that had been there before. There was no place for those people to go, some part of me hoped that the staff would find ways to rehabilitate people like the Red Queen. She may have been beyond help, but at least she'd be well taken care of by people who could help her if she wanted it. Guards were escorting dazed looking patients out. A few people with injuries from falling debris were led to an area that one of the doctors had set up outside. Tremors still shook the building, but they were slowing down, becoming less forceful. I found Denise tending to a hysterical woman, she looked up at me, motioning for someone to take over for her.

"Thanks for your help. There were two people unaccounted for…" She trailed off, a hesitant look on her face.

"Who?" I pushed, the buzz against my skin giving me an answer before she could.

"Frederick Rose, the King of Hearts, and the guard that escorted you never made it outside."

I glanced around, looking for Duchess. She was standing against the wall of the building, her pink dress dirty and stained. "I'm going to go back in and look for them. Please contact this number, they'll be able to provide you additional support." I handed her a piece of paper with Caterpillar's number scrawled on it hastily. I always kept a couple of copies of it for instances like that. "If I haven't returned to you in thirty minutes, please let the man who answers know."

She nodded, gravely. I took a deep breath, making my way toward Duchess. "Your father hasn't been found. I'm going to look for him."

Without a word, she followed me back inside. I beelined toward the elevator, slamming the button, hoping they'd just become stuck inside. When it dinged open, empty, I blew out a breath. I climbed in, pressing the button to return to the basement. The lights were flickering eerily as we exited the elevator. "Let's split up to cover more ground. If we don't find him on this floor we'll move up to the next, and so on until we've found him."

Duchess nodded, and I listened to her heels click away down the hall.

We had been searching tirelessly for two hours with no luck. I had to go out and let Denise know what we were doing after the first two floors yielded no results. Hatter and Caterpillar were outside helping the staff get patients settled into their temporary home across the street at the regular hospital. Teams of cleaners were going to be called in to make sure the building was safe to be occupied before anyone returned. The elevator slid open to the top floor of the building pulling me from my thoughts. Duchess had come up here twenty minutes before, when she hadn't come back down, I decided I needed to come check as well. The top floor was empty, so I turned, noticing a door was cracked open. I pushed it wider, climbing the stairs, finding myself on the roof. What I wasn't prepared to find is the King of Hearts on his knees before the Queen of Hearts. Duchess stood silently beside him.

"You've failed me for the last time, Freddy. I have had enough of your insolence. I allowed you your playtime with Penthea. Allowed you to reproduce and look at you." Her words were venom, "A pathetic man on his knees."

"I'm sorry. You have to understand, Penthea wasn't well when..." His words were cut off when her slim fingers reached down and squeezed his throat. Duchess didn't flinch, didn't move as I stepped out the door. I searched her face, looking for answers, but only blank, brown eyes stared back at me.

"Oh, Alice. I'm sorry but you are interrupting family business. I don't have time for you today." The Queen said without looking from the man turning purple under her grip. "But thank you for bringing me, my dear Duchess. You know how important family is." She reached up, running a gentle hand over Duchess' short curls.

A picture suddenly came together in my mind, images and moments clicking together. "She's been your informant."

The Queen laughed in response to my statement. Duchess still didn't meet my eyes as I glared at her. Rage blinded me as I launched myself at the Queen, forcing her to release her grip on Frederick. My fist caught her cheek, but she was gone before I could land another blow. She appeared to my right, blood trickling down her face where the ring I wore cut her. "I told you I don't have time for this today."

I wasn't prepared when she came at me, but I was able to dodge her blows. "Alice." Duchess' voice broke my concentration, her scream alerting me that I was on the ledge of the building. I glanced over the side noticing the people milling around below. She took two steps before stopping, a strained look on her face, "It...isn't... me."

I ignored her words. I didn't have time to process them when the Queen of Hearts grabbed my shoulder, bringing me in close. "I never thought for a moment, ending you would be this easy. And look, the child of my blood has joined me. At least you won't live to see me take Wonderland from your men." With those words I was falling, grabbing at the air as I went over the edge of the building. A tear rolled down my face knowing she was right. No one could survive a fall like this. I closed my eyes, giving myself over to the wind.

A loud caw had me opening my eyes. I saw Azure flying toward me, wings beating the wind away. I reached my hand toward the white bird, begging the Creator to provide me help, to save my life. Azure swept below me, and I felt her feathers brush the bare skin of my back. She wasn't a large bird, certainly not large enough to carry me. Her caws didn't stop, and suddenly more birds appeared. Hundreds of wings fluttering in the wind, diving toward us. Their small, warm bodies came underneath me, wings flapping as together the birds slowed my fall. It felt like an eternity as they slowly brought me toward the ground. I rolled off their backs, hitting the grass. My breaths coming hard, tears rolling down my face unchecked. Azure landed beside me, pressing her beak against my cheek.

Strong hands suddenly grabbed me, pulling me from up the ground. I was smushed into a chest, the scent of oranges and woods filled my nose. I looked up into Hatter's green eyes as he whispered, "You're alive."

"I'm alive," I responded in disbelief.

"What the fuck just happened?" Caterpillar rumbled from behind Hatter.

I shook my head, struggling to find the words to explain. "Let's get her home. She almost died, Caterpillar." Hatter snapped.

"Where's Duchess?" Caterpillar asked.

My heart caught in my throat at the question, "She was with the Queen of Hearts."

"I fucking knew it." Hatter hissed, "Damn it, we should never have trusted her."

Caterpillar had an odd look on his face, "We still need to go ahead with the plan." I looked at him confused, so he continued. "Duchess could have been the traitor, but I've got a feeling it's not as simple as that. Outing her as the traitor might make anyone else helping the Queen of Hearts sloppier."

"We can talk about this more later. Let's go home." Hatter urged, sweeping me up into his arms. I stared at the roof of the building as he carried me away, wondering why Duchess would have betrayed us. What everything I'd heard the Queen of Hearts say today really meant. Azure flapped her wings, taking off in flight as we departed. Silently, I sent a prayer to the Creator giving my thanks. I had no doubt that Eumonia had been the one to truly save my life, but without the Creator's guiding hand she wouldn't have had the chance.

Chapter 21

✦

March

February 17th, 2159

Alice had insisted that we all take some time to recover. I'd say almost dying after being pushed off a building by the Queen of Hearts hadn't made her feel particularly safe. Revealing Duchess as the traitor hadn't surprised me at all. She was the Red Queen's daughter after all, it was in her blood to be cruel. At least we'd found out who it was and could focus on finding Griffin. Dina had been giving Alice as much space as she could, but with every day that passed I could see her grief that her husband still hadn't been found. I had no hope he was still alive, but I wasn't going to be the one to tell her that.

"Whatcha doing, Marchie?" Cheshire's voice startled me, but I smiled at his approach. He didn't expect that we were planning a late surprise party for his birthday, or else he wouldn't be so cheery. As long as I'd known him, he had hated his birthday. I actually understood, but I agreed with Alice that we all needed a good party to take our minds off of things.

"H-heading out to meet Hatter for lunch." It was an easy lie to tell. Hatter was in the conference room setting up the decorations, and I knew he'd be there until I got back with the cake.

"Oh... okay. Have fun." Cheshire turned on his heel and left without another word. I pulled my phone out, typing out a text.

Bun Bun: Warning, Ches knows something is going on. Told him I'm headed to lunch with Hatter.

Ali: Thanks for the heads up. I'll distract him.

Boss Man: Don't distract him too well. I have plans later.

Ali: Don't threaten me with a good time.

I smiled at the exchange, wondering what Caterpillar had planned for our evening activities. My cock jumped at the thought, imaging all the wicked things he could have up his sleeve. Watching Caterpillar dominant Alice had become one of my favorite past times. Alice and I had found our dynamic early on. She enjoyed pampering my body, loving and teasing me, and I loved letting her do anything she wanted to. Some part of me wanted to take her the way they did, but I was comfortable with what we had. It was safe, which meant more to me than anything else these days. There was more uncertainty now than there had been when we'd been trying to find a way to take down the Red Queen. The difference was the entire city was relying on Alice and Caterpillar now. I could see the toll it was taking on them, but they just pushed forward, working toward the goals we all had without a complaint. I wasn't as good at it as they were, at least Cheshire and I shared that in common. We'd spent a couple of late nights when the others were asleep drinking and complaining about how things were now.

The walk to the bakery Alice had ordered Cheshire's cake from was long, but I couldn't bring myself to ride one of the bikes or ask to borrow someone's car. I like walking, it gave me time to think and enjoy the fresh air. I was surprised when Alice asked me to pick up a cake instead of her making it. She turned red and insisted she didn't have the skill level to make a cake that large. I doubted that but didn't want to argue with her. Alice was a confident woman so seeing any insecurity in her was rare. It wasn't my place to push, but when my birthday came, I was going to insist she make my cake herself. A few people waved at me as we passed, but thankfully no one spoke to me. There was a chill in the air that kept most people inside today, but it didn't bother me.

The bakery was small, a hole in the wall, and only recently opened. The smells wafting from the open doors was delightful. I took a deep breath as I stepped inside, giving the young man at the counter a small smile, before I said. "I'm h-here to pick up a c-cake for Alice Young."

I saw a slight panic on his face as he shuffled through some papers to the side, causing my own anxiety to spike. "Oh here it is." His bright smile turned on me. "Sorry, my sister usually runs the place, but she's been..." He trailed off, a cringe on his face. "Her husband requires more of her time these days."

Something about the way he said it set me on edge, "If she ever needs help, you can always call the number on that order." My words were barely above a whisper. He nodded seriously, before disappearing behind the curtain that I assumed separated the kitchen from the rest of the bakery. I hoped he took me up on the offer, I'd be more than happy to pay her husband a visit. I shook my head. I didn't even know for sure what was happening to his sister. I shouldn't feel like wringing someone's neck just for the suggestion that a stranger might be being mistreated. I paced the small space, taking in the small cakes and pastries behind the glass. I had no doubt that Alice could make every one of them. I knew she'd love to own a little shop like this, wanted to live a simple life. Unfortunately, her power and her morals kept her locked in her role as a leader to Wonderland.

"Here you go!" His voice was shrill, causing me to jump as he rounded the counter with a large white box. "Have a wonderful rest of your day. If you enjoy the cake, please tell your friends about it." It was clear he was trying to get me out of the store, ushering me toward the open door. I didn't intend to make him uncomfortable, but it was clear that I did.

I muttered a quiet thank you and began my trek back to the apartment.

"Maxie!" The voice had cold chills running down my spine. I picked up my pace hoping if I put enough distance between my mother and I she would assume I didn't hear her and leave me alone. "Maxie!" Her voice only came closer, along with the sound of her shoes as she jogged across the pavement.

My steps faltered realizing I was all alone and my mother was going to trap me into a conversation. I could feel my hands shaking as I turned, ensuring I kept a good grip on the cake. I didn't want to ruin Cheshire's birthday party by dropping the cake.

"Oh Maxie, it's been so long. You stopped coming to visit. I know a woman can keep you busy, but really that girl could at least let you out often enough to come see your mother." Her words were fast and sharp. I couldn't even begin to open my mouth to stop her as she continued, "Really Maxton, I'm disappointed. I finally get out of that horrible place, and you are nowhere to be found. You know your grandfather was accosted by the leaders of the city. He insisted I didn't show up to visit you, but no matter. You're here now. I need to discuss my living arrangements with you. I cannot continue to stay in that tiny apartment with your grandfather, it's driving me crazy. I'll come home with you, I'm sure you and Alice have plenty of space for me."

"Wh-what?" I was alarmed by her words, struggling to keep up with her train of thought, "I'm busy, Mom. I can't—"

"You've really put on some weight. I mean I'm glad you're being fed well, but you need to keep your health in mind. I didn't take Alice for a glutton, but I guess I could have misjudged." I snorted. The only weight I'd gained was muscle from spending so much time in the gym running from this exact scenario. Terrified my past was going to ruin my future with the people I loved. I watched my mother's mouth move, but I didn't hear her words. Rage rippled through me, hot and sharp against my insides.

"I never wanted to see you again." I blurted out.

My mother's face went pale and then turned a bright shade of red, "Now Maxie, you don't mean that. I've told you for years not to listen to the nonsense that your little friend and his father spouted on about. I am your mother."

"Stop calling m-me that. I-I-I..." I could almost feel my tongue twisting on itself, my emotions taking over.

"Shh shh. It's okay, honey. Why don't you come with me?" Her hand gripped my shoulder hard.

I jerked away hard, causing the cake to nearly tumble out of my arms, "I'm not going anywhere with you. If I had wanted to see you, I would have c-come." I trailed off, staring her down, "People that love you, don't hurt you. They are accepting and show you love even at your worst. I have that now and I don't need you."

"I see." Her voice was cold, something I'd never seen before in her eyes. Fear had me taking a couple of steps back. As she opened her mouth to continue speaking, I turned on my heel and jogged away, literally running away from her. I didn't slow my pace until the building we lived in was in sight. Then I forced myself to stop, leaning my back against the wall, nearly choking on the oxygen I forced into my lungs.

My arms were aching from the weight of the cake I was carrying, but I ignored that. Trying to find my happy place. Images flashed through my mind, Alice grinning as she took Ilaria to the mat during training, Hatter's warm hugs, Caterpillar's gruff morning voice snapping at Cheshire to shut up. Slowly, my breathing became normal, my anxiety easing. The emotion that filled my chest next shocked me... I was proud. I had stood up to my mother, and no one had been there to protect me. I had done it alone. I didn't know for sure if that would be the end of any harassment from her, but at least I had handled it myself. I wasn't a defenseless child anymore. Finally, I straightened, making my way inside, a smile on my face.

Alice was the first one to greet me, taking the cake from me immediately, "Thank you, honeybuns." She was wearing a lowcut purple dress that ended just above her knees, sheer sleeves ran to her wrists. Her golden hair hung loose around her; my hands itched to run through it. "You didn't have any problems getting it did you?"

I shook my head, about to tell her what happened with my mother, but the expectant look in her blue eyes. The small smile playing across her plump pink lips had me smiling back, "Easy as... cake."

Her smile widened, "We're almost ready. There's a box by the door, could you take it up to Hatter?"

I nodded, placing a soft kiss on her lips, nearly groaning at the slight taste of her. There wasn't an inch of Alice I wasn't completely addicted to, but I forced myself to grab the box and walk back out of the apartment. I could hear glass clinking together as I headed toward the conference room. I pushed the door open with my foot, and setting the box heavily on the table. I glanced around, appreciating Hatter's decorations. He had blown up a bunch of balloons in pink, purple, and blue. A large sheet had been used to paint, '*Happy 28th Ches*' and it hung slightly off center over the windows.

"Oh, good. I can make my dream juice now." Hatter's voice startled me slightly, even though I should have known he was in the room.

When his words processed, I groaned, "You can't seriously be p-planning to make that stuff again. Does Alice know what happened last time Hatter's Dream Juice graced a party?"

His smile was unhinged as he approached me, his hips pressing me into the table. I glanced between us, appreciating the way his slightly larger body covered mine. "We're supposed to be having fun tonight. Cheshire will love it."

My brain guttered out, unable to process what he was saying with his proximity. Hatter could drive me to distraction without even trying. It had only grown worse when we'd started taking our relationship further. I shook my head forcing my mouth to form words, "H-how long do we have before everyone is supposed to get up here?"

"Enough." His breath was hot on my ear as he spoke. That was all the invitation I needed to begin exploring the hard planes of his muscles.

The room was loud, the voices of our family and friends creating a warm environment. Hatter had supplied everyone who came with a cup of his special concoction. The alcohol loosening everyone's inhibitions. I waved to Cheshire, Alice was sitting in his lap, laughing at something he whispered in her ear. I pulled out of my phone, snapping a grainy photo of the moment. It wasn't often we all relaxed and enjoyed each other's company. I wanted to remember it fondly. I glanced around, everyone was caught in conversation or playing a losing game with Caterpillar. So, I stepped out into the hallway. The silence was welcome, I leaned my head against the wall, closing my eyes.

I didn't know how long I stood there, before a quiet voice said, "They can all be a lot."

I glanced down to find Ilaria standing there, holding a half empty cup. I smiled at my old friend, "That they c-can, but it's why we love them."

She nodded thoughtfully, "It's good to see everyone letting off a little steam. Even Dina is in there trying desperately to beat Caterpillar's winning streak."

Alcinda had declined her invitation. Alice's mother hadn't been quite right since the strange incident with her magick. She was more withdrawn, but at least she'd been willing to watch Dina's daughter while she attended. "It's the least they all deserve."

A comfortable silence stretched between us. I studied Ilaria out of the corner of my eye, it was still odd to think of her by her given name rather than Tweedledum. She had her red hair pulled out of her face, giving me a chance to really take in her features. Her brown eyes sparkled a bit from the drink she'd had, but what I noticed more was the deep bags under them. I furrowed my brows, "Are you okay?"

She glanced up at me, her lips pursed as she stared into my eyes, "I will be." For a long moment she didn't say anything else, "March, we've known each other a very long time. I.. I'm glad to see you happier now. I hope you don't let the past ruin your future." Her words were haunting, as if she'd taken one look at me and known all of the struggles I'd faced.

"I d-do my best." I didn't know what else to say, but as she turned to return to the party, I found words tumbling out of my mouth. "You know you can f-find it too. Happiness, I mean. All you have to do is be willing to try."

Her steps faltered, her whispered words floating back to me before she disappeared out of sight, "I am." I stared at the spot she'd left for a long moment, wondering what was haunting her, before eventually deciding to let her come to me when she was ready.

The party was finally winding down, only the five of us and Dina remained in the room. She had her head in Alice's lap as they chatted quietly. I couldn't make out what they were discussing, but every once in a while, I'd see guilt flicker over Alice's features, tugging on my heart. It wasn't her fault we had no leads on Griffin's captors. I knew Hatter and Caterpillar had been combing through every person they could think to interrogate about it, but it wasn't going well. The Queen of Hearts had left no clues or loose ends when she snatched Griffin.

Cheshire stood, stumbling toward Alice. Hatter had managed to get everyone sloshed. I had refused any of the blue liquid, but I know Cheshire had at least three overfilled cups. I watched as he grumbled at Dina, who just laughed at his antics.

"I guess I'd better let you continue your celebration in private." Dina said, as she stood, winking at Alice. Hatter and Caterpillar glanced up from their card game as she exited the room. I saw the gleam in their eyes as they dropped their cards simultaneously. Caterpillar beelined to Alice, yanking her to her feet, and crashing his mouth to hers with no warning. I could hear her quiet moan from here, making me instantly hard. Hatter appeared in front of me, drawing my attention away from them.

"Sh-shouldn't we head to the apartment?" I said, as he reached for me.

He grinned, "I think it will be far more fun to stay here." Before I could argue with him, he gripped the back of my neck, dragging me toward Cheshire, Caterpillar, and Alice. Who had managed to disrobe while Hatter distracted me.

Alice was on her knees, her breasts swaying slightly as Caterpillar thrust into her mouth. I watched some spit roll down her chin, a glistening trail running all the way down her stomach. She locked eyes with me, pulling away from Caterpillar who huffed slightly, before huskily saying. "Do you want to try something new?"

My mouth went dry at the lust in her eyes, but I responded shakily, "Anything for you."

She stood, waving Caterpillar away. She approached me, a small smile on her face as she reached up, pulling my face down to hers. Her blue eyes held me still as she ran a thumb over my lips. I opened my mouth without a thought, and she smiled again, leaning until her warm breath fanned over my face. "Would you like to suck Cheshire's dick while I ride his face?"

I whimpered at the suggestion; I had no idea Cheshire was interested in me. I just nodded, unable to form words. Her face turned serious, "Maxton, you have to give me verbal consent before we go any further. Nothing happens until then."

I took a deep breath, "I would love to."

She grinned, running fingers through my hair, "You're such a good boy." My heart warmed at her praise, "Let's get these clothes off of you." Her hands were gentle but demanding as they tugged my sweater over my head. Her fingers trailed down my chest slowing as they reached the waist band of my jeans.

"Stop teasing him Al. I need to taste your pretty little pussy." Cheshire spoke for the first time, "And we both know how bad Marchie wants a taste of me." I studied his relaxed position on the floor, leaning up on his elbows to watch us. His cock bobbed slightly as I took him in, it was a wider than mine, but similar in length. Hatter was longer than both of us, so I had complete confidence as Alice finally yanked my pants down, leading us toward him. She stood over his head for a long moment, before Caterpillar tangled his fingers in her hair, guiding her down. The sound of her moans as Cheshire began devouring her brought me to my knees. All I could see as I lowered myself down was Cheshire's hand gripping Alice's ass forcing her to move her hips over his tongue.

Fingers tangled into my hair, forcing me to look up at Hatter, who's cock was bobbing, long and proud above my head. "You better finish him off quickly." His growl, and the rough way he shoved my head down harder, had me gagging. Cheshire's hips bucked into my throat harder, bringing tears to my eyes. I heard Caterpillar's loud groan as he emptied himself down Alice's throat. Alice followed him very quickly, Cheshire and his tongue ring making quick work of her. Caterpillar carefully lifted her away, taking her to the couch to watch. My body was warm as everyone's eyes landed on me. Cheshire grabbed my hair, pulling me away from him to stand. I adjusted my stance, taking him completely. In this new position it didn't take long for him to spill down my throat.

When he pulled away, I smiled, "Happy Birthday."

He laughed and stumbled toward Alice and Caterpillar. It looked like Alice had fallen asleep, and I stood glancing around for my clothes. "What do you think you're doing?" Hatter said.

I grinned, an unusual mischievous feeling running through me. "Well the birthday boy is done, so I thought I'd get d-dressed."

Hatter's eyebrows rose comically at my comment, "Are you feeling bratty tonight? You know what happens to Alice when she starts that nonsense."

I did, I quite liked it when Alice decided to have her fun at our expense. I ducked before he could grab me, backing away, "I d-don't know what you're talking about."

"I know it's Cheshire's birthday, but maybe you need a spanking instead." Hatter gruff comment went straight to my dick. I felt my cheeks heat at my reaction to the threat. "Hmm, yes I think that's exactly what you need." Once again, I tried to duck away from him, but his large hand gripped my neck, guiding me toward the windows. He pressed my face against the cool glass, "Maybe someone will look up and see you take your punishment. I know how much you love to be watched." Hatter murmured in my ear just before he yanked my pants and underwear down in one smooth move. His hands skimmed down my sides gently. Even when we played rough Hatter always reminded me in some way just how much he loved me. I closed my eyes, relaxing my body against the window as he continued to touch me. I wasn't prepared when the first blows of his hands came, causing me to shout and dance away. He returned a hand to my neck, holding me in place as he rained blows down on my ass. He stopped suddenly a hand wandering to my dick, gripping it tightly, "Such a good boy, taking Cheshire's spanking for him. So hard for me. What do you want?"

I whimpered, unable to respond with all the blood rushing to my cock as he stroked it lightly. I tried to crane my neck to see if the others were watching, but Hatter held me in place, "You have to use your words, March. What do you want?"

I gasped when he stroked me harder, "I want you to fuck me while I fuck our woman."

"Good boy. Ali come here." I heard Alice's quiet footsteps approach, but I forced my eyes closed, unable to look at her.

Gentle fingers gripped my chin, "Look at me." Alice's melodic voice entranced me, forcing me to do as she said. Her piercing blue eyes bore into my soul, "Are you going to fill me with your cum while Hatter takes you?" The dirty words leaving her mouth made me groan.

I nodded, still unable to form words. Hatter moved me backwards, allowing Alice to slip in front of me. I didn't hesitate to lift her by her thighs, pressing her back into the window. She gripped my face, bringing my lips to hers, as I pressed into her slick entrance. We moaned in unison, her slick heat gripping my cock tightly as I began to move. The pain in my ass was forgotten as I pounded into Alice, but before I could reach my climax, Hatter gripped my hips forcing me to slow. "Not too fast. I want to be inside of you." He worked me efficiently, hitting my g spot, causing me to shake before he'd even gotten his cock in me.

I distracted myself with Alice's beautiful breasts, taking one of her pink nipples into my mouth. She moaned, moving her hips so she could bounce on my cock. "P-please." I groaned.

"We're going to give you exactly what you want, my love." Alice's voice was husky as she reached over me, bringing Hatter's face to hers. Watching them kiss this close did something to me, but I continued to hold off my orgasm. When Hatter pulled away, he gripped my lines, pressing into my entrance. I nearly came from the sensation. "I love you both." Alice groaned, pressing herself down onto me as Hatter set the pace. Every stroke brought me closer to climax, but I wasn't going to finish until I felt Alice cum on my dick. I made sure Hatter was supporting her other leg before moving my hand between us, finding her clit quickly. I pinched the sensitive bud, causing her walls to flutter. I could feel Hatter getting close, so I picked up the pace using my thumb to rub tight circle just above her hood. I watched her face as she came, blonde hair mussed around her head, eyes closed as her body shook around me. The city lights didn't seem nearly as bright when she began to glow. I felt Hatter's hot seed begin to spill into him, and I finally let myself climax. We all stood there for a moment, connected in the afterglow of our orgasms. Hatter moved first, rushing away and coming back with two cloths. He tried to clean me first, but I grunted moving away so he could help Alice first. Her legs shook as I carried her to the table, sitting her down gently. I took the cloth from Hatter, gently wiping away the stickiness between her legs.

Alice kissed me as Hatter did the same for me, before she slipped away. I watched as she redressed herself. The glow on her skin memorizing as she returned to sit between Caterpillar and Cheshire. Hatter pressed a kiss to my head, "You okay?"

I thought for a moment, glancing around the room, "I'm the best I've been in a long time."

Hatter graced me with his beautiful smile, before gathering me up into his arms, "I love you so much Maxton."

"I love you too Hayden," I responded, nuzzling into his neck.

"I know we all love each other, but can we head to bed? I'm exhausted." Cheshire interrupted.

I heard a gentle smack, "Be nice." Alice's scolded him, "It's called aftercare, Cat."

"I know all about aftercare, my devious woman, but it can be performed in a bed." He shot back.

I chuckled at their banter. Things weren't perfect, we still had so much to figure out, but at least we had each other. I had a family that loved and accepted me, even with all of my flaws.

Chapter 22

February 21st, 2159

The river was so clear I could see each rock at the bottom. The water was flowing faster than usual from the rain the past few days. It didn't often rain in Wonderland. I had come to the conclusion that whatever magick kept the dome intact mostly kept the weather mild. It was easy for me to ignore the rain drops running down my face. My nerves kept my attention on the impending situation. If Duchess was the traitor what we were about to do shouldn't cause any problems, but some part of me wasn't certain. The more I turned over that day in my mind the less sense it all made. Footsteps crunching over the dead grass had me turning around, taking in Hatter's expression. I didn't acknowledge his father as Hatter wrapped me in his arms, pressing his lips to my forehead. He whispered, "Everyone is in place. Let's do this."

I stepped away from him, nodding. I finally met Joshua's eye, surprised to find him giving me a small smile. It didn't fit well onto his grizzled face, looking more like he was cringing than anything else, but I appreciated the effort. I gave him a nod before I stripped out of my jacket and boots, leaving me in a tight white tank top and jeans. Once my feet were solidly planted on the ground, I called my magick. It responded eagerly, caressing my mind before flowing down my body, into my arms and feet. I lifted my hands to the sky, sending an arc of electricity straight up. I willed it to reach the barely there shimmer of the magickal dome that protected the city. I wasn't prepared for the way my body seized as soon as my magick connected with the barrier. In my minds eye I could see the golden magick of the barrier race back down toward me, striking me in the chest, sending me to my knees. It twisted violently inside me, fighting my power with invisible claws. I felt warm hands hit my shoulders, ripping me out of the internal battle I was waging. The magick calmed, stretching toward those hands. I opened my eyes, glancing backward, finding Lily standing there, bright and golden.

"W-why?" I coughed out, my throat raw from the sheer force of the magick.

"It called me." Her voice seemed far away, her hands falling away from my shoulders. I stood, grabbing at her, seeing the pain on her face made my heart race faster.

"Let me take it back!" I shouted, digging my nails into her forearms, "It's too much."

Her body was shaking violently, so when the first tremors started, I barely noticed. I grabbed my magick, forcing it into her, but I slammed into a solid wall. I closed my eyes, bending my magick, forcing it to turn golden, to caress that wall gently to become one with my sister. I don't know how long I stood there, the world crashing around me. All I felt was golden magick and the beat of Lily's heart. Slowly I coaxed our magicks together, imagining the magick of the barrier leaving us, stronger a piece of both of us going with it. Imagined it flying like Azure into the sky, slamming back into the barrier, strengthening it.

Suddenly everything stuttered out. My eyes opened to the horrific scene of a long dagger protruding from Lily stomach, mere inches from touching me too. I looked into her shocked blue eyes, trying to grab at her as she fell, barely catching her before she hit the ground. Before I could do anymore the Queen of Hearts appeared, cackling as she yanked the dagger from Lily and dove at me. I managed to get away, calling my magick to the surface, sluggishly throwing electricity out. I looked around, trying to figure out how this happened. Idalia was running toward us, ducking and weaving around men and women that were fighting.

"Do you really believe I'm going to let you undo all my hard work?" The Queen hissed at me.

I furrowed my brows in confusion, but didn't have a chance to respond as Idalia made it to Lily's side, her hands going to cover the wound. Even from my position I could see tears streaking down her face. I dodged another attack from the Queen, running toward my sister. I glanced back to see Hatter engage with her, giving me a moment to focus on my sister. A bit of blood had come from her mouth, and I wiped it away.

"It worked," She choked out, staring up at the sky. I glanced up, surprised to see that the top half of the sky was glowing brightly golden. "We did it."

"Yes, we did," I responded, moving her hair from her face.

"Duchess wasn't the traitor." Idalia snarled at me, "This was too much of a risk. And now my wife is dying."

My mouth fell open, "Your wife... you two..."

She waved me off, "Not important. Your mom is back at base. There's no way Lily is going to make it that long. This exact type of wound is what killed Caterpillar, and Lily isn't going to magickally come back."

I nodded, "We need Hatter." I couldn't do anything else as Idalia jumped up, running full force at the Queen of Hearts. A roar left her throat, as she jumped into the fight. Hatter took his queue and came running toward us, a white streak already starting to form in his hair. No one could figure out why using his magick affected Hatter this way. I made a mental note to ask Eumonia next time the opportunity arose. Idalia's scream drew my attention back to the fight at hand. The Queen of Hearts had her by her short, red hair, her feet dangling slightly above the ground as the Queen drove the same dagger nto Idalia's outstretched hand. My bare feet wanted to sink in the wet ground, but I forced myself forward, trying to get to them before she had a chance to do any further damage. I didn't have a chance before Ilaria appeared from nowhere. A throwing knife releasing from her hand, sinking into the shoulder of the Queen of Hearts in a split second. I didn't stop, barely thinking as I reached into the waist band of my jeans, pulling out one of my own throwing knives. I silently cheered when it sank into her other shoulder. I wasn't prepared when the ground began shaking, causing me to trip, falling onto my knees just a few feet away from the twins.

"At least now I know why they gave you the Tweedledum moniker," The Queen of Hearts snarled at Ilaria.

"You promised you wouldn't touch my sister." Ilaria hissed back. I watched in confusion as they spoke, my mind unable to make sense of the conversation. "I've done everything you've asked and more."

"And yet, I'm still banished. My plans thwarted by a child." She snarled back.

"That isn't my fault." Ilaria responded, her voice shaky.

"No, but you know who I will punish for it." The Queen of Hearts tone changed suddenly. "I think I've had enough of this little game." Her brown eyes cut to me, an evil grin twisting her lips, "Plus you won't be useful to me now."

"Please no, don't—don't hurt her. I'll do anything," Ilaria fell to her knees at the Queen's feet, "She's just a child."

The Queen stared down at her, "I do love it when the underlings beg, but you've made your bed. Enjoy lying in it."

Without another breath she disappeared, along with the people that had come with her. Leaving all of us sitting in stunned silence. Idalia was the first to move, stumbling toward Hatter and Lily. None of them spoke as Hatter continued his healing.

"That's the best I can do. She's still not out of the woods yet. We need to get her to your mother." He finally said, standing.

I nodded, my eyes finding Idalia's strained face. She just shook her head, glancing toward her sister. Her words were careful as she spoke, "I swear to you I didn't know."

"I know." I didn't know what else to say, so we continued to stare at each other. Finally, I did the only thing I could think to, "I'm going home. I guess all of our goals were met today."

"What should we do about?" Hatter nodded to where Ilaria was still on her knees, body shaking from silent sobs.

No one else had come with us. We didn't actually expect the Queen of Hearts to show up, so I turned to Joshua who was carefully avoiding seeming like he was paying any attention to the situation that had unfolded. "Would you escort Ilaria to the basement of our home?"

He seemed surprised that I was speaking to him, "Yes. Anything else?"

"If you can get any information out of her, it would be... easier for us." I said, seeing the cringe that Idalia made at the idea of us interrogating her sister.

"Understood." Without any further discussion we all left. Idalia's trashy green car barely fitting Hatter, Lily, her and I. The tension coming off of Idalia was almost unbearable. I did my best to watch the scenery and not think about any of the events of the last hour of my life.

"She'll be fine, but on bedrest for a couple of weeks." My mother's usually bright skin was dull and grey, her blonde curls pulling harshly out of her face. She smoothed the blanket she'd just laid over Lily, "They got married?"

"Without telling us." I responded, "I'm happy for them, but..."

"Lily was always a private person." She responded, leading me out of Lily's bedroom. Her apartment was smaller than mine but laid out similarly. Small knick-knacks lined almost every surface, ducks and geese in various strange situations. I'd never understood her obsession with them, but I found them heartwarming now.

"They probably had the right idea considering what has happened to me every time." I was only a little hurt that they hadn't told us. Ultimately, I understood that Lily preferred to keep her private life just that. I was glad she had found love. I liked Idalia, even if I had been closer to Ilaria. Just thinking her name made me cringe, causing my mother to grab my arm, "It's not your fault, Ali. You couldn't have known it was Ilaria."

"That may be true, but we should have seen the signs." I'd been thinking on it for hours, turning every interaction over and over in my mind. Ilaria had stopped going on most of our missions' months before, maybe a year.

"You have enough on your plate, blaming yourself for someone else's betrayal doesn't have to be added to it." Her voice was tired. I had thought she was more recovered than this but apparently finishing healing Lily had done its damage.

"You should go lay down." I insisted, nodding to Idalia as she made her way to Lily's bedroom as we passed her in the living room. At this moment, I don't think either one of us knew what to say to each other. Lily was going to live, Ilaria was in one of the two cells we'd created in the basement on our building. Everything else could wait until we'd had more time to process.

"I'm fine." I could tell my mother was annoyed with the way we'd been treating her since the incident, but I couldn't stop. I'd already lost her once, I didn't know what I would do if something happened to her now.

Rab was waiting outside the apartment for us, he'd barely left her side. I gave her one last hug before letting him lead her back to her apartment. I stood in the hallway outside Lily's for a long time, trying to decide what to do. I didn't feel like talking to the men, I knew they would comfort me, but that wasn't what I wanted. I needed to do something, to fix a problem. I just wasn't sure what that was. Lily was going to live. We had succeeded in solidifying the dome around Wonderland even further. We found the traitor. With that thought my decision was made, my feet carried me to the stairs. A shiver ran over my skin as I glanced down the hallway to the door where Caterpillar's body had been kept, but I forced myself to turn away. Toward the cells that had been unused until now. As I stepped into the room, I wondered why we called them cells. Honestly, they were more like small bedrooms. The only difference was they locked from the outside. I looked into the large window, staring at Ilaria's small dejected form. I grabbed the key from above the door and opened it, her green eyes meeting mine. They were filled with unshed tears, but she didn't speak as I took a seat in the chair across from the bed she sat on.

I tried for a long time to find words, to ask some deeper question. Finally the word that came tumbling from my lips was, "Why?"

Ilaria didn't answer immediately, picking at some invisible thread on her pants. It was so long that I stood, making my way toward the door before thinking better of leaving. Instead, I paced, trying to find an outlet for the energy that had been buzzing under my skin for hours now.

"She has my daughter." Ilaria revealed. I had no idea she had a child, and I doubted anyone else knew either.

"Your daughter." I echoed back, "Why didn't you come to me?"

"The Queen of Hearts has had Caroline since just a few days after she was born. Idalia doesn't know. No one knows." She paused, tears running down her face. "After Idalia and I went through Suit training, I was assigned to the boonies. Idalia stayed in the city, she was their next up and coming commander. I was nothing…" She trailed off again, the bitterness in her voice surprising me, "It was a stupid drunken night. I don't even know who her father is, but when my commander at the time found out I was pregnant he sent me before the King of Hearts. I don't remember a lot, but he took me off to her. I can't tell you a lot of details. They kept me blindfolded or drugged the entire time, but once I gave birth to Caroline…" She finally met my eyes. "She took her from me just a couple days after she was born. I've only gotten glimpses of her since. I thought when we helped you take down the Red Party, I would have the chance to go get her, but I couldn't find her. After she crashed your wedding, saw me there, she put the pieces together. I began receiving letters. Threats against me, against Idalia, against Caroline. I had to help her Alice. You have to understand."

"You knew about the Queen of Hearts and never mentioned it?" Rage and pity warred inside of me. If Ilaria had just come to me in the beginning I could have used the information, we could have worked together. Instead, the Queen of Hearts now has her daughter and Griffin. My heart sank into my stomach, "There's no way for us to win is there?" I flopped down into the chair.

"I always thought you'd find a way." Ilaria muttered.

I laughed bitterly, "All while people I trusted were feeding our enemy information."

"I tried not to give her too much." She shot back, "What would you have me do? Caroline is only four. She has no way to defend herself."

"You gave her Caterpillar's funeral!" I screamed back. When she deflated, guilt ate at me, "I'll do what I can to get her out. I can't trust you any longer. You'll have to stay here until we've found a way to deal with the Queen of Hearts."

"Thank you." Ilaria whispered as I stood.

"Don't thank me yet. Caterpillar and Hatter will have more questions for you than I do." I shot back.

"I've always had faith in you, Alice. You'll find a way."

"I wish I believed that." I muttered as I closed and locked the door behind me. I trudged back up the stairs, pausing at my apartment door. Not quite ready to face my men yet. I didn't know why, but knowing they'd want to talk made my stomach roll. I didn't have anything but questions right now. The apartment was silent as I entered. I checked the kitchen first, surprised to find it empty aside from a plate of food with a small note.

Eat Me

Ali, I know you're struggling. I made your favorite meal. Enjoy and get some rest. We can deal with everything tomorrow. You are not alone.

March's handwriting brought a smile to my face. I was truly blessed by the Creator to have him in my life. I pulled the lid off and grinned down at the steaming bowl of potato soup that lie underneath. I devoured it quickly, unaware of just how hungry I was until I was tilting the bowl back to drink the last few drops. I sat it in the sink, tucking the note into my pocket.

The bedroom was also empty, but another note sat on top of some clothes on the bed.

Wear Me

GO INTO THE BATHROOM, GET OUT YOUR VANILLA SOAP, AND ENJOY A HOT BATH. AFTER YOU ARE DONE, PUT ON MY SHIRT AND GET SOME SLEEP PRINCESS.

Caterpillar had picked out his favorite shirt. A green faded one that at some point had advertised some band from before the world had changed. I held it to my nose for a moment before making my way to the bathroom.

I soaked until my fingers were pruned, and the water had gone completely cold. I climbed out, patting my body dry and pulling caterpillar's shirt over my head. When I made it to the bedroom another note had appeared along with a steaming cup of tea.

Drink Me
I couldn't be left out of spoiling our girl, so
I made your favorite chamomile tea. Get some
sleep, sweetheart.

I went to sit the note down, but another small paper fell out of it. I picked it up grinning as I read it.

These four suck. They didn't clue me in on the plan until it was already done, but I promise I'll wake you up just the way you like.

Cheshire left a surprisingly detailed lewd drawing on the other side of his note. I chuckled as I climbed into bed. These men knew exactly what I needed even when I was unable to express it myself. I sipped the tea slowly, letting it warm the parts of me that had grown cold from the stress of the last few hours. Finally, I curled up under the covers letting myself drift off into a peaceful sleep.

Chapter 23

February 25th, 2159

"I'm fine. You all are being ridiculous." Lily snapped at Mom as she sat beside me. I cringed at the sharpness in her tone.

I didn't want to be on the receiving end, but I did force myself to speak up, "Seriously, Lil. It's only been a few days. You were badly injured and your magick was completely depleted."

She rolled her eyes. "I understand that, but we need to talk about how we are going to handle Ilaria's betrayal and getting Griffin and her daughter out of this bitch's hands." My eyebrows met my hairline at her words. Lily had always been the calm and sensible of us, but the rage painted on her pale face was unmistakable.

I nodded, "Do you have any suggestions?"

"Actually I do." Idalia said as she came sweeping into the room, dropping in the seat next to Lily, "I've been talking to my sister. I think we need to send her to the Queen of Hearts."

"What?" Hatter said, "You think sending someone who has already betrayed us into her hands is a good idea."

"No, but it would be if I went in her place." Idalia offered.

I considered her idea for a moment, "How would you get to her?"

"I think I know where her base is." She said, surprising all of us.

"Where?" Caterpillar growled, "If we know where it is, we could just form a team and go take her down."

"She can obviously disappear not only herself but several other people with her. If we go in guns blazing there's a chance she'll run with Griffin and my niece." Her logic was sound, but she hadn't answered the question.

"Where do you think her base is." I asked again.

She sighed, "You're really not going to like this... outside the dome."

"She's right." Joshua spoke for the first time since he had arrived hours before. "There are some strange things right outside the city, buildings that should have been destroyed but weren't. I can't say for certain, because I didn't investigate them, but it would make sense."

"Why didn't you?" Hatter asked.

"It wasn't what I was looking for." His answer was cryptic, but no one seemed to want to push for more, so we moved on.

"If there's a chance to get Griffin out of there, we do it." Dina said, standing in the corner. Elsie was asleep in her arms, her red hair a stark contrast to her mother's dark skin.

"I want to get Griffin home too, but we need a solid plan. Idalia can't go without back up. We'll need a team on standby once she's gotten in." I pointed out.

"Plan it." Dina insisted, her voice hard as she stared back at me.

I took a deep breath and nodded. "Joshua, we're going to need as much information as you can give on what to expect immediately outside the dome."

He looked to Hatter seeming hesitant to speak, but when Hatter gave him a sharp nod, he spoke. "I can't say exactly where her base would be, if it's close to the dome you may not run into much aside from the carnivorous plant life. I have a gel I made it ward those off. I can try to whip some more up..." He trailed off, leaving all of us to imagine what carnivorous plants could be like. A shiver went down my spine, I couldn't imagine what he'd endured out there for ten years. "Animals and the weather are the most dangerous things. Sometimes the rain is acidic enough to give third degree burns. All the animals are huge and vicious if they see a human.”

“Is there any way to protect ourselves from them?” Idalia asked.

“Be faster. Obviously, I wasn’t at one point,” He patted his just above his missing leg, a slight chuckle leaving him. “I should just go with you. It’ll be far easier to lead out there than to try to explain what it’s like from here.”

I glanced to Caterpillar, unsure about that proposition. I didn’t really know hatter’s father, and it wasn’t like I’d had to best impression from him in the beginning. Caterpillar inclined his head, “You would need to train with us.”

Joshua nodded, “Understood. The less of us that go the better, it isn’t safe out there for one human. Much less a small army.”

“I’m going.” Idalia insisted.

“So am I.” Lily said, surprising us. No’s echoed from nearly everyone, but Lily’s determination remained unchanged. “This is my niece we’re talking about, and I’ve known Griffin just as long as Alice has. Plus there’s no one else with shielding abilities.”

I grimaced at her reasoning, “You need more time for your body to heal.”

“Magick healed me, Ali. I think by the time we have this put together I’ll be perfectly fine. I’ll train with Joshua.”

“Cheshire and March will stay here.” Rab piped in, “Cheshire can monitor the city from the cameras, make sure nothing happens. March can be the contact for the team.”

“My m-medic training could come in handy.” March argued.

“I was the one who gave you that training originally.” Joshua chimed in.

“You’re not ready for another big mission.” Caterpillar added. When he saw the look on March’s face he rushed to say, “We know you’re capable, but we need some of us hear to watch over the city. If something happens to me or Alice someone has to step in for us.”

I watched as the argument continued, everyone wanted to go, to help save Ilaria’s child and Griffin. The faces of all the people that I loved were lined with stress and exhaustion. Eventually I chimed in, "We train for two weeks. Caterpillar, Joshua, Hatter, Lily, Idalia, and I will go. It's not up for further discussion, that is the largest team that's reasonable to take outside of the protection of Wonderland. Tillie, March, and Mom will wait at our departure point, in case we need back up."

I could see arguments starting so I raised a hand, "There's another thing I have to do. No one here is going to like it." Cheshire groaned, forcing me to stifle a laugh, "I'm going to talk to the Red Queen." The room was silent, awaiting an explanation. "Something about the Queen of Hearts, about Duchess, everything about that day doesn't make any sense. I need to see if Penthea has any answers."

"I don't like it." Caterpillar growled, "You almost died the last time you were there."

"I know, but what if she has information that I could use? She has no power left, I'll be fine." I reasoned.

"One of us should go with you." Hatter said, trying to bring compromise to the situation. "She's right that speaking to her aunt could be useful."

Caterpillar glared at him for several beats before sighing, "Fine, but I don't like it."

"Is there anything else we need to discuss?" Idalia asked, "Lily should go lay back down, and Rab and I were planning to go have another chat with Ilaria."

As everyone shook their head, people began to exit the room. I stood as well, but a hand wrapping around my bicep stopped me. I looked to March, surprised at his firm grip, "I made p-plans tonight." I could tell he was feeling a bit nervous to spring this on me, so I smiled, "Is it like the plans we made for Cheshire's birthday?"

He chuckled, "No, I thought we all needed a date night before we get wrapped up in training and planning."

"Apparently, March has been plotting this behind our backs for a while. He gave the owner the permit to open." Hatter said, coming to wrap an arm around his shoulders.

"What kind of restaurant is it?" I asked, curious about what March was doing while the rest of us went about our duties.

"You'll have to g-go with us to find out." March teased. "Go get dressed. Wear that white dress Cheshire bought you." He shouted after me as I left. I grinned at his instructions; March rarely took such a lead. I was excited about this new side of him.

I showered and changed as quickly as I could, finding all of the men waiting for me in the living room, each of them dressed in trousers and a button up shirt. March had paired his with a soft green sweater that complimented his honey brown eyes. Cheshire had left the top buttons of his dark blue pinstripe shirt open, revealing the top of his new tattoo. It was still red and healing, but it was the most realistic image of a lioness I'd ever seen outside of textbooks. When I'd asked him why he'd gotten his first tattoo on his chest, he'd told me that I needed to be as close to his heart as possible. I felt my face warm at the memory. I still couldn't believe he'd gotten a tattoo for me. Caterpillar had grumbled about having the most ink. I was sure he was looking for some way to outdo Cheshire, and I couldn't wait to see what it was.

"Are we ready to go?" Hatter asked, his eyes roving over me. The dress I wore hugged every inch of me. From the front it seemed modest, reach up to my neck and down to my wrists, but the back was completely open, barely covering my butt crack. "Lead the way, March."

We didn't have a far walk surprisingly. Which was perfect in my book, since I'd elected to wear silver heels tonight. The building we came to was short, not fitting in well with the others around it. Clearly it had a fresh coat of dark blue paint, a sign hung just over the top of the door welcoming us to Alice's Tavern. I looked from the sign to March, eyebrows raised, "I-I-I... I didn't know what they were going to name it."

"Do we know these people?" Trepidation filled me, I shouldn't feel weirded out that this place had my name, Alice wasn't even an uncommon name...

"No." He opened the door for me, letting all of us file in the small entry way. A bubbly girl with bright blue hair greeted us. "Welcome to Al--" She cut off when she got sight of me, squealing, "Oh my god, you're her. You're--"

I held up my hand to stop her screeching, "We're just here for a date night, I'd like to keep it as low profile as possible."

"Of course. Of course, right this way." She led the way, though it was difficult for her, since she kept bumping into tables and other guests to crane her neck to look at me. Finally, we made it to a round booth tucked in the corner of the restaurant. It was quiet in this area, and I appreciated her thoughtfulness.

"Thank you..." I paused, waiting for her name.

"Sheridan, my name is Sheridan. Seriously, I want to thank you so much for all you've done for the city. You saved my family from one of the Red Queen's labor camps. That why-"

I put my hand on her slim shoulder, stopping her, "It's my duty to the people of Wonderland."

I saw tears form in her brown eyes, "You don't know what it was like to be a magick user in those conditions. We were drugged for days to keep our powers active. You saved a lot of people, Alice."

A knot formed in my throat. I didn't come across many people who felt that way. Most of Wonderland hadn't felt good about the change in power, and the ones who did weren't especially vocal about it. "I... Thank you. I'm glad you can live in a safe place now."

"Only because of you. If you ever need any help, please come here. My family and I would be honored to do anything for you... any of you." She nodded toward the men who had already taken their seats.

"I'll remember that." I smiled at her, before climbing into the booth next to Caterpillar. Who immediately forced me to stand, so I could slide in to sit between him and Hatter. Sheridan stood there for another moment, staring at us, before a small shake of her head. She almost sprinted to the front of the restaurant, leaving us in silence.

"I didn't know you had fans, princess." Caterpillar smirked at me, noting the redness in my face.

"Really, because all of you follow me around like obsessed fans." I shot back at him.

"Oh do we?" He leaned closer, his minty breath fanning across my face, "Or do I have to follow you around to keep you out of trouble."

Before I could respond, a young man approached our table, asking what we'd like to drink. I decided to order a cocktail, though Caterpillar immediately insisted I order a water as well. Once everyone else had ordered and the young man had disappeared again, I picked up the menus. My eyes widened as I browsed over it, my mouth starting to water. "They have braised lamb? The Grove doesn't even serve lamb."

"They're from the labor camps, I'd say they have a power that lets them work with animals." Cheshire pointed out.

"Do you know how those powers work?" March asked, looking to me.

I shook my head, "Honestly no. I have no idea how it works. The best explanation I've ever heard was that they're able to help the animals propagate."

"They can make the animals fuck?" Cheshire snorted, "What a fancy power."

"They keep us fed. Have some respect." Caterpillar snapped at him. "You can't imagine how they were treated by the Red Party."

Cheshire had the wherewithal to look embarrassed as Caterpillar continued to lecture him on all the things he'd learned helping to save the magick users after we'd removed the laws that kept them as slave labor for the city. I hadn't known when we'd taken the Red Party down just how badly those magick users had been treated, but it was abhorrent. Just thinking about it now made my stomach roil. The conditions they'd been kept in. I glanced toward the front of the restaurant where I could see Sheridan's blue head bouncing around. Thank the Creator that young girl was free and happy now.

The young man returned, sitting our drinks down in front of us, before taking our order. He turned to walk away, before pausing, "Are you.... h-her?" His stutter had me looking to March whose face was full of sympathy. I nodded, unsure what to say, "I w-wanted to... say... th-thank you."

"No, thank you. For everything you do for the city without any recognition." I reached up, patting his shaking hand, "Will you do me a favor?" He nodded, an excited look in his eyes. "If there's anyone else who wants to come speak to us, let them know they are more than welcome to, but I don't need any more thank you's."

He gave me a small smile, "Miss Alice, everyone here is a magick user. We... all want to thank you."

"It's really not necessary. I just did what was right." I insisted.

"That means more than anything to us. Most people don't do what is right in this city." His voice was stronger as he said those words. "You could have... protected yourself... instead you helped us. Saved us, when keeping us in... chains would have benefitted you." I was speechless as he smiled again, "I'll have the chef g-get your food started."

After he'd walked away, I looked toward the men I loved all of them were in varying stages of surprise and emotion. I felt tears prick my eyes, "I love this place."

"This is the b-best thing I've ever done." March had a small tear running down his cheek. Hatter reached over, wiping it away before pressing a small kiss to his temple.

"Did you know they were magick users?" Caterpillar asked.

He shook his head, "I only ever met--"

"Maxton!" A voice boomed through the restaurant drawing attention to us. A huge burly man came charging toward us. I felt Caterpillar tense next to me. I grabbed his hand as it reached for the gun resting under his shirt on his hip, "You brought your woman! Alice Young." He grinned, showing all of his bright white teeth, "I am Clinton, owner and head chef of this place. It's an honor to be hosting the leaders of Wonderland this evening."

"Thank you, Clinton. This place honors me far more than I deserve." I said, shifting to reach over and shake his outstretched hand.

"Beautiful, powerful, and modest. If only I was twenty years younger." His warm belly laugh was infectious, and I joined him. Ignoring the tension in the men surrounding me.

"Clint, have you looked at the men surrounding our leader? You wouldn't have stood a chance even if you were thirty years younger and a hundred pounds lighter." A woman said.

"You wound me woman." He laid a meaty hand over his heart, "And what does that say about the fact you married me."

"Nothing good. Sorry about my husband. I'm Sara." She introduced herself, "We're not going to harass you your entire meal, I promise."

"You're not bothering us at all. Honestly, hearing from all of you has really improved my day." I responded.

"You are welcome here anytime. Please don't hesitate to contact us if you need anything. Let me give you, our number." Sara reached into the apron she was wearing, pulling out a small book and scrawling a number in it before ripping the page away and handing it to me. "Your meal is on the house tonight."

"Absolutely not," I said, sternly, "Please let us pay you for all your hard work."

She looked up at her husband, "I... If you insist but at least let me give you complimentary desert. I make all the cakes by hand each day."

"That's perfect." Cheshire said, stopping me from refusing her.

Sara and Clinton stayed for a few more moments, telling us a bit about their dream for the restaurant and continuing to profusely thank us for saving their lives. Finally, Sara ushered them away promising us the rest of our meal in peace. The smile wouldn't leave my face as I watched them walk away. People like them made all that we did worth it. When our food came out, it wasn't long before we were all making obscene noises. The meat was tender and juicy, an explosion of flavor in my mouth. Even the simple potatoes and carrots that had been paired with it were perfectly seasoned. Hatter and Caterpillar had both ordered steaks. When Hatter offered me a bite, I moaned the moment it met my tongue, earning me a heated look that promised I'd be making those sounds later for a different reason. Cheshire slid a creamy pasta dish toward me, letting me sample it as well, cheese and lemon burst in my mouth. "Is there a bite of this that isn't perfection?"

"This is some of the best food I've ever tasted in my life." Caterpillar responded.

"Someone is going to have to roll me out of here." Hatter joked, patting his perfectly flat stomach. Suddenly, his eyes darkened, "You've got to be fucking kidding me."

I glanced in the direction he was looking to see Claudia and Dodo making their way toward us. I looked at March, who looked surprisingly unconcerned, taking another bite of the chicken he had ordered. "Maxie! Maxie!" Claudia's screeching ended the peace I'd been feeling for the last hour. None of us moved as they approached our table. I made eye contact with Dodo, promising all the pain in the world that I'd warned him of last time we'd seen each other. I saw him flinch, but he did nothing to stop his daughter from speaking to us. "Hayden." She sneered at Hatter, "You're still letting the mop on your head grow out."

"Something for your son to grab onto when I'm inside him." He snarled back shocking me. March couldn't stop himself from laughing, causing him to snort his drink out of his nose.

"Well I..." She sputtered, looking for a response, "That's just... gross and inappropriate. How could you allow this?" She swung on me, glaring.

"You'd be even more disgusted by all the other things I allow." I shot back, "What do you want? Your father has already been warned that any contact with us was not allowed."

"You can't keep me away from my son. Maxton, is this why you were rude to me the other day? A partner should never keep you from your true family." She said. I furrowed my brows wondering when she'd spoken to him. Why would March hide seeing his mother from us?

"A true family wouldn't have l-let me be sold to the highest bidder." March snarled at her, standing up. Cheshire scrambled out of the way as March exited the booth. "Or do you want to keep pretending that d-didn't happen?"

Claudia's mouth was hanging open. Dodo was pale glancing between his daughter and grandson, "What?" He finally said.

"Oh don't pretend like you didn't know what Martin and your daughter d-did to me." March snapped at him. "Get the fuck out of here. You aren't welcome in this establishment."

"You don't own this place." Claudia said haughtily, recovering from his words.

"No, but I do. If Maxton wants you gone, you aren't welcome in my business." Clinton's voice boomed out of nowhere. I turned in my seat, seeing him approaching with a large piece of cake held aloft.

"I'll ruin you." Claudia screamed, face turning a concerning shade of red.

"You'll do no such thing." Dodo growled at her, shocking all of us, "Come, Claudia. I believe there's some things you need to tell me." He gripped her bicep, nodding his head to us, "I apologize for ruining your meal. You won't have any more issues out of us."

We watched them exit the restaurant in silence, staring after them. Clinton interrupted our silence, placing the piece of cake in the middle of the table. "I apologize for that. If I had known there was anyone you had issues with they'd have already been banned."

"You can't d-do that, Clint." March said. I could see his hands shaking slightly, but he continued to speak, "Just don't let them in when we're here."

"No Maxton, I heard more of that conversation than I'd have liked. People like that aren't welcome in my place." The burly man said, before yanking March into a bear hug. When he finally pulled away, I swore he wiped away a tear. "Enjoy your cake." He walked away before any of us could respond.

March climbed back into the booth, all of us staring at him. It was obvious to me that he'd had some kind of interaction with his mother that he hadn't shared with the rest of us. None of us spoke, waiting for him.

Finally he said, "I ran into her when I went to get Cheshire's c-cake. I told her I was done. I didn't think it would come up again, and I didn't want to ruin Cheshire's birthday party."

"We always tell each other when something happens." Caterpillar growled.

"You didn't tell me until after you'd threatened Dodo." March pointed out.

He was right, we had purposefully kept him out of the loop, "Yes, but we did tell you. Would you have told us about that confrontation if they hadn't shown up here?" I asked. I could tell just from the look on his face that the answer was no, "We can't be supportive if you don't tell us what's going on." I paused, "But I'm proud of you for handling that bitch on your own. The next time she crosses paths with me, she's getting zapped."

"Did Dodo really not know what happened to March?" Cheshire asked, pulling the decadent cake toward him.

I snatched a fork, and leaned over grabbing myself a bite before I responded, "I think it's possible, but how did he not know?" I groaned as the chocolate cake hit my taste buds. I was going to marry Sara and Clinton and indulge my every food fantasy if I didn't leave here soon.

"I never t-told him." March muttered. "He already hated me because of my stutter. Seemed pointless to give him more reasons to hate me."

"Even if he didn't know it doesn't excuse how he's treated you." Hatter said.

We all fell into thoughtful silence as we finished our food. Our waiter brought the check over, and I could tell they hadn't charged us for everything we'd ordered. I left a tip that was triple the bill. Sheridan waved us out the door, begging us to come back soon.

We walked slowly, enjoying the cool evening. A few people waved, but no one interrupted our journey home. I took in each of the men I'd been in love with for over a year. Cheshire was whistling, a smile on his face. He'd been more relaxed lately, seeming happy despite the Queen of Hearts shenanigans. Caterpillar had his hand on my lower back, I could tell he was scanning for threats. Forever my strong protector. When he noticed me studying him, he stopped me, pressing his lips to mine in the middle of the street. I was out of the breath when he let me go, my lips puffy. Hatter grabbed me before I could fall back into step, kissing me, a hand tangled into my hair. When he finally pulled away, March grabbed my hand, continuing our walk. Even with Claudia's appearance at dinner, I was going home feeling ready to take on the next mission. Together we could take down the Queen of Hearts, then we'd get married. Hopefully our happily ever after was right around the corner.

Chapter 24

March 1st, 2159

"How the hell did you convince Caterpillar that you only needed me here?" Hatter asked as we walked toward the building. They had moved the patients back in just a couple of days ago, there were no signs of the quakes that had done the damage.

"You don't want to know." I joked, giving a fake shiver. In all reality, it hadn't been as difficult as I'd expected, Caterpillar knew I could handle myself.

He rolled his eyes but sobered as we approached the reception desk. Denise nodded, "She's already been moved into a room. We didn't tell her that you were coming."

"Thank you." I took the key she offered me, letting a guard lead us down the corridor.

"I'll be right outside. One knock and I'll come inside. Two knocks and I'll bring back up. Three knocks we lock the building down." He explained.

I nodded, pushing the key into the lock. Once the door was cracked, I handed the key to the guard knowing it was a bad idea to have it with us.

"Of course it's you." Penthea sneered as I took the seat across from her. Hatter stood behind me, surveying the situation.

"I have some questions for you." I started, "I need to know more about the Queen of Hearts."

She snorted, "I'm sure you do. What's in it for me?"

"She took Duchess." I revealed. I watched her jaw clench slightly at that reveal, but otherwise, her face remained unimpressed. "She also took Frederick." At that, Penthea leaned toward me, "If you can give us any information we don't already know. I will move you and Frederick into the same cell." I had thought the offer over for several days. I hoped that it was tempting enough that she would help. Based on what my grandfather had written in his letters there was a chance Penthea actually cared for her husband.

She was silent for a moment, "I want a room with windows."

I looked to Hatter, who nodded, "We can do that, but only if you give us useful information." Penthea pursed her lips, waiting for me to begin my questioning. "What is her relationship to your husband."

She chuckled, "Oh you really don't know anything. Let me just tell you what I know. Her real name is Rosyn Rose. She's a powerful magick user, more powerful than you are certainly." She smirked at me for a long moment, but when I didn't react to the comment she continued. "I'm not exactly sure what her relation is. She looks young, but maybe an aunt of his."

"What are her abilities?" I asked. While knowing the actual relationship between Frederick and the Queen of Hearts could be useful, it wasn't my biggest priority. Obviously, Frederick hadn't been totally honest with his wife.

"She can cause seismic activity. I know she's got more power than that, but she's always very hush-hush about what exactly she can do." She answered.

I knew she had some ability to affect time, something that caused it to slow down when she wanted. I hadn't seen her use that much, so I didn't have a good grasp on what exactly she could actually do. "Why does she want Wonderland so badly?"

Penthea stared at me for a moment, clearly trying to decipher the question, "It was part of the plan."

"What plan?" Hatter asked.

She didn't respond immediately, leaving me on the edge of my seat. "Do you know why I became the Red Queen?' I raised an eyebrow, shaking my head. She gave a small huff; it was the most human thing I'd ever seen her do. Usually, my aunt was tightlipped and perfectly poised. "I wanted to punish your grandfather for ruining my life. If my whore mother had never gotten pregnant with Cindy, I would have continued to have the perfect childhood..." She trailed off, a vacant look in her eye, "Maybe I wouldn't have become... this." She gestured to herself, "They were too happy. While I suffered Oran, my mother, and Cindy had love and joy. I had nothing. I was nothing... until my powers manifested. Then I had fear, respect." I hated the pity that came to my heart as I watched her stare at her long nails. "Frederick was the first person to show me something different. Love is probably what you'd call it. I called it devotion, loyalty. I had control of him. He would do anything for me. When I told him that I wanted to hurt my family... He introduced me to Rosyn. He knew that Wonderland was Oran's priority. Taking it away, molding it into a world that I could prosper in. That would hurt him most. Rosyn already had the framework for the Red Party and already was close to taking over. Killing him, putting Frederick in charge. It was easy to put in motion with everything she'd been doing behind the scenes. Honestly, the fact you were able to topple it as easily as you did... I've been wondering for a year now if it was by design."

I had to stop my mouth from dropping open at her revelation, "By design? You think she let it happen? Let us take Wonderland from you? Why?"

She met my eyes, "I wasn't going to give up what I had gained to that red-headed bitch."

"What is she going to do to Wonderland?" I asked, pressing for more.

She shrugged her shoulders, "I have no clue, but if she has my husband and daughter... you should be afraid."

"Why?" Hatter spoke this time, "Duchess is powerless."

"I always thought so too, but Rosyn always had an interest in her, always tried to get her hands on her. Frederick and I made every excuse to avoid her having contact." She responded, at the look on my face she began to defend herself. "Duchess may not have liked my parenting style, but I did care for her. I certainly wasn't going to let some other woman use her."

"How would you take her down?" I changed the subject, uncomfortable with the direction we were going. I didn't want to feel pity for Penthea if I could avoid it.

She snorted, "Do you know your biggest flaw, niece? You're arrogant."

I rolled my eyes, "And you aren't?"

"You're too young to have that amount of arrogance. I can't deny you're powerful, but there is always someone bigger and stronger than us. And sometimes they win." Her words reflected one of my greatest fears, but I forced myself to ignore it.

"It's called confidence." I shot back, "You just don't have any idea how to defeat her."

"You're right. I wouldn't put myself in your position, even if I still had my powers. Rosyn will end you." It wasn't a threat. She said it as if she was telling me the sky was blue.

I stood, "And if she does. Your husband and daughter will forever be at her mercy. I wonder how she would feel if she knew what was said here today."

Her red eyes widened just enough that I noticed, but she was careful to keep her composure. "If you're here asking for my help, you're either desperate or you know something. Which is it?"

I thought for a moment. I'd wanted to talk to her for many reasons. The letters from my grandfather had shed new light on who she was. For a long time, my aunt was just the villain of our story... now she was something else. Not a victim. No, she would still be causing pain and suffering if she had the option. But she was... broken. Some part of me saw a bit of March in her, saw that the things they suffered as children had shaped their magick into a weapon against others. Unlike Penthea, March didn't want to make others suffer the way he had. Penthea's past gave me an even bigger appreciation for what an amazing, strong man I had been blessed by the Creator to know and love. I glanced back at Hatter, but his face was blank. He was playing his part as the guard. I realized I had let the room fall into silence for too long, "I hoped you'd want to save the only person you seem attached to." With that, I made my way toward the door, "But since you aren't interested. We'll go."

I opened the door, but before I could step over the threshold she said. "She's ruthless and after something, the rest of us don't understand. I can't help you because I wouldn't put myself in your shoes if I had all your power and mine combined. The woman is... terrifying. If she's got Frederick and Duchess... she's going to do something big."

I gave a tight nod, "If I can save them I will." Without another word, I exited the room. I had a little more information than before, but still not enough that I felt confident about our plan. name... Rosyn, at least let me humanize her.

Hatter and I walked in silence back to the bike we'd ridden here. I climbed on behind him, wrapping my arms around him. Pressing my cheek to the soft material of the jacket he was wearing I closed my eyes. Letting the wind and the hum of the engine lull my mind. I always felt like I had more questions than answers. I knew we would find a way, if Penthea wanted to call that arrogance then fine. I had faith in us, had faith that no matter what happened we would come out on the other side together and stronger.

When the bike stopped, I expected to be back home, but Hatter had driven out of the city pulling off on a dirt road in a wooded area. I didn't recognize the area so when he climbed off, offering me his hand I took it tentatively. He pulled his helmet off, flashing me a smile, "I think we need some time together. I can almost hear the thoughts running through that big, beautiful brain of yours."

I snorted, "I don't know why I thought Penthea would have more to tell me."

"It wasn't nothing Alice. We've confirmed her name, we know she has at least two powers. It wasn't easy to sit down and talk to her, you don't have to pretend it is." He pulled me into a hug, "You don't have to be stronger than us. We can take some of the weight off your shoulders."

"You're dealing with enough. Your dad—" I started.

"My dad is fine. We've got an understanding now. Once Jabberwocky took you, he started to understand. I don't believe he's truly okay with it, but he at least has learned to shut up about it." He argued, "Let me take care of you." There was an edge in his voice I hadn't heard before, something about it gave me pause. I nodded slightly, unsure what I was even agreeing to. He nodded, yanking me down the path we were on. "I come out here to run sometimes when I need the time away."

"Please tell me you didn't bring me out here for a run," I whined. I was in shape, and I did spend plenty of time in the gym, but I hated running. A light jog was about as much as I would do willingly.

"No, I don't want you that worn out." He winked at me, his green eyes sparkling with mischievousness.

Warmth flooded my entire body, my mind spinning with possibilities of what he had planned. What I didn't expect was for us to come to the end of the path and find a small table and chairs set up, just a few feet away from an overlook. I jogged to the edge of the area, realizing I could see the entire city from up here. It took my breath away, seeming so far above everything else. "It's beautiful," I muttered.

"Not as beautiful as you." Hatter breathed against my neck, before turning me away from the view. "I don't know how we got blessed with you, but the Creator makes my dreams come true every morning when I wake up with you in our bed."

My breath hitched, "I'm the one the Creator blessed. I have the four most dedicated, beautiful men in the entire city. I just wish I could actually enjoy it."

A sad look passed across his face, "Joy can only be felt because we know what pain is like. I would go through all of the pain a hundred times over if it means I get to stand here with you at the end."

My eyes welled with tears, but instead of letting them fall, I reached up, pulling his lips to mine. I poured every worry, every unspoken fear I had into that kiss. Hatter took the weight of my body, one hand on my face while the other arm wrapped around my back. I lost track of time as he cradled me, exploring my mouth. When we pulled apart, we were both panting, "I love you."

"I love you too. Let's get you fed." He said, leading me toward the small setup.

"How did you make this happen?" I asked as I sat.

"Cheshire and March took care of it while we were talking to Penthea." He revealed. I smiled; my men were an amazing team. Hatter leaned down, pulling a small basket out from under the table. Slowly he revealed a rather extravagant meal for a picnic, wine and bread came first. Then two bowls that when he opened steamed, the smell of tomatoes and cheese filling my nose. Finally, he pulled out a small plate that held a red fruit I didn't recognize covered in chocolate. "Lily was pretty sure you'd never had strawberries, so I had Cheshire hunt a few down. We have some more at the house that are just plain."

I was speechless, unable to find the words to express my gratitude. "I wanted to spoil you one last time before we go on this mission." Even his mention of our impending plans did nothing to take away from just how amazing this was. "Eat, sweetheart."

I didn't hesitate, digging my fork into the pasta he'd sat in front of me. Flavors burst across my tongue, causing me to moan, "S'good."

He laughed, "I'm glad you like it."

We didn't speak as we continued to eat. I slowed down a bit, looking over at our view between bites. If I could ever get Wonderland to a good place, we could do this more often, step away from the duties we hadn't been entirely prepared to take on. "Do you think we'll ever be done?"

He didn't respond immediately, his eyes roving across the sky, "You are destined for something more. I don't know what exactly that is, but Alice... I'm going to be right beside you no matter what. You just have to be willing to accept that our lives are never going to be quiet and peaceful."

"I don't think I'm anything special truthfully," I held my hand up to stop him from arguing. "Seriously, I'm just a woman with magick. It could have been Lily or my mother just as easily as me. Because here's the thing, if just one person steps up there's a ripple. We've seen it go both ways. The only reason we were able to take down the Red Party was because we encouraged others to join us. Rosyn Rose is doing the same thing."

"So why didn't everything your mother did before she was 'killed' change things?" He countered.

I thought for a moment, "Maybe enough people weren't discontent with their treatment. Maybe it's because my mother isn't a fighter. She's a politician like her father." I hadn't spoken those words aloud before now, but they felt right. My mother's strength was diplomacy, but you needed soldiers to fight a war, not politicians. "In any case, we're going to keep fighting."

"Hell, yes we are." He raised his glass, clinking it against mine, "Until the very end."

"Until the very end," I murmured back, a strange feeling causing my magick to buzz under my skin. I shook it away, assuming it was the wine.

We finished our dinner, and Hatter pulled his chair around, picking up one of the strawberries for me to try. He pressed it gently against my lips and I opened my mouth taking a small bite. The flavor wasn't exactly what I was expecting. The fruit was just a bit tart against the sweetness of the chocolate but it was amazing. He held it up to my mouth again and

I took a bigger bite. A bit of juice dribbled down my chin, and he leaned closer using his tongue to lick it away. It should have been disgusting, but everything Hatter did was seductive. That was why I fell for him first. I glanced up noticing that the sky was turning dark. "Oh, we need to head home. How are we packing this stuff onto the bike?"

Hatter shook his head, "I've already set up for someone to come get it." He still carefully placed everything back into the basket, leaving no mess for someone else to clean up.

We meandered down to the bike, enjoying each other's company as long as we could. When we got home the real world was waiting. We'd let the Queen of Heart's problem go on long enough. It was time to make our move.

Once the bike was in view, Hatter stopped me, pulling me against him. "I need just a few more minutes with you." He breathed as he kissed my neck. I wrapped my arms around him, soaking in his body heat as he trailed kisses down my neck. His hands slipped under my shirt, yanking at my bra until it landed on the ground beside us. He pushed my shirt up, sucking one of my nipples into his mouth causing me to moan loudly. Suddenly he stopped, glancing around. I whined at the loss of his mouth on me, "Sh sh, sweetheart." He picked me up, and walked toward the bike. He sat me down long enough to swing his long legs over the machine. I furrowed my brow confused as to his intention. He motioned for me to come to him, and I didn't hesitate. I wasn't prepared for him to grab me by my jeans, unbuttoning them and pushing them down before he lifted me onto the bike, straddling him. A few moments of maneuvering had his cock slapping against my leg. I grinned, reaching between us to stroke the head gently. He growled, "Now isn't the time to tease me."

"But you love it." I shot back. I yelped when he gripped my thighs, slamming me down onto him without warning. The feeling of being filled so suddenly caused my vision to go white for a moment.

"Reach behind you and grip the handlebars." He commanded. I rushed to follow his instructions; he moved my shirt out of the way. The new position pressed my breasts into his face as I rode him. "You feel so good wrapped around me." I couldn't respond as he reached down, rubbing my clit. "I've never been so glad the Hummer got wrecked." He murmured to himself before he began to slam up into me. The bike rocked hard under our movements, but Hatter managed to keep it stable as he slammed into me one last time spilling inside me. The feeling of his hot seed filling me pushed me over the edge.

"I had no idea sex on a motorcycle was on my bucket list," I said as Hatter helped me to my feet.

"Neither did I, but we'll be doing it again soon." He joked, picking my bra up from the ground and tucking it into his pocket.

"Caterpillar is going to be jealous he didn't insist on joining us," I said, pulling the helmet onto my head. Hatter stepped up, buckling my helmet to ensure it was tight enough.

"I'm sure the old man will live. He got to have you in the wildflowers last year." He pointed out, climbing onto the bike again. I climbed on behind him, resting my head against his bike as he took off.

Chapter 25

March 10th, 2159

Nothing Penthea gave us changed our plan. Idalia and Caterpillar spent hours every day with Ilaria grilling her on every interaction she'd had with Rosyn. I stopped by occasionally, but seeing my friend in that cell made me hate myself. How was I different from my aunt when I was holding someone in a cage? Even if she had betrayed us, her daughter was a good enough reason. The fact she hadn't felt like we would or could help made me sick. I spent the rest of my time talking to Lily and my mother about what we could do magickal or in our gym training as hard as I could. When we all finally made it to the apartment at night we were too exhausted to do much more than fall into a pile on the bed.

"How much more time do we need?" I asked as I stepped out of the shower, glancing toward Caterpillar's naked form. He climbed under the hot water I'd just left.

"Not long. I think we should be ready in just a few days. We need a couple of group sessions." He explained. I forced myself not to stare at his body as he scrubbed himself.

"I'll set them up. Anything else?" I asked.

He shook his head, splattering me with water and soap. I giggled, "Now look at me. I have to get back in."

He just smirked at me, as I climbed in behind him.

Coordinating schedules for seven people who helped run a city was harder than I expected it to be. Joshua had been training with Hatter and Caterpillar privately, ensuring that he would be able to work with us. I was lucky enough that everyone in our group was available today. The group that would be waiting for us inside the city was going to train in a few days. I'd left the responsibility of dealing with that to my mother. She was doing better. I could tell she wasn't exactly back to normal, but at least she no longer looked like a ghost walking through our home.

Idalia was already in the training room when Hatter, Caterpillar, and I walked in. I could see the droplets of sweat dripping down from her hairline, but she kept pushing her body. Throwing punch after punch at the bag. I would have expected Lily to already be here since her wife was, but as I glanced around, she was nowhere to be seen. "She's upstairs." Idalia bit out, seeing me glance around.

"Everything okay?" I muttered to her as I stripped off the shirt I was wearing. Leaving me in a sports bra and workout shorts. She didn't immediately respond so I began stretching. Hatter had insisted that I learn yoga and stretches to ease my body after workout sessions. I hated to admit that he was right, but it had all but ended the pain I experienced each time I came down here.

"She shouldn't go." Idalia finally snapped, "That woman almost killed her once. She's holding my niece and your best friend hostage. This isn't something Lily needs to be involved in."

I let her rant. When she finally stopped trying to catch her breath I said. "I don't want to risk my sister either, but she's a grown woman Dalia. Her shielding could save any of our lives."

"Lily isn't a soldier." Idalia said, snapping at me, "She's soft, sweet. She might know how to defend herself, but we both know that's different."

"She doesn't fight. She defends. Some part of our magick is about who we are. My mother is a healer. Lily is a protector. I... I can't tell you what I am." I trailed off. I hadn't thought too deeply about what I'd said, but I knew without a doubt it was true.

"You are a Queen," Hatter said, coming to join us. "The rules will always be a little different for you."

I glanced at Idalia, catching the look on her face. I hadn't told everyone what Eumonia had revealed to me. I wasn't sure if Lily had shared the information. "Hatter, there are no queens in Wonderland," I said, brushing him off.

He just grinned down at me, knowing the truth. There was at least one queen in Wonderland, my immortal great times a million grandmother. Her line ran in my veins, but we didn't live in the same world she did when she was made a queen.

"What's the goal for today?" Joshua asked, striding into the room.

Caterpillar glanced around, noting Lily's absence, "Just warm up. We're still missing one."

Thirty minutes passed before Lily finally arrived. Her eyes were rimmed in red, but she held her head high, "I'm sorry for being late."

Hatter waved her off, "Gave us time to grill your wife."

I chuckled. We hadn't, but it was a good way to ease the tension that radiated off of the two of them.

Caterpillar motioned for everyone to gather around him. "The six of us are going to be going outside of the city in three days. Joshua has found a spot he believes is most likely close to where her hideout might be. We still expect a few miles of walking before we find it. I know all six of us are in good shape, so I'm not worried about stamina. We're here today to discuss our strategy. Joshua will also be giving us a few tips on how he survived out there."

"Ilaria needs to go with us." Idalia blurted out.

My eyebrows reached for my hairline at the comment, "She has already betrayed us once."

"I know, but the more I've spoken to her. There's no way the Queen of Hearts won't realize she's being tricked if I try to go in her place." She argued.

"I could use some of my illusion magick." I pointed out.

"And if it fails? Ilaria has to seem alone. We get her there, and then we sneak in another way." Idalia offered.

"We don't even know if there will be another way." Hatter pointed out. "If Cheshire could extend his ability to others I'd switch places with him."

"That would be useful. If we are unseen, it might be safer out there." Joshua added.

"Why can't Alice use her illusion magick to make everyone but Ilaria invisible?" Lily asked.

I hadn't considered it. Honestly, I didn't use my illusion magick as much as my electricity. It wasn't as useful in day-to-day life. "I'd need to try it. See how long I can hold it."

"Let's do that." Caterpillar pointed to me.

I dropped to the floor groaning. Sweat was dripping down my back. My magick was straining under my skin. I felt used and abused from trying to hold the illusion magick under all of Caterpillar's tests. We'd been at it for four hours, checking every downside and hole in our plan. "Can't. Go. On." I bit out, before releasing my illusion magick. Hatter, Idalia, Lily, and Joshua all sat down once the magick I'd wrapped around them disappeared.

"It won't work on me." Caterpillar pointed out again. We'd been going round and round about how to handle Caterpillar's resistance to my illusion magick.

"Why did it before?" I asked, causing everyone to look at me, "Remember, in Griffin's apartment. I used illusion magick to leave."

Caterpillar considered that, "I didn't rest enough, and I wasn't aware that I was a void. Maybe like everyone else with magick, I wasn't charged enough for my void ability to work."

I nodded, agreeing that that was a possibility. We hadn't deeply explored Caterpillar's ability, but it was going to be a hindrance on this mission. "So you need to switch out with one of the others."

Caterpillar shook his head, turning a dark look on me, "You are not going out of the city without me."

"So, we take you in as a prisoner." Joshua offered.

Everyone looked at him, considering the idea. When I couldn't find any holes in it I said, "That would work. If Idalia, disguised as Ilaria, offers Caterpillar up as penance for being caught it might give us enough time to get Griffin and Caroline out of there."

"We need to take my sister." Idalia insisted again, "I know we can't trust her, but if all of us are there how much damage can she really do?"

"We are going to save her daughter. She's unlikely to betray us in the process." Joshua pointed out.

I considered his point, glancing at Caterpillar to gauge his thoughts. He gave me a subtle nod, and I sighed, "Okay... but Idalia. You have to be by her side the entire time. If she tries something, you have to end it before she can betray us again."

"Are you asking me to kill my twin sister?" She quirked an eyebrow at me.

"No-"

"If it comes to that." Caterpillar and I spoke at the same time. My mouth dropped open at his words, "You can't honestly expect her to take her sister's life?"

"If it saves this city, I do." He continued, "That is the role we have as leaders."

I bit my tongue, unwilling to argue with him in front of everyone else. Idalia didn't feel the same way. She stepped into his personal space. Her small height was even more obvious against his huge frame, "Fuck that and fuck Wonderland. Punishing Ilaria when she's a victim of that bitch is a mistake. If you can't see that maybe you should consider if you are really the leader, you think you are."

The room was silent as they stared at each other, her words like knives against us. I considered her point. Yes, Ilaria had been victimized by the Queen of Hearts, but she could have come to any of us at any time and told us the truth. I shook my head, she was protecting her child. A mother would do anything for their babies. Including betraying people they care for. "Ilaria is being protected," Caterpillar growled. "What you might not know is that Alcinda and I worked together to protect that room against all magick users. The Queen of Hearts cannot get to your sister where she sits right now." Idalia's mouth dropped open, but he continued. "If you question my dedication to this city maybe you'd like to spend some time in my role. I could certainly use the time off."

I stepped toward them, but Hatter grabbed my arm to stop me. Idalia found her words, "The five of you are keeping secrets from the rest of us. I know Lily has information that she has been sworn to secrecy on. Have you considered that keeping the people who are supposed to help you in the dark doesn't inspire trust?"

"We can't risk some of what we know getting out." I defended, causing Hatter to sigh behind me. I pulled my arm out of his grip, stepping toward them, "I know you're upset, but don't let them divide us. We're only trying to protect everyone." Idalia's eyes cut to mine, and I could see the unshed tears there, but I continued. "I'm willing to bring the option of Ilaria coming with us before the rest of the group, but I want to talk to her first. Make sure she knows the risks. There's a chance that even with a prisoner her usefulness to Rosyn has run out. She might be killed."

"That's true if I go in her place." Idalia pointed out.

"I know, but I believe you want to protect your sister. What would you rather risk?" I asked.

"Take it to everyone. I will accept whatever they decide." She responded, avoiding my question.

The tension in the room eased some as she left, Lily running after her. Joshua stood from his spot on the floor, "I think I'll go grab some lunch. I'll see y'all in three days."

Hatter, Caterpillar, and I didn't speak as we reset the gym for the next person to use. My mind was spinning with thoughts. If Idalia went in Ilaria's place there was a possibility she'd be killed the moment the Queen of Hearts laid eyes on her. They might be identical twins, but we all managed to tell them apart. It was a risk to take someone who had already betrayed us to our biggest enemy, but if what Caterpillar said was true, he didn't believe she was a threat. My mind couldn't process that he'd worked with my mother with his abilities and hadn't told me. I felt my anger rising, and before I knew it I whirled toward him, "Why the fuck didn't you tell me about your magick?" His grey eyes widened just a bit at the rage in my voice, but I continued before he could respond, "We're supposed to be a team."

"You didn't tell me about sector six which got you kidnapped by Jabberwocky." He shot back, leaving the fact that my omission had ultimately gotten him killed.

I felt heat rush to my cheeks, but I couldn't find the words to express what I was feeling so I threw my hands in the air. "I'm going to talk to Ilaria."

Neither of them stopped me as I stormed out of the room, making my way down to the cell Ilaria was being kept in. She was dressed in a linen jumpsuit. Her red hair pulled away from her face while she went through a series of exercises, I'd seen her do a hundred times before. I pushed the door open, and she glanced up, a tentative smile on her face, "Alice, you haven't been to visit much. What can I do for you?"

I was surprised by how at peace she seemed when she was a prisoner, "Idalia wants you to go on the mission with us."

"I know." Her smile faded and she moved away taking a seat on the small cot.

"Caterpillar is against it," I added.

"I know." She murmured. We watched each other in silence for a moment before she finally asked, "What do you think?"

"I've got no fucking idea. They both have good points. I came to figure out what you think." I admitted, leaning against the wall.

She was silent, her face giving away none of her thoughts, "Caterpillar thinks she'll kill me. I actually agree with him. If we do this, I probably won't come home…" She trailed off, "I'm okay with that. I want my daughter to have the same life that Lewis and Elsie are getting here. I want to go, but if you make me stay here, I won't fight."

I nodded, "I'll see what I can do." I turned to leave the room, but stopped, "I want you to know that I'll do everything in my power to keep you alive if you go with us."

I had refused to go back to the apartment after my fight with Caterpillar and my conversation with Ilaria. So I found myself on the roof of our building, shivering from the cold air that caressed my skin. My pride was wounded. I couldn't bring myself to face the accusation he'd leveled at me when he mentioned Jabberwocky. Some part of me knew he was right. If I had told them about any of the suspicions that had led me to that day, it wouldn't have happened.

"It's cold as fuck up here." Cheshire groaned from behind me, causing me to jump. "Creator, get away from the edge. You need to stay the hell away from the roofs of buildings after what happened last time."

I snorted, stepping into his open arms to absorb some of his body heat, "Why are you up here?"

"Caterpillar is in the apartment brooding over a glass of whiskey like some kind of mafia boss. You've been gone for hours, but Hatter is determined to stay out of it so it looks like it's up to me to smooth things over." He explained, rolling his eyes. "Really, you're both so dramatic. That's why you need the rest of us. Things would get too intense if you didn't have your comedic relief."

"You know you're not just comedic relief." I said, pressing my lips against his, "But I do appreciate you trying to play mediator."

"Trying, please. You know I'm going to succeed. So don't fight back. Let's go down to the apartment so the two of you can kiss and make up."

"It's not that simple, Ches. He threw Jabberwocky in my face." I pulled away, pacing in front of him, "Not to mention that he told Idalia she would have to kill Ilaria if it came to it. That's heartless. We all know that Ilaria wasn't betraying us just for funsies."

"But she did betray us. You, especially." He argued, "I don't think Caterpillar was trying to throw Jabberwocky in your face. You were tortured by that psychopath."

"He killed him," I murmured, "And we can pretend all day that no one is at fault for that, but I knew I was being followed. I knew going to sector six alone was a risk. I could have done anything different and none of that would have happened."

A tear rolled down my face, and Cheshire reached up to wipe it away, "You could have." His words were like a slap in the face, but before I could respond he continued, "But you didn't. You are powerful, Al. We all know that you don't know how to stop being the badass you are. All I need you to learn is to clue us in when you're about to do something risky in the future."

"I'll do my best." I conceded, his speech taking away some of my anger.

"That's all any of us can do." He kissed my forehead, "Now can we please go in, so I don't freeze my balls off?"

I laughed but allowed him to lead me down the stairs and into our apartment. Caterpillar looked up from his glass as I walked toward him. Before I could say anything he stood sweeping me up in his arms and slamming his lips into mine. The kiss was harsh, filled with anger and other emotions I couldn't identify. When he pulled away I was panting. He smirked, but said, "Throwing Jabberwocky at you was fucked up, but I need you to understand that--"

I cut him off, "It's okay. We're allowed to argue sometimes. In the future, if it has to do with magick I'd like you to include me."

"I can do that." He agreed before reaching to lift me by my thighs, "Now it's time for a proper apology."

Chapter 26

❧❦

March 13th, 2024

After a short discussion Caterpillar and I had agreed that Ilaria would join us on the mission. It was her daughter in danger. It didn't seem right to keep her from helping us. There was nothing left to do now but step outside the protection of Wonderland. Everyone was standing at the edge of the dome, miles from the city or even the boonies.

"If we haven't come back in six hours do not come looking for us. Return home and start the backup plan. Keep Wonderland safe for us." Caterpillar commanded the small gathering of people that would be staying behind. I could see the anger on Cheshire's face at that direction. There was no doubt in my mind that he would be the first to step outside the dome if we didn't return.

"You know we won't abandon you," Mom said, coming to wrap her arms around Lily and then me. "No matter how much you grow you will always be my little girls. I am sorry for all the responsibility that has been laid at your feet." Her last words were aimed at me, but I waved her off forcing myself not to get emotional. I would come back; we would win the day today.

"It's time," Hatter said, grabbing my hand to walk toward the shimmering wall. It was hard to see, I'm not sure that anyone would notice it if they weren't looking for it.

March and Cheshire stepped over, sandwiching me in between their bodies. "When you get back, I have a surprise for you," Cheshire muttered in my ear before releasing me. I appreciated his confidence that we'd be back, unfortunately, I wasn't quite as certain.

I turned giving March a good squeeze, "I love you."

"L-love you too, Ali." He responded before kissing me passionately. I was a bit taken aback since he preferred to be more private in his affections.

Everyone stood waiting for me. Joshua looked extremely uncomfortable, but at least he didn't comment on it. "I'll go through first. Alice and Caterpillar should follow me. Hatter is going to bring up the rear." He instructed.

I watched as he stepped through, only to find that he immediately disappeared from sight. I glanced to Caterpillar who shrugged and followed through disappearing as well. I took a deep breath and stepped through. I could feel the magick of the shield bending around me, an uncomfortable pressure on my skin until I stumbled, falling into a solid mass. I glanced up to find Joshua had caught me, "Thanks."

"It can be jarring, try to take shallow breaths. The air out here isn't as clean as it is inside of Wonderland." He said before stepping away to assist Lily and Idalia who had appeared holding hands. Ilaria came through behind them, immediately losing her breakfast. Idalia pulled a bottle of water out of the backpack she carried, handing it to her sister. Hatter was the last to step through, and while he looked a bit pale, he managed to avoid losing his lunch.

"Should I make us invisible now?" I asked.

"Save your energy. I'd say we have at least an hour of walking before we're even close to where she is." Joshua said, "I know of a building that she might be using. I never approached any of the ones around the city because of how many animals make their homes out here."

I motioned for him to lead on. As we walked, I took in our surroundings. Grass grew as tall as my hips, making it hard to know exactly what I was stepping on. At one point Joshua stopped us all and we watched as a snake slithered by. It was huge, but thankfully ignored us completely. How he'd known it was in our path I couldn't figure out but I was thankful for his help. Hatter's father was a gruff man, but slowly he was warming up to our group. He'd even laughed at a joke I'd made as we walked. The sun beat down on us, and even with the cold air sweat had begun to drip down my spine when Joshua brought everyone to a stop. "We're getting close."

"This isn't as bad as I expected." Hatter mused, joining our small huddle.

"I survived out here for ten years. I know how to avoid most of the things that would kill us. I don't think the entire city could relocate. There are too many dangers for the average citizen, but it's not as bad out here as I expected. The air and the predators are the biggest problems." Joshua explained.

The air was different, thinner as if we were standing on top of the tallest mountain. I could breathe, but it wasn't comfortable. "Alice go ahead and mask all of us but Ilaria and Caterpillar."

While I began calling my magick to the surface Ilaria stepped up to Caterpillar, wrapping rope around his wrists. Before I began actually working the magick I said, "Rough him up a bit. If he looks perfectly fine, it's not believable that you dragged him this far." They both nodded at me, and I turned away ignoring the sounds of skin slapping. I closed my eyes, letting myself fall into the well of my magick that lived deep inside of me. Once I was fully immersed, I opened my eyes, casting a hand out toward Lily, Idalia, Hatter, and Joshua willing my magick to coat each of them.

"That's freaky as fuck." Ilaria said once my magick had covered everyone, hiding us from view.

"I can still see all of you. Once we're inside, split up, and find Griffin and Caroline. Ilaria and I will keep her distracted as long as possible. We need to do this quickly." Caterpillar commanded. I tried to ignore the blood that dripped from his lip and the bruises already forming on his face. Ilaria had certainly ensured that it looked real.

Joshua made his way ahead of them, leading us even though he wasn't seen. I gasped as the building came into view. It looked like a tower out of a fairytale, covered in vines. Two armed men stood at the entrance, dressed in all black. Joshua moved out of the way, letting Ilaria approach them. Neither moved as she came forward, "I'm here to speak to the Queen."

"The Queen doesn't take visitors." One of the men barked, "Get out of here girl."

"She'll want to see me. Do you not know who this is?" She motioned to Caterpillar who was putting on a fantastic performance of seeming beaten down. "This is Caterpillar."

The men glanced at each other, and one disappeared from the door they guarded. None of us spoke, but I motioned toward Hatter getting as close as we could to the door. We would need to sneak inside without drawing any attention. The door swung open, the man seeming panicked, "The Queen wants them up there now."

He held the door open as the other guard escorted Ilaria and Caterpillar inside. We all slipped in, but when I glanced back, I noticed that Joshua hadn't been able to make it. I wanted to curse, but there was nothing to be done now. I motioned for Hatter, Lily, and Idalia. Before we'd come we had found a few hand signals to use so we could communicate without speaking. I sent Hatter to follow Ilaria and Caterpillar to the Queen. I knew I needed to be there too, but finding Griffin was my biggest priority. Lily and Idalia I sent down the stairs in the main entrance as I began climbing up them. Very few people milled around, but enough that I could easily open doors without drawing attention to myself. I didn't want to risk being caught so early in the plan. I found a room with an open door and stepped through, exploring the large room. A bed took up most of the space, a wardrobe was the only other furniture in the room. I opened a couple of drawers before I heard the creak of a door opening. I turned to find Duchess standing there, water dripping down her naked body. She was covered in bruises and had clearly lost weight. I watched as she opened the wardrobe, dressing in simple black pants and a tank top. I debated my options for a long moment before I dropped the illusion hiding me from her sight. I reached out with my magick, suring up the illusions around the others. Duchess gasped, brown eyes wide as she took me in. "You can't be here."

"Well, I am. I've got one question." I took a deep breath, "Did you betray us?"

Her face mottled red, and I could see a spark of her mother as she snapped, "Gee Alice no idea. I'm sure being a prisoner as a crazy woman tries to torture me was in my plans for this year."

"Sorry, I just needed to make sure. Do you know where they're holding your father and Griffin?" I asked.

"She killed my father the day she brought us here." Duchess eyes were distant, voice flat as she continued. "Apparently he had refused to bring me to her just before you took down the city."

"Why does she want you so badly?" I pressed, needing more information.

Duchess' eyes cut away from me and she muttered, "I have no idea." I knew she was hiding something, but now wasn't the time to demand the information.

I sighed, "Okay, it doesn't matter right now. We need to get out of here. I can make you invisible if you want."

She nodded and I stretched my magick feeling the strain of covering so many people. I forced it to extend to me, hiding both of us from sight. I motioned for her to stay quiet, but she led me out of the room. I let Duchess lead me back down the stairs but stopped when I heard a small giggle. I noticed a door cracked open just enough to reveal a tiny girl with red hair. She held a strange-looking horse in her hands. I was taken aback when she raised her hazel eyes and looked directly at me. "' Lo pretty lady. Was your name? I'm Cara."

Duchess realized I wasn't following and came to grab my arm, but I stepped further into the room letting the illusion around me drop. "Hi, Cara. My name is Ali, would you like to go on an adventure with me?"

She clapped her hands together, "Like the stories Mr. Turtle tells me at night?"

"Just like that." I smiled, "But you have to be very, very quiet, okay? Cause we're hiding from a mean old witch."

Her voice dropped to a whisper, "Is it Auntie Ros?"

The little girl was far more intelligent than I was prepared to deal with, "Yes. I'm a good witch, and I came here to rescue you." Cara's smile grew, and she reminded me of Ilaria as she bounded toward me, wrapping tiny arms around one of my legs.

I reached my magick down toward her, coating her in it gently. She giggled and said, "That tickles." I held my finger to my lips reminding her to be quiet and headed back out the door. Duchess stood outside eyes darting up and down the hall. She glanced down at the little girl giving me a nod before she continued her trek down the stairs. She led us down the winding stairs, pausing when we reached the bottom. I strained my ears, hoping to hear any of my team, but only eerie silence reigned. Duchess turned, heading down the stairs I'd sent Lily and Idalia down. It was dark, nearly impossible to see if not the torches on the wall. Caroline gripped my hand tighter, fear crossing her features. I was relieved when we stepped onto flat ground, finding rows of metal bars, and rusting cells. The smell was dank, a mix of human excretions and mildew. We walked quickly, glancing into empty cell after empty cell. We came to the end of the hallway, and I tried to push away the disappointment that we hadn't found Griffin, but Duchess distracted me from the thoughts pointing toward a heavy wooden door.

I left Duchess with Cara and stepped toward the door, using my weight to push it open. There was no light in the room, so I turned around, grabbing a torch off the wall. I stepped into the room but couldn't stop myself from gasping when I saw Griffin. His ginger hair was tangled around his head, his shirt ripped open revealing every rib. I rushed to him forgetting that I was invisible.

"Griff, Griffin." I shook him slightly.

He groaned, but blinked his eyes open, "A floating torch… great now I've started hallucinating."

I dropped the magick hiding me, "Alice!" He hissed, trying to lift his body off the cot, "You have to get out of here. She'll kill you."

"Shh, shhh. I would never leave you. Dina and Elsie need you. I need you." I checked him over. He actually didn't look injured like Duchess, just starving, "Can you walk?"

He nodded, standing. He swayed slightly but managed to stay on his feet, "Okay. I'm going to make you invisible. Don't freak out Duchess and Ilaria's daughter are right outside."

"Ilaria's daughter?" He asked.

"Long story. Can you keep an eye on them? Duchess can lead you all out of the tower. Joshua is outside." I instructed, "I sent Lily and Idalia down here to find you. We didn't find them on the way. I'm going to get everyone out of here."

"You've got to be careful. This woman has a huge grudge against you." Griffin cautioned.

Adding Griffin into the illusion made my skin burn from the effort, but I pushed through. I made sure they made it up the stairs, leaving Duchess and Griffin to get out on their own I headed in the direction the guards had taken Ilaria and Caterpillar. The halls were empty, but I finally came upon a large open room that was filled with people. The Queen of Hearts sat on a chair raised above everyone else. Ilaria and Caterpillar were kneeling in front of her. I scanned the crowd for any familiar faces but didn't find anyone of note. I moved carefully, ensuring not to brush against anyone as the Queen of Hearts continued speaking. "Today is a good day my lovelies. Our favorite little traitor has brought me a present in penance for being caught." She giggled, her blood-red curls bouncing around her ageless face. "I wonder just how pissed Alice Young is. You've stolen her favorite cadre member."

A few chuckles filtered through the hall, but Ilaria started speaking. "I hope you can forgive my grave error, my Queen."

She tsked but didn't speak as she stood. She ran a hand down Caterpillar's chest, "Bringing me the void is useful, but what I really need is the woman herself. You see, I can use her like a battery."

I stiffened. I'd never let this woman use me like that, but I couldn't do anything at this moment. I glanced toward her chair again, forcing myself not to rage at the way she was touching Caterpillar. Lily and Idalia were waving their arms behind her chair, trying to get my attention. I couldn't figure out what they were trying to tell me, so I moved closer. Unfortunately, a large man bumped into me, causing the magick to stall out. Every eye in the room swung to me, shouts of my name ringing out. I scrambled away from the hands that grabbed at me. I caught Ilaria's eyes letting her know to release Caterpillar. She dropped the rope, yanking it just right to make the rope fall away completely. He reached up, grabbing at the Queen, but missed her by just an inch as she winked out of existence.

Lily and Idalia ran toward me, "We have to get out of here. We found—" Idalia's words were cut off as the ground beneath us shook. Ilaria and Caterpillar stumbled toward us just as we were surrounded by the Queen of Heart's people.

I released all the illusion magick I'd been holding, calling my electricity, "This isn't my first mob." I muttered shocking the people directly in front of me, "Everyone should be out of the tower. Come on."

My skin tingled as I felt Lily shield us. Caterpillar, Idalia, and Ilaria spun around me fists and legs a jumble as they took down everyone that came after us. I felt my magick lagging, I'd used too much but I forced my body to continue, zapping anyone who got in my way. I saw the door that would get us out of the tower, a lone man standing in front of it. My steps slowed as Jabberwocky grinned, "You owe me something." I glanced toward where his arm should have been, a knot tied in his shirt just under his shoulder.

"Sorry, I'm all out of fucks to give." I took two running steps, gathering every ounce of magick into my fist. Electricity crackling I slammed my first into Jabberwocky's sternum sending him flying into the door. It crumbled under his weight flooding the hall with sunlight. I stepped over his choking, breathless form, my strength waning. Arms grabbed me, and I was tossed over Caterpillar's shoulders as he began to run.

"Great job, princess." He spoke as he ran, legs eating up the ground. I didn't complain as my stomach jumped up and down on his shoulder.

"Roman, over here," Joshua yelled. He was standing with Duchess, Griffin, and Caroline who were all pale under the light of the sun, "This way." The ground shook harder causing Caterpillar to stumble, but he managed to stay upright.

"Is there somewhere we can hide?" He shouted.

"No, we need to get back into the city," Joshua said, matching pace with us. "She'll bring her tower down at this rate." I glanced back, noticing the debris that fell from the roof.

"It's a long run. There's no way we'll make it back to where we entered." I heaved out.

"We're not going to." Joshua panted, "If we can make it a half mile that way we can enter where the river flows into out of the city. Well, where it should."

"Caterpillar put me down. Carrying me will make this take longer." I said, pressing against his back.

"Ilaria is carrying her daughter. Idalia and Lily are helping Griffin. Duchess is managing right now, we can't stop." He ground out. I knew arguing wouldn't help so I kept quiet, ten minutes later we came to a stop, and he set me on my feet. Everyone was breathing hard, dripping sweat, but at least we were all in one piece. The ground still shook slightly, but not too badly.

"Get them in first, I'll go through last," Caterpillar ordered.

"I can shield us. I'll go through last." Lily insisted, pushing Idalia and Ilaria through the wall, Cara clutched to her mother's chest.

Griffin followed them when I realized something, "Where is Hatter?"

Joshua turned glancing around, "He didn't come out with you?"

I shook my head, turning, "We have to go back and get him."

"You've got no juice. Joshua and I will go, get back in the city." Caterpillar ground out.

I ignored him, marching back the way we'd came. I didn't make it far before I saw Hatter come running toward us, panting, "Really appreciate y'all waiting up for me."

"I'm sorry son. We didn't have time to do a head count." Joshua said, "What happened?"

"Did Lily and Idalia tell you what they found?" Hatter asked.

I shook my head, stress lined his forehead, "They didn't have a chance."

"Strange machinery, looked like something from before the end." Lily said, "Hatter, I'm sorry I thought you'd made it out to your father."

"It's fine. I managed to get here, didn't I." Hatter winked at me, "But I did see the Queen headed this way. Let's get inside."

I nodded, watching as Joshua and Hatter stepped through the barrier. As they disappeared the ground shook harder, and just over the hill that Hatter had come from appeared the Queen of Hearts. Her hair flew behind her as she ran toward us, rage twisting her face. Caterpillar tried to scoop me up, but I pointed toward Lily, "Get her out of here."

"You're not fighting her in your condition." Caterpillar snapped, reaching for me again.

"No, I'm not. Get inside the city." With those words, I shoved at his chest causing him to fall back into the wall.

I grabbed Lily's shoulders, "Wrap me up?" She nodded, wrapping her golden shield over me, as soon as I felt it click into place I shoved her into the wall as well. Facing off with the Queen of Hearts alone.

Chapter 27

"Did they leave you for me? You've got to be weak from all that magick you've used." The Queen of Hearts said as she came to a stop before me.

I kept my body relaxed, "No, they knew I could handle you alone."

Fury lit up in her eyes, "You've taken things from me, girl. I'd like them back."

"People aren't things for you to own." I snapped at her, "Let's settle this. You want Wonderland. You have to get through me."

"I'm not plebian like Penthea, child. I'm not going to fight you." She snapped her fingers, a dagger falling into her waiting palm, "You're going to end your own life here today."

I furrowed my eyebrows, but she continued, "You see I've figured something out. You'll do anything for what you love. Even die I'd guess. If you don't want me to take your city, to kill every person you've loved all you have to do is plunge this dagger into your own heart."

"What's the catch? Once I'm dead you can do whatever you want." I asked.

"I have honor. I'm a Queen. If you give your life here today, I will leave your precious Wonderland in peace for fifty years. I'd say that's a pretty good deal myself." She pressed the dagger into my palm.

I turned it over in my hand, taking in the strange inscriptions. The handle glittered with an odd purple gem. I could almost feel the magick coming off of it. I turned it toward myself, glancing up at her. I let a feral smile curl across my features, "Rosyn right?" Her face paled slightly at my use of her name, "I'm just going to call you Ro I think. You see, I want to believe that you would honor that bargain, but here's the thing…" I reached for her faster than she could stop me, I dug my fingers into her arm, punctuating each word with a stab. "You. Are. A. Liar." On the last word I dug the dagger into her stomach. I let her fall to her knees before me, "Wonderland is my city. So long as I draw breath you will never have it."

Strange sounds left her, at first, I thought they might be sobs, but when she stood throwing the dagger I'd left buried in her I had no words. "I could have seen us as friends in a different world."

I didn't have a chance to process that she hadn't even bled before she was on me, raining blows down on me. Her words are venomous, "You are nothing. Even with all that power you waste it. I've watched you. You care more about falling into bed with those four men than anything else. You're nothing more than whore playing a queen's game."

Before she could land another punch, I felt a hand wrap around my wrist, and I was once again surrounded by pressure. I gasped, falling to my knees as I was yanked back into Wonderland. I looked up finding Eumonia standing above me, "Give me your hands, girl. I need your power."

"I'm tapped out." I squeaked.

"You are a Lyon; your power is endless." Her usually soft voice boomed in my ears. She took my hands, "Close your eyes and just feel. I will lead."

I did as she said, but I gasped as I felt myself pulling toward her. Her magick was golden like Lily's but different, older. I felt it reach inside me, toward my own sleeping magick. The moment they touched I felt my back bow. Power and electricity shooting through me. Eumonia's warm hands kept mine in a rough grip, refusing to let me pull away as she yanked my magick to the surface. "Someday you'll learn how to do this and so much more. One day you will surpass even me in power, Alice. Today, we stop anyone from entering this city."

I had no idea how she planned to do that, but I couldn't ask. My voice was frozen in my throat as I felt her send our combined magick away. I wanted to open my eyes to see what she was doing, but I couldn't. I couldn't do anything but kneel before her. I had no sense of time, but eventually, the pull stopped, my magick returning to its slumber. "Sleep, my child. The city is now protected."

March 14th, 2159

My eyes blinked open to complete darkness, my body was cradled by something soft. I tried to move, but something was holding me down. A soft snore had me turning my head to find Caterpillar's brutally handsome face next to mine. I breathed a small sigh before I tried to scoot out from under his arm. It took way too long, but eventually, I managed to get out from under him, making my way to the bathroom. I did my business and found myself staring in the mirror. My skin was silver, and my entire body ached with a bone-deep pain I'd never felt before. I glanced toward the tub, deciding a hot soak would be best. As soon as the water turned on I heard noise from the other room. I peeked my head out and saw Caterpillar sitting up, looking panicked.

"Hey, I'm right here," I said, softly.

He stalked toward me, "If you ever push me like that again I'm going to take you over my knee."

I huffed out a laugh, "I'm glad you're alright."

He pulled me into arms, "When Eumonia brought you in I thought you were dead."

"I'm okay, just very sore." I winced as he squeezed me.

"Sorry." He muttered, motioning for me to head back into the bathroom. I climbed into the tub, letting the warm water begin to wash away my pain. "Eumonia is still here. We all needed to sleep."

"Where are the guys?" I asked as he began to wash my hair.

"In the guest room. We didn't know how you would be once you woke up. We'd been switching off every few hours." He explained.

"How long have I been out?" I asked.

"Just a day. Now that you're awake I'll have everyone gather in the conference room."

"Did everyone make it home?"

"Ilaria is back in her cell but we've made it comfortable enough that Cara can stay with her. I'm not ready to risk the Queen of Hearts figuring out a way in and straight to them. Duchess has been staying with Griffin and Dina. He's okay, malnourished, but happy to be home with his family again." Caterpillar explained, rinsing the soap off of me.

"Thank the Creator." I murmured, sleep weighing on me heavily, "Could I go back to sleep for a bit."

"Of course, princess." He helped me out of the tub, drying me off. He stepped out of the room, returning with a t-shirt and shorts. He helped me dress before leading me back to bed. "Eumonia says you may feel drained for a few more days."

I couldn't respond to his words because I had already been pulled back into peaceful darkness.

"Just sit down and listen." Mom instructed as I walked into the conference room, "You shouldn't even be out of bed yet."

"I'm fine, Mother." I joked, taking my seat. I wasn't lying, I'd woken up feeling a hundred times better, my magick was still slumbering, but I was no longer in any pain.

"Let her fuss over you." Eumonia said from her seat at the other end of the table, "It's part of the joys of being a mother."

Mom laughed, pressing a kiss to the top of my head, "Before everyone gets here, I just want you to know that I am so proud of you."

"It was all Eumonia," I said, feeling a blush reach my cheeks.

"It wasn't if you weren't helping, I couldn't have performed the feat I did," Eumonia argued.

"Which was what exactly?" I asked.

"Be patient." She chided.

Slowly everyone filed into the room, only Dina and Griffin were missing as they'd been tasked with taking care of Lewis, Elsie, and Caroline today. Tillie arrived last, flanked by Jackson and Cahir. All three stopped off, giving me hugs and apologizing for not doing more. I waved them off, it certainly wasn't their fault things hadn't gone to plan.

"Thank you for coming everyone. I want to introduce myself; I am Eumonia Lyon. Alcinda, Alice, and Lily are my descendants. Yes, I founded Wonderland. Yes, I'm immortal. Yes, I come from Undraland. No, I'm not looking to lead any of you or the city." She got to the point, "I just wanted to explain to everyone here what I've done." Everyone nodded, waiting with rapt attention for her explanation. "With Alice's help, I altered my shield, no one will be able to enter or exit the city anymore. This will keep any of the Queen of Hearts people out, but it also keeps all of us in. If the city were ever to fail it would take a great feat of magick to undo this." Her voice was grave as she finished.

A mix of emotions showed on the faces of my family, but I stood, "Thank you. Not just for saving my life. Again. You've done more for this city than anyone else, I hope you're willing to join our rag-tag group here. We could certainly use your knowledge."

"I'd be honored to get to know my grandchildren better." Tears misted in her eyes, "But if we could keep my secret in this room, I'd appreciate it. I went to a lot of work to hide my existence. I don't want to undo all that work."

My mother spoke up. "Whatever you wish, but just know that today's Wonderland would rejoice to meet their fearless benefactor. None of us would be here without your sacrifices."

"Sacrifice is the greatest gift that we can give. I gave it freely." Pride shown on Eumonia's face. "But I know that isn't the only reason we're all gathered here today." She turned her eyes toward Cheshire.

"Alice, I told you that I had a little surprise for you," He was nervous as he came to kneel beside me. He pulled a small velvet box from his pocket, "Rab helped me gather everything I needed for this." He opened the box to reveal a beautiful silver ring, four gems sparkled up at me, one in purple, an amethyst. I knew without a doubt that was for Cheshire. The next one was a light green, it took longer for me to realize it was a jade for March. Next to that, a blood-red ruby reminded me of Caterpillar's intensity. Finally, a diamond sparkled last, catching the light it filtered between orange and pink. I knew that it was meant to represent Hatter. Tears welled in my eyes as the beautiful piece, but he wasn't done, "Tomorrow would you please marry us? Third times a charm."

"Yes!" I nearly shouted, throwing myself onto the floor to wrap my arms around his neck, "I love this. Thank you so much." I slipped the ring onto my finger. It was the perfect fit, and even with the four gems it wasn't overly large. Cheshire stood passing me to Caterpillar who kissed me before passing me off to March and Hatter who held me between them for a long moment.

I turned to ask questions, but my mother held up her hand, "We have everything prepared. All you have to do is show up tomorrow."

I smiled, so glad she knew exactly what I was going to ask. "Thank you all so much. I want you to know how touched I am."

"You've done everything you can for all of us. Marrying your men is the least we can do." Duchess said, "Not that I had much to do with any of this." She looked better, but I noticed she'd cut her already short hair up to her ears. The curls were riotous around her head, but she made it look glamorous.

"Go relax today, Ali. Tomorrow you're getting married." Tillie said, waving me out of the room.

Chapter 28

March 15th, 2159

When Mom said they'd planned everything she was being literal. The men had all disappeared from our room in the early morning hours, going to get dressed. A dress bag was laid out for me when I stepped out of the shower and Dina waited to help me with it. We didn't speak, but she wrapped her arms around me, her squeeze said everything I knew she wasn't able to verbalize.

The dress was familiar, but someone had it altered to add a corset that lifted my chest and pulled my waist in more. A pale blue soft material fell to my feet in thin, tulle layers. Once Dina had finished lacing the back, she started on my hair braiding in around my head. I wore minimal makeup, but as I looked in the mirror, I barely recognized myself. "One last thing," Dina said, a mischievous grin on her face. She pulled a velvet bag out of her purse, carefully removing a silver tiara that was studded with diamonds. When I took a closer look, I saw that the tiara was made of twisted vines. "A Lyon Queen needs her crown."

"Where did you get that?" I asked, a bit breathless as she placed it on my head.

"Eumonia gave it to me." She explained, "God you look amazing!"

I turned, wrapping my arms around her, "Thank you. Seriously, thank you for putting up with all my bullshit. I'm sorry it took so long to get Griffin home. I'm sorry I'm a terribly neglectful friend these days."

"Stop. You're going to make me cry. I love you. We don't have to spend every day together for me to still be your best friend." She said, "Now let's get you married!"

We made our way down to the main entrance, but she stopped me as I went to leave, leading me toward the back, opening a door I'd never noticed before. She led me through a short hallway, Rab was waiting in a traditional suit at the end. "I hope this is the last time I have to walk you down the aisle. It's starting to lose its excitement." He said by way of greeting.

I chuckled, "It will be."

Dina opened the door, revealing a small courtyard that was tucked in the back of our building. My mouth dropped open as I saw that they had cleaned it up, bringing down chairs for everyone to sit in. I glanced down to see that red roses covered the ground to the altar. I let my eyes rove over my men. They were all wearing the same suits they had the last time we'd tried to get married, but they looked even better. I was surprised to see Eumonia standing next to them, but she motioned for us to begin our walk, so I didn't have time to wander. Once we stood in front of her, Caterpillar and Hatter kneeled before her, followed quickly by Cheshire and March. I looked at Eumonia in confusion, but she just began to speak. "My favorite part of being a Queen was blessing love matches. I haven't done this in far longer than I'd like to admit, but hopefully, I'm not too rusty." She cleared her throat, motioning for me to take the spot they'd left open before her. I went to kneel as well, but she stopped me. "A queen never kneels." She whispered, a glint in her eyes, "Today we are all here to watch as these five souls become one in the eyes of the Creator. It is my honor to lead them through this ceremony." She turned, picking up a small knife from a cushion to her left. "These Knights wish to bind themselves to my granddaughter, Alice Young. We stand here as witnesses to their devotion."

She handed the knife to Caterpillar who stood, bowing his head to her before turning to me. "I am Roman Ainsworth and I vow my life, my love, and my loins to Alice Lyon." I raised my eyebrows at the change to my name, but didn't argue "May I be her shield to the end of my days." He sliced his palm and reached for my arm. I didn't even feel the prick as he opened a small cut on my left forearm. "Will you have me, princess?"

"Forever," I whispered, pressing my lips to his as he pressed his bleeding hand to my forearm.

He stepped away, handing the knife to Cheshire next. "I am Sinclair Malone, and I vow my life, my love, and my loins to Alice Lyon." His smirk as he said loins had me giggling, but he didn't stop, "May I provide her laughter to the end of my days." He repeated the same process as Caterpillar, kissing me soundly, before handing the knife off to Hatter.

"I am Hayden O'Hare, and I vow my life, my love, and my loins to Alice Lyon. May I be her healer to the end of my days." Hatter's voice was like butter as he spoke, entrancing me. I nearly fell into his arms letting him kiss me before he passed me and the knife off to March.

"I am Maxton Danara and I-I..." March stopped for a moment, clearly frustrated he restarted. "I am Maxton Danara, and I vow my life, my love, and my loins to Alice Lyon. May I be soft for her to the end of my days." Tears filled my eyes at his vow, and I crushed my mouth to his as soon as he'd finished cutting his hand.

I turned to the crowd, a strange feeling propelling me, "I am Alice Lyon, and I accept my Knights vows... And I make one myself. May I be a wife to them first and a Queen second." As soon as the words left my mouth, I turned throwing myself at my husbands.

"As the Queen of Undraland and the grandmother to Alice Lyon. I bless this union and all the fruits it will bear," Eumonia said. Shouts of joy and clapping filled my ears, but I was enveloped in the arms of the people I loved most.

Tables of food had seemingly appeared out of thin air soon after the ceremony was over. We'd all eaten and talked for hours.

"It's time for cake!" Dina shouted over the crush of voices that surrounded me.

She opened a door and Sheridan's blue head appeared just over the top of a huge blue and white cake. "Congratulations to the happy couple!" She bounced, making the cake wobble slightly. She managed to recover slightly, placing the cake on the table. "Thank you for letting me come." She said as I approached.

"I'm glad you could be here. Did your dad make this?" I asked.

"He did. Says it's the greatest honor of his life." She said, "You look so beautiful."

"Thank you—" Before I could say anything else, Cheshire appeared, "Give me some of that cake."

I laughed, "Okay. Okay." Together we cut the cake, handing out pieces to all of our family. When I finally took a bite of it the creamy taste almost brought me to my knees. "This is the best thing I've ever put in my mouth."

"No, it isn't." Cheshire winked at me, wiping a bit of frosting from my mouth.

The sun had started setting when my mother began to call for all of us to come and get pictures taken. My cheeks were sore from smiling, but I was so happy I couldn't complain. "Just one more. Dina, Duchess get over here and stand with Alice."

I wrapped my arms around both of them holding the pose. A flash caused me to blink and when I opened my eyes chaos reigned. The screams of a little girl had me turning my head. Ilaria stood just a few feet away, a sword through her neck as blood ran down the pale purple dress she was wearing.

I couldn't move, my feet stuck in place I just watched in horror as the Queen of Hearts stepped out from behind her. Her sword dripping blood as she walked toward me.

"Rhosyn?" Eumonia's voice echoed like I was underwater.

I watched as the woman turned, face going pale, but she smirked, "My, my Eu. You haven't aged well at all." I fisted my hands in the dresses of Duchess and Dina trying to do anything to force myself to move.

"How are you—No no. That doesn't matter. Why are you doing this?" Eumonia was struggling with her words. I couldn't even speak to tell her something was wrong with me. I just watched on in horror, Caroline's screams still echoing in my ears.

"You always were stupid. Never did figure out who I really was." She growled, "I am Rhoysn Black, the last living child of the Red King."

None of her words meant anything to me, but Eumonia looked stricken, "We were friends."

"Fool. I was trying to take your crown. I thought getting you stuck in this dismal place would work, but as you can tell it hasn't. Now, if you'll excuse me, I have something to take care of." Rhosyn or Rosyn, at this point I had no idea what her name really was turned toward us. A black cast on her fingers clued me in that something horrible was about to happen, but I was helpless to stop it. "Bye-bye, little lioness."

The ground fell out from under us, I glanced down finding only blackness. The last thing I heard as Dina, Duchess, and I fell into the blackness was the roars of the men I loved.

Acknowledgements

Blue Dreams was not an easy book for me to write, it tested my abilities as an author at every turn. You see Code Red was the first book I ever finished; this book was the test of my dedication to this career path. Being an author is all I've ever wanted. I can't express all of the emotions that I have about sharing my work with the world... again. I hope to have many, many more stories out soon. With that let's start actually acknowledging all of the wonderful people who made this journey possible.

As always, my family is the net to catch me when I start to fall off the ledge, without their unerring support I could never have managed to get this far. Thank you, Dad, Papaw, Whitneigh, and even Teagan.

My fiancé, Tyler, deserves so much recognition for supporting me through the moments where I was sure I was going to quit. Everything he does for me does not go unnoticed though I'm sure he sometimes feels that it does. I love you so much, you have my unending gratitude.

To my cover artist, and more importantly, my bestie, Leah. I can't wait to keep working with you for many more years to come. You've introduced me to so many wonderful people, authors and readers alike. I'll also take a second to plug The Reading Lounge, since it has been such a big part of my author journey so far.

To my Beta, Alpha, and ARC readers, none of this could happen without you. Thank you for dealing with all of my questions. This book wouldn't be half as good without your contributions.

And finally, to my street team, everything you do to help market my books is so helpful. I couldn't ask for a better group of people to be working with. Y'all rock!

If you aren't mentioned by name, I promise I still love and appreciate you. These acknowledgements would probably be longer than the book if I listed each and every person who supported and helped on my journey with Blue Dreams. Thank you!

Coming Soon

One Bloody Night- June 13, 2025
Book Two of The Austral Witches- October 2025
Secret Reclaiming Wonderland Novella- December 2025
Emerald Knights (Reclaiming Wonderland #3)- Spring 2026

About the author

Taila has always had an obsession with stories, cultivated by a loving grandmother. She always had her nose in some book or another, but at fourteen she began writing her own stories. Code Red may be the first to publication, but you can expect many, many more to come. Taila lives in the hills of East Tennessee. Where she can often be found cuddling naughty kittens, reading, or working her day job. Occasionally, her family or partner will convince her to leave her cave to see the outside world.

If you want to chat with Taila or stalk the socials for book updates:

Facebook Page: Taila Cantrell Author

Facebook Group: Taila Cantrell's Cuties

Instagram: tcantrellauthor

TikTok: @tailatalks

www.ingramcontent.com/pod-product-compliance
Lightning Source LLC
Chambersburg PA
CBHW060259310726
48976CB00007B/2129